Three Graces

Victoria Connelly

To Mum – remembering all our wonderful visits to country houses.

ACKNOWLEDGMENTS

Thank you to the following people who have helped during the writing of this book: Lady Montagu, The Honourable Rebecca Howard, Lady Victoria Leatham, and Elizabeth Howard.

Thanks also to Pia Tapper Fenton, Sue Haasler and Stephen Bowden.

And, as ever, a big thank you to my dear husband, Roy, a tireless chauffeur who hardly ever grumbles at taking me to yet another stately home!

I found the following helpful in the writing of this novel:

Deborah Devonshire, *Counting My Chickens and Other Home Thoughts*
Tiger Aspect's *Country House* series
The Duke of Bedford's *How to Run a Stately Home*
Marchioness of Tavistock and Angela Levin's *A Chance to Live*
Woburn Abbey Guidebook
Castle Howard Guidebook

PROLOGUE

Deep in the English countryside, at least three train rides away from London, lies the forgotten county of Cuthland. It's not the first choice of tourists but those who discover it revisit it until they know every perfect mile.

It's a county of winding roads, gently sloping hills and river valleys. Beech woods sprawl luxuriously, rivers flow calmly, and the brilliant purple moors spread to the very heavens.

In the heart of this landscape lies Amberley Court. For most of the year, it's hidden by a dense emerald veil of trees but, during the winter months, you can catch a glimpse of it from the road. It looks something like a honeycomb with its warm golden stone but it's anything but symmetrical. Added to down the centuries with a wing here and a turret there, it is a wonderfully higgledy-piggledy sort of house. No two towers are the same height and no two windows are the same shape. If one was comparing it to a human face, one would, perhaps, think of a Picasso and yet it has all the grace of a Gainsborough.

Inside, it is a perfect jamboree of Medieval, Tudor, Jacobean and Georgian with fourteenth century alcoves and sixteenth century fireplaces. Mahogany vies with walnut, and rosewood with satinwood. There are Chippendales and Hepplewhites, Sheratons and Gillows. There are cellarets and chaise longues, davenports and dressers. There are tapestries to take your breath away, galleries that will make you gasp and ceilings that will have you reeling.

There are …

Hang on …

You're not interested in all that, are you? You don't want me to tell you the strange story about the dining room doors or how long the ornate plaster work in the Long Gallery took. You have no desire to know how much the sixth duke paid for a bust of himself or how long the enfilade is. You want to know if it's haunted, don't you? That's why everyone visits these old houses. They're not interested in the furnishings. They don't want to know dates. They all have but one question to ask the tour guides and room stewards.

Is the house haunted?

Georgiana? Do you care to answer this question?

No?

Are you *sure*? This could be your big moment.

Not yet?

Oh. All right then.

CHAPTER 1

'I'm not at all sure about this,' Carys said to Louise, looking up at the grand country house as they finally reached the top of the driveway. Three storeys high, with windows the size of swimming pools, it was the biggest house they'd ever seen.

'Oh, come on! How often do we get to go to a bash like this?' Louise giggled, running her other hand through her hair and opening up a tiny gold compact in order to check her lipstick.

'Where shall I park?' Carys asked, noticing that all the cars were Jaguars, BMWs and Range Rovers.

'Yours will fit in there, won't it?'

'Mine would fit in to the boot of any of these,' Carys said, eyeing up the enormous cars with immaculate paintwork gleaming in the evening sunlight. She was incredibly fond of the old Marlva she'd inherited from her uncle but she couldn't help feeling it was a little out of place at Roseberry Hall. Although Marlva cars were the county of Cuthland's most celebrated industry, Carys wished she could boast the latest model, the sleek Marlva Panache, instead of her rotund 1960s Marlva Prima.

'I'll reverse in, I think,' Carys said. She had a habit of talking through every manoeuvre she made. 'Straight over here,' she'd announce as they approached a roundabout. 'Left turn after the hospital,' she'd inform whoever was in the passenger seat as she drove into town to work.

'What was that?' Carys suddenly asked as she heard a bump.

Louise looked out of the back window. 'Some sort of wall, I think.'

'Oh, God!' Carys inched the car forward slowly, hoping she wouldn't hear the sound of old brickwork collapsing

'Don't worry. It's probably already seen out the Civil War; it can survive you.'

Carys wasn't so sure. There were areas of her life in which she demanded perfection but driving wasn't one of them. She wasn't a public hazard or anything; it was just that her car received more than

3

its fair share of bumps and bruises.

'I'd better take a look,' she said, getting out of the car and hoping nobody was watching from one of the hall's many windows.

A light breeze caught her long, pale hair, sending it floating behind her like a golden comet's tail and inviting the hem of her light summer dress to dance up, revealing slender legs encased in pale stockings.

Thankfully, the dark red paintwork and the wall were unmarked and Carys breathed a sigh of relief.

'All right?' Louise asked, getting out of the car and straightening her dress. Carys hadn't seen her looking so lovely for months. Her chestnut hair had recently been cut and it clung to the contours of her faces making her look quite bewitching, and her sky-blue dress reminded Carys of a mermaid.

'Do I look okay?' she asked, noticing Carys looking at her.

'You look gorgeous,' Carys told her, remembering the old baggy jumpers and washed-out jeans her friend had been sporting ever since the break-up of her last relationship.

'How did you get invited to this party, anyway?' Carys asked.

'I told you. It was some business colleague of Martin's who got invites to distribute to whomever he chose.'

Carys narrowed her eyes. This was the very man who had turned Louise into the queen of grunge overnight. 'I thought you two had broken up.'

Louise looked sheepish for a moment. 'We have. But we still see each other from time to time.'

'I don't understand you, Lou. When I break up with someone, we can't even share the same town.'

Louise laughed. 'I got over him,' she said.

'And is he going to be here tonight?'

'Would I be looking so gorgeous if he wasn't?'

'You're not getting back with him, are you?' It was a question but Carys made it sound like a command.

Louise smiled. 'Of course I'm not. I just want him to realise what he's missing out on.'

'He was an absolute idiot to let you go.'

'All exes are absolute idiots.'

'Quite right,' Carys said, locking her car and linking arms for the walk across the enormous gravel driveway. Both of them knew what they were up to, of course. It was the unspoken' rule between girlfriends of a certain age that a night out would mean they were on the lookout for that most elusive thing: a potential boyfriend.

Carys shook her head at the word *boyfriend*. It just didn't sound grown-up. *Partner* sounded too business-like, *beau* was too old-fashioned, and *date* was too temporary. Anyway, that's why they were both there. They hadn't spent hours agonising over their appearances just so they could feel good about themselves. They were in full hummingbird-attire, hoping against hope that they'd find some rare nectar to hover around that evening.

They crossed the driveway, their shoes, as light as butterflies, crunching softly on the gravel. However, as they approached the house, Carys couldn't help feeling out of her depth.

'Look at the size of this place,' she said, each of her words filled to bursting with awe and anxiety.

'I know. It's wonderful, isn't it?'

'Who owns it?' Carys asked.

'I have absolutely no idea,' Louise confessed. 'Oh my goodness!' she suddenly burst in excitement.

'What?'

'I've just seen a deer - look!'

Carys looked out across the parkland which rolled gently into the distance and spotted a solitary deer moving like a ballerina amongst the long grass.

'The only wildlife you can see from my house is at chucking out time at The King's Head.'

Louise laughed. 'It is beautiful, isn't it? Can you imagine living in a place like this?'

Carys shook her head. 'Absolutely not. No point trying, either. I might get ideas above my station.'

'But just imagine,' Louise enthused, her smile filling her face and her eyes sparkling with mischief. 'Lady Carys Miller cordially invites *Cuthland Life* to her sumptuous home, Roseberry Hall.'

Carys had to laugh. *Cuthland Life* was the county's home-spun version of *Hello!* and each issue boasted some member of the landed gentry, eager to show off their twenty bedroomed palatial home with swimming pool, gymnasium, and paddock filled with horses.

'Heaven forbid,' Carys said. 'I could never be one of those even if I won the lottery.'

Reaching the front of the house, they craned their necks to gaze in wonder at three storeys of symmetrical beauty, the dozen or so windows winking in the last of the evening light. The stone was the rich red-gold that was used for all the fine houses of Cuthland and, on summer evenings, it seemed to glow from within as if it had been paid a compliment and was blushing with pride.

'Are you sure we've come to the right place?' Carys whispered, as they dared to approach the front door.

Louise nodded. She was still smiling like an over-excited child but Carys's smile was refusing to make an appearance. It had been chased away to some unknown corner of her body by her nerves.

'Come on,' Louise said. 'Time to make an appearance.'

They pulled an old-fashioned bell and the door was opened by a woman wearing a black dress and cape with frilly white sleeves. Drinks were offered and they were left to mingle.

'These aren't our sort of people,' Carys whispered.

'How do you know until you get to talk to them?'

'I just know,' Carys said. 'Their names, for example. I bet they've all got really pompous names - like Ophelia and Horatio.'

'Oh, and your name is so normal, I suppose?'

'It's Welsh - as well you know.'

'I know,' Louise grinned. 'It means *love*,' she said, batting her eyelashes like a cartoon character.

'Louise!' a voice suddenly shouted from the staircase.

'Martin!' Louise shouted back, her obvious joy at seeing him worrying Carys. 'Carys, I must just say hello for a moment.'

'Don't be long,' Carys said, anxious that her friend should not be sucked back into the vortex that was Martin Bradbury. She watched as Martin bent down to peck Louise on the cheek in greeting. Louise blushed prettily - a little too prettily for Carys's liking. When Louise caught Carys's eyes, it was she who was blushing and she turned away quickly, trying to find some diversion.

The entrance hall, where most of the people seemed to be gathered, was like no other Carys had ever seen. The hall of her own Victorian terrace was narrow and dark but this was wide, light and elegant. A staircase swept up from the centre of the hallway before curving right, its bright wooden banister rail polished so that it gleamed like a mirror. The walls were a pale butter and covered with paintings, mostly landscapes but there were portraits too.

Carys leant forward to get a better view then, wine glass in hand, began to climb the stairs, her heels clicking pleasantly on the white stone which had been left bare, its simple beauty glowing like fresh snow.

She passed a landscape of a ruined monastery overlooking a river; a pastoral scene in dark oils; and a number of hunting scenes with dogs carrying dead birds in their mouths. Carys winced. She'd never understood how people could gain pleasure from killing things. But she couldn't deny how impressive the pictures were, hanging in fine gold frames which caught the light. How incredible, she thought, to live in a house like this. For a moment, she wondered what it would be like to come home to a place such as Roseberry Hall. Imagine turning off the road into the long, winding driveway lined with trees, and parking in the huge sweep of driveway at the front of the house. It would certainly beat fighting for a car parking space in her street: a crowded suburb of Carminster. And how strange and wonderful to be surrounded by beautiful things all the time. She wondered if the owners ever got bored. What if the paintings weren't their choice but handed down from a forgotten ancestor whose taste didn't match theirs?

Pondering these thoughts, she climbed a few more steps and gazed appreciatively at more of the landscapes. It was all so magnificent, elegant and opulent. She thought of her cheaply framed floral prints hanging on the walls of her own house and smiled. Not that she'd swap them. The gold framed oils she was admiring just wouldn't look right in her place.

'You like the paintings?' a male voice suddenly broke into her thoughts.

Carys looked up but was quite unable to make out the face of her questioner who was silhouetted against a huge window on the landing.

'Some of them,' she said.

'These ones are better,' the dark man said.

Carys hesitated. It sounded like the worst of chat-up lines but, as Louise was still occupied with Martin and she had nobody else to talk to, she walked up a few more steps.

'Which ones?' she asked. 'I don't want to see any more dead birds.'

'Well, they're dead birds of a kind,' the gentleman said, nodding to the portraits which Carys had spied from the bottom of the stairs.

Her eyes adjusted and, before she took in the portraits, she saw that the dark man was dark indeed: he had dark hair which was thick and short and eyes which Carys couldn't quite make out. Were they a particularly dark shade of brown or were they actually black? But it was his smile which demanded her attention. There was a sweetness in it as if he held a secret: a ripe, juicy secret which he was about to impart, and Carys felt herself smiling back at him.

'Charlotte,' he said.

Carys raised her eyebrows. 'I've never met a man called Charlotte before.'

His smile broadened and he nodded towards the painting. Carys turned and saw a pale beauty staring out of a gaudy gold frame. The eyes were bewitchingly bright in her pale face and she wore a silver dress which was low cut, exposing acres of luminous skin. Her hair was fair and had been swept away from her face with just a few tendrils curling over her left shoulder.

'She's beautiful,' Carys said.

'Lady Charlotte de Montfort,' the gentleman said.

Carys nodded. She was none the wiser for the information.

'She had two husbands, nine children and an uncountable number of lovers.'

Carys grinned. 'Good for her.'

'And him-' the gentleman began, pointing to a portrait of a handsome man adjacent to Lady Charlotte, 'was Lord Nicholas de Montfort, her husband.'

'You seem to know these people,' Carys pointed out.

The gentleman shrugged. 'You could say I have an interest in them.'

Carys nodded. 'I'm afraid I've never really had much time for the aristocracy. I mean, they're a bit of a waste of space, don't you think?'

The gentleman smiled. 'You think this house is a waste of space?'

Carys's eyes widened. 'Oh no! I didn't say that. This house is beautiful.'

'But who do you think built it?'

'Probably somebody who once leant the king of England a sovereign.'

The gentleman gave another smile that seemed very knowing. 'I take it you don't agree with the monarchy either?'

'Let's face it,' Carys said, 'they're all rather outdated and useless. I think the French had the right idea - *off with their heads*!' she laughed, and then she wondered why she'd said it. She wasn't usually so opinionated at parties and she'd surprised herself with the strength of her feelings. Perhaps it was the wine talking.

'I see,' the gentleman said, good-humouredly.

Carys bit her lip. 'All I'm saying is that titles are outdated. They don't really provide a use today, do they?'

The gentleman shrugged. 'I imagine you could get a table at a restaurant in a hurry, or a free upgrade on a plane.'

'That's outrageous! How could anyone behave like that?'

'People do.'

'But they shouldn't.'

'I agree.'

There was a moment's pause. Carys looked down into her glass of wine, aware of the gentleman's eyes upon her.

'What's your name?' he asked in a low voice.

'Carys.'

'Carys?'

She looked up and smiled. She was used to the baffled response her name always caused. 'Like Paris but with a C instead of a P and a Y instead of an I.'

'C instead of a P and a Y instead of an I,' he repeated.

'That's right.'

'That's pretty.'

She felt herself blushing which was ridiculous. She wasn't the sort of woman to fall prey to blushes. She cleared her throat, determined to take charge of the situation.

'So,' she began, 'are you going to tell me-'

'Carys!' a voice shouted up from the foot of the stairs. Louise's voice. 'Where are you?'

Carys gave an apologetic half-smile to the gentleman whose name she'd probably never know now.

'Carys, come on. I want to introduce you to someone,' Louise said, her voice childlike with insistence.

'I've got to go,' she said, pausing for a moment. What did she think would happen? Did she think he'd beg her to stay? Did she even want to? He was still smiling at her: that knowing smile that was warm and unnerving at the same time.

And then she felt Louise's hand clasping her arm. 'There you are. Oh,' she said, suddenly seeing the gentleman, 'hello.'

'Hello,' the gentleman replied.

'Come on, then,' Carys said, giving Louise her full attention at last. 'Who's this person you want to introduce me to?'

They went downstairs, their dainty summer shoes tapping musically on each beautiful white step. Once in the hallway, Carys was ushered over to Martin and introduced to one of his friends. His face filled with uncontainable excitement as soon as he saw her approaching him but the feeling wasn't reciprocated. Carys forgot his name as soon as it was told to her but managed to make polite conversation despite the fact that she knew Louise was trying to match-make her, and the fact that her mind was still on the mysterious gentleman at the top of the stairs.

As Martin's friend told her about his favourite garden centre for bargain bulbs for spring colour, Carys found her gaze wandering to the top of the stairs but the gentleman had gone. She scanned the groups of people in the hallway and in the main room off the hall but couldn't see him.

'They can be extremely difficult to grow, of course,' Martin's friend was telling her, 'and it's best if you dig the bulbs up each year to stop rot.'

Carys nodded, feeling that her brain was rotting with his topic of conversation. Where was the gentleman? Had he made an early departure? She might never find out who he was.

'You can't beat a decent tulip for a spot of colour, of course…'

She'd never been smiled at before like that. She'd felt it in her very stomach.

'My mother used to have the most glorious auriculas you've ever seen.'

His eyes too. They'd looked at her in a way she'd never been looked at before.

'Most people believe they're native to Britain but they're not,' Martin continued, completely absorbed in a world of bulbs, buds and blooms.

Carys swallowed the last of her wine and then had a thought. 'I need another drink,' she said with a smile.

'Oh, allow me,' Martin's friend said, taking her class and disappearing across the room.

Carys looked around. Where on earth was Louise? It wasn't bad enough that she was probably getting back together with Martin but Carys would never forgive her for dragging her away from the gentleman at the top of the stairs to listen to Martin's friend going on about mulching and fertilizers.

She pushed by a group of people in the middle of a grand living room and spotted Louise standing in front of one of the enormous windows that had made them whistle when they'd first arrived. Sure enough, she was in deep conversation with Martin, her smile bright and eager, and her fingers running coquettishly through her hair.

'There you are,' Carys called, deciding she was going to break this meeting up as quickly as Louise had broken hers.

'Carys! Where's Martin's friend?' Louise, it appeared, had also forgotten his name.

'I've sent him away to get me a drink,' she said with great meaning.

'Oh,' Louise said.

Carys glared at Martin.

'Good to see you again, Karen,' he said.

'Carys,' she corrected, noticing Louise wince at his mistake.

He cleared his throat but didn't apologise. 'I'll, er, see you later, Louise,' he stuttered, before disappearing through the crowd.

Louise sighed. 'I don't suppose he will.'

'Good,' Carys said. 'I'm not having you getting back together with him.'

'We were just talking,' Louise insisted. 'There's nobody else here to talk to,' she said, scanning the room. 'They're all in their own little groups. Look!'

It was then that Carys saw him. He was stood on the other side of the living room talking to a beautiful red-head.

'Who's that man in the corner?' she asked Louise casually.

'Where?'

'By the table.'

'The one with his fingers in the nut bowl?'

'No,' Carys sighed in exasperation.

'Oh! You mean the man you were talking to on the landing?' Louise said, spotting the dark-haired gentleman. 'Fancy not knowing who he is. He's probably the most famous man here. He's certainly the only one other than Martin that I've actually heard of.'

'Well, who is he?'

'Richard Bretton, Marquess of Amberley. Heir to the Duke of Cuthland.'

'No!'

'Yes. His father's Henry Bretton, the eleventh Duke, no less. He's the one who's always banging on about bringing back the House of Lords.'

Carys knew, instantly, whom she meant. Henry Bretton was something of a local celebrity in Cuthland. If he wasn't on local television, he was on the radio, busting a blood vessel at how England was *Going to the dogs*.

'Fancy you talking to a marquess and not knowing it.'

Carys rolled her eyes. It was just like Louise to get all star-struck.

'What's so special about being a marquess?' she said but she could feel herself blushing from head to toe with shame as she remembered everything she'd said. She'd said she was a sympathiser of the French Revolution, for goodness' sake!

'Tell me he's not related to the de Montforts.'

Louise's forehead puckered into a frown as she mentally trawled through the many society pages of the many glossy magazines she'd ever flicked through. 'de Montfort, let me see-'

Carys's heart hammered.

'Yes. I do believe that's his mother's maiden name. *Something* de Montfort. Some sort of society belle, if I remember correctly. One of those masculine turned feminine names. Georgina or Willamina or something.'

'Oh God!'

'I know, awful names. *Francesca!* Louise suddenly shouted. That's it. Francesca de Montfort.'

'Great,' Carys sighed. Now it turned out that she'd unwittingly suggested his ancestors should have been beheaded.

'You like him!' Louise chimed.

Carys tutted. 'I never said that. But he was a little more interesting than Martin's friend.'

'What were you two talking about, anyway?'

'I don't know. He was going on about auriculas or something.'

'No, not Martin's friend. I mean the handsome Marquess of Amberley. He is handsome, isn't he?'

Carys nodded. He certainly was. Movie star looks were rare in

Cuthland.

'You know his wife left him?' Louise continued. 'Stark raving mad, they say. Amanda. I remember reading somewhere that she swore Amberley Court was haunted and packed her bags one day and just left - demanding a divorce.'

'Really?' Carys looked across the room at Richard with new eyes. 'He's single?'

Louise nodded. 'And a single marquess in possession of a large fortune must be in want of a wife,' Louise giggled.

Carys play-punched her and then, just as she looked across the room at Richard, he glanced up and caught her eye. And smiled.

'Wow!' Louise said in an excited whisper. 'Why don't you go over? He's smiling right at you.'

'We're leaving.'

'What? Well at least say goodbye, then,' Louise pleaded.

'What's the point? I made a complete fool of myself in front of him and I'm not going to see him again.'

'I think you might,' Louise smiled.

Carys looked up. He was walking towards them.

'I think I'll just go and get myself another drink,' Louise said.

'Louise - no-'

But it was too late. Louise had gone and Richard, Marquess of Amberley, heir to the dukedom of Cuthland, was standing before her.

'I'm sorry,' he said, extending a hand towards Carys. 'I should have introduced myself properly before.'

'Yes, you should have,' Carys agreed.

'Richard-'

'Marquess of Amberley,' Carys finished.

'You know?'

'I do now,' she said. 'I'm afraid I didn't before.'

'And would that have made a difference?'

Carys's eyes widened. 'Of course. I wouldn't have been so rude.'

'You mean, you'd have lied to me?'

'No!'

'Just not told me what you were really thinking?' he asked. 'Don't worry,' he assured her, noticing her frown. 'I wasn't offended.'

'I'm sorry. I really shouldn't have said those things - not in front of anyone. I don't know what came over me.'

He smiled at her. 'I think a lot of people are of your opinion.'

There was an awkward pause when neither knew what to say next.

'I was thinking of getting out of here,' Richard said at last. 'Get a spot of dinner somewhere. Maybe at Venezia. What do you think? It would be my very great pleasure if you would accompany me.'

'Oh,' Carys said, rather taken aback. 'It's getting a bit late, isn't it?' she added, knowing that Venezia was one of the most popular restaurants in Carminster.

'You're worried about not having a reservation,' he said as a statement rather than a fact. 'I can always explain who I am.'

'You wouldn't!' Carys said in undisguised horror.

He smiled at her, his eyes full of warmth and laughter. 'For you, I believe I'd do anything.'

CHAPTER 2

'I'm afraid there are no tables left at Venezia,' he said a moment later after ringing on his mobile. 'I could ring back and tell them who I am.'

'No way! I can't believe you'd really do that.'

He shrugged as if it was no big deal. 'I'd do it because I'd really like to take you there.'

'Well, I'm afraid I don't want to go that much.'

For a moment, Richard looked somewhat crestfallen. 'Come on,' he said, leaving Roseberry House and walking across the driveway. 'I've got an idea.'

Carys followed him. 'Wait a minute,' she said.

He stopped and turned around.

'Whose car are we going in?'

'Oh, I'm sorry,' he said. 'Do you have a car here?'

Carys nodded and pointed towards it.

Richard's eyes widened. 'Is that really yours? I was admiring it from the window just before. I haven't seen a Prima for years.'

'No, they're a dying breed.'

'Like the aristocracy,' Richard said grinning, causing Carys to blush.

They approached Carys's car and Richard ran a hand over the curved bonnet.

'So,' Carys said, 'which is your car?'

He nodded across the driveway. Of course, his car was a Marlva Country. Big as a tank but far more beautiful.

Carys looked back at her Prima. 'Maybe we should go in yours,' she said. 'Slightly more room.'

'Okay,' he said, 'but you must promise to take me out in your Prima some time.'

Carys laughed. 'If you insist.'

A few minutes later, they were sat in Richard's car. It felt strange to be so high up after being used to her tiny car. They left Roseberry House via the driveway where the trees stood deep in shadow.

'Amberley's driveway beats this one,' Richard suddenly said.

Carys looked at him.

'Have you ever been to Amberley Court?'

'No,' Carys said. 'I haven't.'

'Well, I'm not just being conceited; I'm being honest: it's the most beautiful place in the world and it's at its best at the moment although I do have a fondness for autumn when the colours mellow and deepen and great, ghostly banks of mist roll across the valley.'

Carys looked at him. He wasn't being conceited; he was very much in love with Amberley, she could feel that.

'I guess I'll have to visit, then,' she said.

'And let me know when you do and I'll give you a personal tour.'

Carys bit her lip. This was all moving at a pace a little faster than she was used to. 'I have a garden too,' she said. 'It's a ten foot by fifteen yard which just about fits a dustbin, a collection of potted plants and a deck chair.'

Richard smiled. 'It sounds great.'

She laughed. 'Rather like my car, it's a bit on the small side.'

'But small can be beautiful. You know, large estates come with a lot of problems. Sometimes, I wish that things were simpler: that there was only a limited amount of space to worry about and manage - not often, but sometimes.'

'What sort of things do you have to worry about?'

Richard turned left onto the main road that led to Carminster. 'Well, the deer in the park are a big responsibility. Gardens need constant work, especially old gardens where walls are apt to crumble, and ancient trees have to be monitored. Last year, for example, we lost several trees in the gales and they're our responsibility. We can't just ring the council up and complain.'

'I suppose not. But it must be incredible to actually own a tree.'

'Are you making fun of me?'

'No,' Carys assured him. 'I'm not. I really mean that it's just an odd thing owning something so special.'

Richard glanced at her as if gauging her.

For a moment, they drove in silence, starring out at the darkening sky, the last streaks of apricot cloud fading to indigo.

'Doesn't it seem a bit obscene owning so much land?' Carys asked at last.

'Are you trying to pick a fight with me?'

'No,' Carys said.

Richard frowned but he was smiling too. 'First, you recommend that I have all my ancestors beheaded, then you think I should turn all my trees loose-'

Carys laughed. 'No!'

'It sounds as if you are.'

'I'm not - honestly. It's just, I've never met anyone who owns so much land.'

Richard slowed the car down and pulled over into a passing place. 'Okay,' he said, 'let's get some things sorted out. Firstly, I don't own so much land. At the moment, the Amberley estate belongs to my father - as far as anything like that can actually *belong* to anyone. We've grown accustomed to thinking of ourselves as custodians rather than owners. Secondly, I didn't choose the circumstances of my birth. Yes, I'm well aware that some believe I was born with a silver spoon in my mouth but they are thoroughly misguided.'

Carys's eyebrows rose.

'We sold the family silver two generations back,' he explained.

They looked at each other for a moment and then they both burst out laughing.

'I'm really sorry that you think I'm making fun of you,' Carys said at last. 'It's just, well, I must admit to having a problem with inherited wealth.'

'Then what are you doing letting the heir to the dukedom of Cuthland run off with you into the middle of the night?'

'Because I like you,' she said simply.

He waited for a moment before replying. 'And I like you,' he said at last, 'but I can't change who I am.'

'I know; I don't expect you to,' Carys said. 'Anyway, I don't even know why we're getting so worked up about all this. We're only going out for dinner, aren't we?'

Richard nodded and indicated to pull out into the road again. 'You're right.'

Carys bit her lip. She could feel her heart racing. This was very strange. Why was she getting herself all worked up like this? This wasn't the way she normally behaved on a first date. Come to think of it, this wasn't even a first date, was it? They'd merely done a runner from a party together.

Suddenly, she felt rather uncomfortable and fidgeted in her seat.

'You okay?' he asked.

'Fine,' she said. 'Where are we going?'

'Surprise,' he said, 'but I promise I won't try to influence anyone into giving us better service by revealing who I am.'

Carys managed a smile which turned into a broad grin when they parked outside Perfect Pizza in Carminster.

'I could have got us seats at Venezia,' Richard said, 'but this is the next best thing. How about a takeaway? We can eat up on Solworth Hill and watch the sunset.'

Carys nodded. She really couldn't believe this man and his talk of trees and clouds and sunsets. She realised that she'd probably discovered the last gentleman poet in Cuthland.

Twenty minutes later, they were parked and eating pizza on their laps, an apricot and indigo sunset bathing the valley below them and making their skin glow.

'Are you going back to the party?' Carys said in between mouthfuls of Margherita.

'Only to drop you off. I'm not going back in.'

'Me neither.'

'What about your friend?'

'Louise? She'll be long gone by now.'

'Oh.'

After nearly burning the roof of her mouth on a particularly hot piece of tomato, Carys added, 'I was double-crossed tonight.'

Richard frowned.

'Louise - my friend - knew her ex would be there and I have a horrible feeling she'll start seeing him again.'

'And that's not good?'

Carys shook her head. 'It's terrible. He's a pig and a bore.'

Richard nodded. 'Too many of those around.'

'You're not wrong,' she said philosophically, her teeth pulling at a strip of cheese the length of an anaconda.

'And have you a pig and a bore of your own?'

Carys smiled. 'I'm not seeing anyone, if that's what you mean.'

The sunset was deepening into a soft, shadowy mauve and the valley was slowly disappearing behind a veil of night.

'We'd better get back,' he said, wiping his fingers on his paper napkin.

'I suppose we should,' Carys said, feeling somehow flat that this was how things were ending. She'd been so hopeful for Solworth Hill.

'Unless-' he stopped.

'What?' she said, a little too eagerly. She mustn't sound too eager!

'Unless you want to go for a walk.'

'But it's getting dark,' she said and, as soon as the words were out, she could have kicked herself. Why had she said that?

She sneaked a sideways glance at him. He was disappointed, wasn't he?

'We could, though,' she added tentatively.

He shook his head. 'No, you're right. It's getting late,' he said, chucking his pizza box onto the back seat and starting the car.

CHAPTER 3

Carys groaned. She'd screwed up. If she hadn't been so stupid, she might have been wonderfully seduced under a summer oak tree in the darkening shadows of evening. And heaven only knew that she could have done with some of that to liven up her world at the moment. She couldn't remember the last time she'd been kissed properly.

So why had she turned down the possibility of passion tonight? She couldn't deny that Richard Bretton was a very attractive man. He was also very respectable. He'd probably meant nothing by suggesting a walk at dusk at all. He may only have wanted to hold her hand. But she couldn't help wondering what might have happened if she'd only got out of the car and taken his hand as he'd led her through a shady grove of oak trees before stopping to kiss her neck, luminous in the gathering dusk …

Shaking an image of passion in the undergrowth out of her mind, Carys went upstairs and switched on the lamp at the side of her desk and turned on her computer. As she spent most of her working days gazing at a computer, the one at home was only occasionally used but it was handy to have access to the internet and this was one occasion when it was most welcome.

For a moment, she wondered if what she was doing could be classed as stalking but shook the idea from her mind as she typed *Richard Bretton* into a search engine. She'd never gone out with anyone who'd had an internet presence before. It was quite exciting, really, seeing page after page on the man who'd abducted her.

She hit the images button and bit her lip as the photographs downloaded. There he was. Richard Bretton, Marquess of Amberley, opens a new wing at a children's hospital in Carminster. Richard Bretton with Lady Electra Hewett at the summer ball. Richard Bretton with a boring line of dignitaries. Richard Bretton with Eustacia Viner, daughter of some lord or other. Richard Bretton with the Honourable Miranda Selby.

Carys frowned. He seemed to spend half his life with a beautiful girl draped over his arm, and they were all strikingly similar: willowy tall with costly manes of hair and clothes which Carys had always referred to as the *unimaginative designer* look: clean lines, neutral colours and showing absolutely no individuality.

Well, if that was the type of woman he went for, perhaps it was a good thing she'd nipped things in the bud before they'd really begun. It would only have ended in disaster, with her flowery, flouncy wardrobe of rainbow-coloured dresses in cheap fabrics. She'd never be seen dead in beige or wishy-washy pastels. She loved sherberty yellows, cornflower blues, deep lilacs and poppy-bright reds. Her job in the office, of course, frowned upon such displays of vibrancy so she toned it down by wearing close-fitting skirts and neat jackets, but there was always the hint of the rebel about her: a beaded hemline, an embroidered waistband or a stunning piece of silver jewellery to defy the dullness of office life.

So, what on earth had attracted Richard to her? Perhaps it was because she was so different from the women he normally mingled with. They wore pearls; she wore marquisate. They bought from boutiques; she bought from the market. They were expensive; she was cheap - no, not cheap - just not so high-maintenance as they were.

She paused, staring at Richard's face which gazed out at her from her computer screen. She should stop this right now, she thought. Switch the computer off and go to bed. Forget she'd ever met him. But she couldn't resist looking for more. Her fingers tapped effortlessly over the keyboards as she confided her nosiness to Google, wondering how on earth the world had managed before its creation.

Amberley Court.

It was the first website to come up and Carys clicked on the link and then her eyes widened at the site that greeted her. It was one of the worst websites she'd ever seen: unimaginative, unattractive and - well - amateur. It was obviously done on the cheap, Carys thought. But there was no getting away from the fact that Amberley was beautiful. All mellow red brick and barley-twist chimneys, it looked straight out of a children's fairytale book. No wonder Richard felt so passionate about it. A house like that got into your blood whether you owned it or not. She could imagine how hard it would be to think of leaving such a place to the ravages of time and how hard you would fight in order to save it.

The house was photographed from the driveway, peeping shyly through an avenue of brilliant green trees. It was pictured from the rose garden with blushing blooms making the prettiest of foregrounds. And it was pictured from the wood on the hill, making it look tiny and vulnerable as if the merest puff of wind might blow it away.

There were photographs of the interior too: the rooms looked sumptuous but slightly shabby around the edges. The colours were extraordinary: wine-red carpets, gilded ceilings, floors of multi-coloured marble, brilliant chintz bedding with flowers bursting in bright blooms, and curtains of every imaginable colour from brightest yellow to darkest emerald. Then there were plates and bowls, chandeliers and chaise longues, cabinets and candelabras, and things Carys couldn't even begin to name. And, everywhere, there were portraits: the Bretton family peered down on the unsuspecting visitor from almost every wall in the house. Centuries of eyes - some looking stern and severe as if they were trying to frighten the visitor away; others looking kindly, perhaps curious at their new home in cyberspace.

Carys was in love. She'd never seen such an incredible place, and to think that this was the very place that Richard Bretton called home.

Open: Wednesday - Sunday; Grounds: 10:00 am - 17:00 pm; House: 11:00 - 16:00 pm

Tomorrow was Saturday. She could go there tomorrow. Richard had told her she should go. But would tomorrow be too soon? Would that make her appear too keen? Hang that, she thought. She couldn't wait to see it. It was the most beautiful place she'd ever seen and she probably wouldn't even run into Richard anyway. She could sneak in and out without him ever knowing.

CHAPTER 4

It was ten o'clock on Saturday morning and there was only one car parked in the visitors' car park at Amberley Court and that was Carys's Marlva Prima. She'd paid her £4.50 to a little old man who sat in a hut inside the gate.

'I'd like to go inside the house too,' she'd said.

'That ticket will get you into both,' he'd explained.

Four pounds and fifty pence. No wonder the estate was short of money, Carys thought, leaving her car and taking a footpath towards the walled garden. It was a long time since she'd visited an historic house but she was sure it should cost more than she'd just paid.

It was a beautiful summer's morning. The air was cotton-soft and filled with the delicate perfumes of flowers as she entered the walled garden. The walls were a rosy red, like those of the house, and had the mellowed look that time and weather bring. There were a few low-lying box hedges and a token bed of vegetables and a few fruit trees but, overall, it had the look of somewhere that could do with an extra gardener or two.

As Carys wandered around, she started trying to picture the garden as it should be: bursting with blooms: great fat roses launching their perfume into the air, rows of neat cabbages in the beds whose borders would be neatly trimmed with box hedgerows which didn't look as if a pack of Jack Russell Terriers had been playing hide and seek in them. There'd be bucket loads of apples and pears, and gooseberries - fat and crunchy - would glow greenly. It would be the perfect kitchen garden: a blend of the pretty and the practical.

As it was, it looked as if somebody had thrown a couple of packets of wildflower mix across the soil and hoped for the best. It was very pretty but it wasn't fulfilling its potential. It was like a supermodel before make-up and Carys felt desperate to get going with a bit of foundation and blusher.

As she turned a corner at a bed of flowers that looked as if they could do with a good sorting out, she saw a dog hurtling towards her, its long ears flapping and its tail rotating like a mini windmill

'Hello, there,' she said, bending down to ruffle the silky-soft head. 'What's your name, then?'

The bright chestnut eyes peered up at her from a brown and white face.

'You're a beauty, aren't you?' she said, smiling at the cheeky freckles. 'Is this your garden, then? You lucky dog. I bet you have fun in here, don't you?'

'Carys?'

Carys stood back up to full height and turned around, seeing Richard walking towards her.

'What are you doing here?' he asked and she couldn't tell if he looked happy or perplexed at seeing her there.

For a moment, she was tongue-tied. She felt like a thief that had been caught red-handed.

'You told me I should visit so here I am,' she said, managing to keep calm.

'I didn't think you would. But I'm glad you did. You didn't give me your phone number.'

'You didn't ask for it,' she said and then wished she hadn't. It sounded as if she'd minded that he hadn't asked for it which wasn't true, of course.

'You gave me the impression that you wouldn't have given it if I had asked.'

'Did I?'

He nodded. 'Yes.'

'I didn't mean to.'

The brief exchange dried up and both seemed at a loss as to what to say next.

'She's a gorgeous dog,' Carys said at last, bending down to ruffle the long fur on the top of her head.

'She's Phoebe's. My sister. One of my sisters, I should say.'

'How many do you have?'

'Two: Phoebe and Serena. There's a brother too: Jamie.'

'You're lucky. I'm an only child.'

'I think you're the lucky one.'

They smiled at each other and the tension was instantly dispelled.

'You should have told me you were coming.'

'Well, I didn't know myself. It was kind of a spontaneous

decision,' Carys lied.

'You didn't pay, did you?'

'Of course I did.'

'Then we must get you a refund.'

'Don't be silly,' she argued. 'You're charging little enough as it is, by the way. You really should think about increasing your entrance fee.'

Richard frowned. 'You think so?'

'Absolutely! You can't buy anything for four pounds fifty any more.

'The only thing is, Barston Hall only charges £6 and they have a lot more to offer. More rooms, grander gardens, an animal park, a playground for the kids-'

'So? That's their business.'

Richard smiled. 'You're very-'

'What?'

'Direct.'

'No point being indirect, is there?'

'I don't suppose there is,' he said.

They began to walk towards the arch in the wall which would lead out into the main gardens.

'Dizzy!' Richard called, as the spaniel hurtled towards the exit. 'Wait.' The dog came to a halt and looked around, tongue flopping pinkly out of the side of her mouth.

'Dizzy?'

'That's Phoebe for you,' Richard explained.

'I like it.'

'She didn't think how silly I'd feel yelling that name across the estate.'

Carys grinned. 'Maybe she did.'

This made Richard smile.

They left the walled garden and turned right. There were a few more cars in the car park now but it was still quiet.

'Will you please allow me the honour of showing you the house?'

'Haven't you got things you should be doing?'

'Nothing that can't be postponed,' he said.

Carys looked at her watch.

'Unless you have somewhere else you should be?'

'No,' she said. She wasn't sure why she'd looked at her watch. It must have been a nervous reaction because she had absolutely nothing to do with her time other than tidy up and that could wait for another month.

'I'd love to see the house,' she said.

'We'll sneak in the back way.'

'The tradesman's entrance?' Carys teased.

'The owner's entrance,' Richard corrected her. 'We won't be told to wipe our feet if we go in that way.'

They followed Dizzy down a gravelled pathway and Richard produced a key from a pocket as they approached a door.

'This is the private part of the house, of course, so we won't run into any coach loads of pensioners.'

He opened one of the double doors and Carys followed him inside, her mouth dropping open at the enormous hallway which greeted her.

'You could fit my whole house in here,' she said, looking around the huge open space, its flagstone floor taking up acres of ground. A long row of boots and shoes stood on sentry duty by the door, quietly flaking mud, and a coat rack was hung with more coats than Carys had ever seen outside a department store. The smell of wax was quite overpowering. There was also a fascinating collection of hats. Most were flat caps in various shades of green and grey but most were woolly, shapeless creations - fiercely practical and terribly unattractive.

'Big family - big hallway essential,' Richard said. 'I'm one of four. Dizzy's one of five. Add parents and other relations and friends and, if you all decide to come in at once, it's chaos.'

Carys noticed a huge Ali Baba pot stuffed full of walking sticks of every shape and height. Some were curved, others were dead straight. One looked as if its handle was made of horn and others were carved and painted to look like birds, badgers and foxes. There was also a rifle.

Richard followed her gaze. 'Don't worry,' he said. 'It's broken. Father uses it to scratch his back.'

Carys frowned. That sounded awfully dangerous to her, broken or not, but she didn't say anything.

There was a beautiful fireplace and Carys could imagine how wonderful it would be to come home to: to walk through the door, throw your coat onto the rack, kick your boots across the floor and toast yourself in front of a real fire. There were two large, arched windows at the far end of the hall through which Carys could see a small enclosed courtyard and columned walkway resembling a cloister. Was the house old enough to have a cloister? She wasn't sure about dates and architecture but it was very pretty nevertheless.

There was also a fabulous barometer in a rich chestnut-coloured wood. Carys had always been fascinated by them even though she wasn't at all sure how they worked. Something to do with air pressure, she thought. But did they tell you what the weather was like now? Or was it a way of predicting what weather was on its way? Reading left to right, it read: stormy, rain, change, fair and very dry. It was pointing to 'change' at the moment, which sounded about right for a summer's day in England. She was tempted to reach out and touch it - it had such a wonderfully curvy smooth look about it but she didn't want to risk his disapproval by fingering antiques before they'd even left the hallway.

'Should I take my shoes off?' Carys asked, noticing a beautiful rug in front of them.

'Good heavens, no! Your feet will freeze and you'll most likely catch a nasty case of carpet beetle.'

She grimaced. Could you really catch carpet beetle? Carys wasn't sure what carpet beetles were but imagined something like a cockroach crossed with a dung beetle scurrying up her bare legs.

'Come on,' he said, leading the way through to a small drawing room which looked like any drawing room in the country but for a collection of spectacular portraits hanging on the walls.

'Wow!' Carys said.

'Ah! The dreaded relations. I'm afraid there's no escaping them. Very vain family, the Brettons. Lost count of how many portraits were commissioned down the centuries but it's enough to fill a hundred country houses and they invariably end up hanging in the oddest of places. There are even one or two,' he said in a whisper, 'in the guest lavatories.'

'Most off-putting,' Carys said with a grin.

'So I'm told.'

'And this is one of the private rooms?'

Richard nodded. 'The Yellow Drawing Room. Reserved for naps after walks and arguments after dinner.'

There were two large yellow sofas on which sat fat red cushions, squashed and dented by happy bottoms. Newspapers lay scattered over coffee tables and there were neat piles of *Country Life*, *Cuthland Life*, *Social Whirl* and *The Field* on the coffee tables. It was a cosy, comfortable room. Dizzy certainly seemed to be making herself at home: leaping up onto an armchair and snuggling into a large red cushion.

'That's the dog chair,' Richard said by way of explaining why he hadn't reprimanded the animal.

As they walked through the room, Carys saw a shoal of silver photo frames standing on a sideboard which looked more Habitat than Chippendale, and a herd of wooden deer marched across the mantelpiece of a fireplace.

'My mother's,' Richard said. 'Dotty about deer.'

A large window looked out onto a private lawn where a motley collection of deck chairs stood waiting for the sun to find them.

Carys felt she could have spent all day in the room but was aware that Richard was probably en route to something grander and far less homely.

'This way,' he said, opening a door which led into a narrow passageway.

Carys got completely lost after that. They walked down corridors, up staircases, through endless rooms hung with silks and tapestries, down staircases, along passages lined with portraits, passages lined with cabinets of china, under ceilings decked with plaster garlands, through rooms inhabited by ginormous beds, and ante-rooms hiding tiny baths and washstands.

Her head spun with portraits, busts, screens, tables, chairs and chandeliers. She heard terms she'd never heard before: acanthus, ormolu, japanning, bollworm. She sat on a balloon-back chair:

'I feel like a queen!'

'You look like one too.

She looked at her reflection in a pier glass mirror:

'It's very flattering.'

'It doesn't need to be.'

She stroked a piece of William Morris wallpaper.

'Don't tell mother I let you do that.'

'I won't.'

And had even been allowed to lie down on a full tester bed.

And neither of them had dared say a word.

When she got up, he led her down another staircase and into a corridor.

'Stay there,' he told her.

'Why?'

'Stay right where you are,' Richard added, almost running ahead to open the door in front of them.

'Where are you going?'

'You'll see.'

'What are you doing?'

She watched in bemusement as, after opening one door, he walked through the next room and opened another door. Then another. Then another. Before walking back with a huge grin on his face.

'It's an enfilade. A series of interior doors arranged to provide a kind of vista when the doors are open.'

'Ah, yes! I remember now. I have one just like it at home.'

Richard laughed. 'Then you'll know what fun they are,' he said. 'When we were growing up, we used to open all the doors and roller skate down it.'

Carys smiled as she tried to imagine Richard on roller skates. The funny thing was, she really could. He still had that boyishness about him: that edge of fun which followed you into adulthood and made sure you didn't turn into a funless frump.

'Sometimes, we'd even risk a scooter or one of those go-carts. And Serena would journey down the corridor on her space hopper.'

Carys laughed, staring down the seemingly endless runway of fun. She'd never thought of ancient houses as being places of fun before but she was beginning to see them in a new light now. She could imagine rainy days being no obstacle to having the time of your life. There were miles of corridors and acre upon acre of space inside the old walls of Amberley. How different it must have been from her own childhood in her mother's immaculate apartment where everything was white, forbidding any activities which might have been deemed fun like painting or baking or owning a pet.

'Don't leave that there!' was a regularly shouted command from her mother if Carys dared to leave her toys out.

Carys had always had a sneaking suspicion that she'd remained an only child because her mother couldn't have coped with any more mess.

'The mirror at the end gives the illusion of infinity. You can imagine it reaching right to the edge of the world,' Richard said, bringing Carys back to the present.

She looked up at him. 'You love it here, don't you?'

He turned around to face her, his eyes still sparkling with reflections of his childhood antics.

'There's nowhere else in the world I'd rather be.'

'Just as well, I suppose.'

'What do you mean?'

'Because you're lumbered with it, aren't you? I mean - one day-' she stopped. What on earth had made her say that? She could feel a blush creeping over her face like a dark cloud.

'Is this the aristocracy-basher again?'

'I'm sorry,' she said quickly. 'I don't know why I said that.'

'Because it's true?' he suggested. 'You're right - I am lumbered with it. Although lumbered isn't quite the word I'd have chosen. But I'm the first son. I will take on the responsibility of seeing that the old pile doesn't crumble into the ground whilst I'm alive.'

'Isn't that an awful duty? Doesn't it make you want to run away and-'

'And what?'

'I don't know,' Carys said. 'Join a circus? Or an insurance company or something - *any*thing else?'

'It's strange,' he said. 'There must be something in the genes that makes you stay. It's as if you're born with the blood of the house running through your veins. It's air is the only air you can breathe. It's bricks, its foundations - they're a kind of extra skin you wear. There's no getting away from it even if you wanted to; it's a part of you.'

There was a moment's silence before he continued.

'I'm sorry. I'm being boring, aren't I?'

'No. It's all so fascinating - to be so attached to a place. I've never had that experience before. I mean, I'm Cuthland born and bred but I don't have that connection to a place as specific as Amberley. I think you're very lucky.'

'You do?'

'I really do. I didn't realise how passionate you could get about an old pile of bricks,' she said with a little laugh.

Richard's eyes widened. 'I object to the word *pile*!' he said.

'Amberley may not be in a perfect state of repair but I like to think of her as being a few stops up from a pile.'

'Oh, she is. I was just teasing.'

'Then you like the house?'

Carys looked down the length of the enfilade again. Its rich chestnut floor stretched for what seemed like miles, highlighted, at intervals, by sunlight spilling in from the windows. She caught a glimpse of golden mirror from the next room and could just make out a brilliant jade urn in the room after that.

'I love the house,' she said at last. 'I really love it.'

And she did. It was the most beautiful place she'd ever seen and she couldn't stop thinking about it all evening. It was as if it had woven a wonderful spell over her. It had spoken to her.

'Carys.'

She remembered hearing the voice distinctly as she'd left Amberley.

'This is your home now.'

At first, she thought she'd imagined it and then she thought it must have been a voice from deep within her, telling her of her future.

She bit her lip as she remembered it. Yes, that must have been it: she must have had some sort of premonition. What else could it possibly have been - a ghost? Carys smiled. She didn't believe in ghosts and, anyway, Amberley wasn't haunted, was it?

CHAPTER 5

'I don't understand what you mean,' Louise said, her nose scrunched up in consternation.

'I'm engaged!' Carys said again, her eyes dancing with a light one rarely sees north of the Mediterranean. 'Well, it's not official yet. Obviously.' She gave a half-laugh. 'We haven't told anyone and we haven't got a ring yet but -'

'Carys! Have you gone absolutely mad? You've only just met this guy. God! I was with you. You were only talking to him for a few minutes. How could you possibly know him?'

'I know him better than I know anyone else. And you can trace his family back about eleven generations if you want to. There are no skeletons in his English oak cupboards.' She giggled at her own joke.

'English oak-' Louise's nose was in danger of disappearing altogether if she scrunched it up any more. 'Ah!' she said at last. 'I'm beginning to understand now. You've fallen in love with this man's house, haven't you? Just like Elizabeth Bennet in *Pride and Prejudice* when she sees Darcy's estate for the first time. Remember?'

'I don't know what you're talking about.'

'Oh, yes you do. Look - you're blushing.'

'I am not!'

'You are. You face is all red.'

'That's rubbish. Love has got nothing to do with possessions or titles or estates. You don't marry a man because he has a title or a few acres of land.'

'He's got more than a few acres.'

'You marry him because you love him. You don't live with a title. You live with a man. Anyway, I don't see what's wrong with a whirlwind romance.'

'Whirlwind? This is more like a tornado!'

'Oh, Louise! I'm not going to talk to you any more if you're going to be so impossible.' Carys got up to go.

'No, don't go,' Louise said quickly. 'I didn't mean to upset you. I'm just trying to understand, that's all. It's rather a lot to take in.'

Carys sat back down. Her friend was right, of course. She realised how surprised she'd be if the roles had been reversed.

'Now,' Louise said. 'Start from the beginning and tell me what happened.'

Carys sighed and began to tell Louise about her extraordinary visit to Amberley: the walled garden, Dizzy the spaniel, and the tour of the house.

'You should have seen the rooms. You would have loved them.'

'Yes, yes! I'm sure I would have but when did he propose? What did he say?'

Carys smiled. She'd been doing a lot of smiling since she'd met Richard.

'We were in the library. It was the last room in the house that we visited,' Carys said, replaying the scene once more.

'Do you like books?' Richard asked.

'I love them,' Carys said, trying to remember the last time she'd sat down with a good novel. A few months ago, perhaps? On holiday? She wouldn't let on.

He opened a door and Carys gasped.

'It's the old Long Gallery. Once used for walking in on a winter's day and dancing in on a summer's evening but Amberley's ever-expanding library had to be housed somewhere.'

'It's amazing,' Carys said.

Dark shelves crammed with books filled every inch of wall space. Spines of muted reds and greens greeted her eyes and she took a step closer to read the titles.

'There are around fifteen thousand books in here and I've not read a single one,' Richard announced.

Carys turned to look at him, her eyes searching his for humour but he was deadly serious.

'Being told to read with gloves on when you're a kid doesn't exactly inspire enthusiasm. Give me a modern paperback whose spine I can crack. I like a book I can drop in the bath and not worry if it's a valuable first edition or not.'

'Me too,' Carys said. 'My first edition Charles Dickens novels aren't allowed to leave my library either.'

Richard looked at her.

Oh, dear. Had she gone too far with the jokes? Had she

overstepped the boundary of humour and insulted him and his way of life - again?

And then he smiled. 'Will you marry me?'

Carys's mouth dropped open. Had he just proposed? Hadn't they just been talking about books and baths and ... how had they got onto this subject all of a sudden?

'What?'

'Will you marry me, Carys?'

She frowned. What was going on here? They hadn't even been on a date. Their drive out into the country with a pizza could hardly be called a date and, anyway, it had ended disastrously. They hadn't even kissed. She didn't know anything about him.

Actually, that wasn't true. She'd learnt more about this man in that last couple of hours than she knew about some members of her own family. She knew all about his family history: two sisters and a brother and generations of devious dukes before that. She knew that he didn't think much of mahogany but couldn't imagine life without walnut - particularly a simple little side table he had in his bedroom. She knew that he never watched soap operas but was a huge fan of *Countryfile* and watched most wildlife programmes as long as they weren't about bats of which he had an irrational fear. He was born on the thirteenth of July which, she'd worked out made him a Cancerian. He liked marshmallows, copper beaches, mullioned windows and, she'd just discovered, cracking the spines of new paperbacks whilst in the bath.

Was it enough?

'You don't know anything about me,' she said.

'But I do,' he said. 'you're unhappy in your job-'

'I never said that!'

'But you are, aren't you?'

Carys frowned again. How had he worked that out? What had she said? She couldn't quite remember.

'You love beautiful things but don't think you have a right to them.'

'What do you mean?'

'You're well-versed in literature but haven't read much modern fiction.'

'I never-'

'And you're beginning to think more kindly of my way of life.'

Carys's hands were on her hips and her brow was furrowed with consternation.

'I never said anything-'

He kissed her and the rest of her protestation was silenced.

'Marry me,' he said once he'd let her go.

'And I said yes,' Carys told Louise. 'That was it. He asked me and I said yes.'

Louise's face was a picture of puzzlement. 'Nothing like that's ever happened to me.' And then something occurred to her. 'My God! You'll be a *duchess*.'

'Not at first. A marchioness to begin with.'

'A marchioness?' Louise's tongue stumbled over the foreign word. 'But you hate the aristocracy. How can you suddenly become a recruit?'

Carys sighed. 'I might have hated most of them at one point but I think, now, that I'm rather in love with one specific member.'

Louise rubbed her head in her hands. 'My brain aches. I can't take all this in. Are you sure you're not winding me up?'

Carys shook her head. 'You'll be my bridesmaid, won't you?'

Suddenly, Louise's face lit up with joy. 'Oh, yes! Oh wow! Where will you be getting married? Will it be in the cathedral? Just imagine! It will be in all the glossy mags, won't it? When will the wedding be? Have you bought any bridal magazines yet? Oh, this is so exciting!'

Carys grinned. It hadn't taken long to win her friend over.

CHAPTER 6

It was only after Carys had accepted Richard's proposal of marriage that he introduced her to Cecily and Evelyn - his two daughters.

She'd driven out to Amberley to be officially introduced to Richard's parents, the duke and duchess. As though that wasn't enough of a nerve-wracking experience for one day, he'd taken her into the private drawing room and sat her down.

'There's something I should have told you,' he said.

'It's all right,' Carys said. 'I know you've been married before.'

'You do?'

'You don't live in a complete bubble here, you know.'

A look of enormous relief passed across his face.

'Then you'll know about Cecily and Evelyn?' he said. 'Girls! You can come in now.' The drawing room door opened and two young girls, aged about eight and ten, walked in. They were a pair of perfect blonde bookends and had the kind of complexions which made them ripe for creamy soap commercials.

'These are my two beautiful daughters,' he announced proudly.

Carys's eyes stretched in surprise. She had known about the wife but she hadn't known about the two children. How had he managed to keep them a secret, she wondered? And then she realised, once again, that they really hadn't known each other very long and that such things as children could be hidden away and forgotten about.

'Hello,' Carys said, standing up as the two girls approached. 'I'm Carys.' She wondered whether to shake their hands but they were a bit young for that, weren't they?

'Are you going to be our new mama?' the younger girl asked.

Carys blushed and Richard cleared his throat in obvious embarrassment.

'Don't be silly,' the elder girl said. 'Nobody can replace mama.'

There was a very awkward silence as Carys began to realise the enormity of the situation. She glanced at Richard who gave her a look as if to say, I won't blame you if you run away right this minute.

'Cecily, Evelyn,' he began, 'Carys is going to be my wife, yes.'

Carys swallowed hard. The term *wife* was alienating enough; the title *marchioness* would be odd in the extreme, but the position of *mama* was positively daunting.

She bit her lip. 'And I'm hoping you two will be my bridesmaids,' she suddenly said, wondering how she'd come up with such a bribe. Well, it had worked wonders with Louise.

'Can we?' the younger girl said.

The older girl, whose expression seemed set in stone, said nothing.

Richard knelt down and took the little girl's hands in his. 'Of course you can be a bridesmaid, Evie.' He turned to face Cecily. 'And you can too, my love.'

Cecily didn't say anything but remained resolutely silent.

'Now,' Richard said, 'hadn't you two better get ready for lunch?'

Cecily and Evelyn nodded in unison and left the room.

Richard stood back up to full height and dared to turn to Carys.

'I meant to tell you earlier,' he said, his face creasing in anxiety.

Carys's eyebrows rose. 'Don't tell me, they slipped your mind.'

'Of course they didn't. It just didn't seem to be the right moment.'

'Didn't seem right to warn me that I'd be taking on two step-daughters?'

'Well, you won't really. They have a nanny and a tutor. You don't have to have anything to do with them if you don't want to.'

'What do you mean?'

'I mean, they're well looked-after.'

Carys frowned. 'But they're children, and I'm going to become their surrogate mother. What kind of a woman do you think I am?'

Richard sighed.

Carys shook her head. This was going badly. 'Look,' she said, 'they're adorable. I'm sure we're all going to get on really well. It's just - well - they're a bit of a surprise.'

'Then you're still going to take me on?'

Carys couldn't help but smile even though her head was spinning. 'Of course I am! But don't go presenting me with any more surprises.'

'Okay,' he said, his face flushing with relief. 'But there are two more surprises.'

'What?' Carys said, envisioning mad wives in the attic.

'Mother and father.'

Nothing could have prepared Carys for the Duke and Duchess of Cuthland. Before entering the dining room, Richard took her through to an ante-room filled with dark, oppressive tapestries.

'So,' a gruff voice greeted her. 'This is Miss Miller, is it?'

Carys stepped forward.

'This is Carys, father, mother. Carys, please meet my father and mother.'

Carys held her hand out to shake the duke's. He wasn't as tall as she had expected but he was solidly built and had the kind of expression which made one feel instantly ill at ease.

He shook her hand, crushing her fingers into a slim sausage. 'Carys. Welcome to Amberley,' he said, doing his best to avoid eye-contact.

'Pleased to meet you, your grace,' she said quietly.

'How do you do, Miss Miller?' the duchess said, stepping forward. She was slightly taller than her husband and stood with the grace of a ballerina, her slender frame and elegant clothing making her look as if she'd stepped out of the pages of a glossy magazine. She had raven-dark hair which was thick and lustrous and swept up into a perfect chignon. Carys also couldn't help noticing the most exquisite amethyst broach she was wearing - its jewels winking darkly at her.

'Very pleased to meet you,' Carys said with a smile. 'Your grace,' she added quickly. Oh, dear. Had she lost brownie points even before sitting down to lunch?

'And you,' her grace said simply, quietly and with very little emotion as she shook Carys's hand.

'Great,' Richard said, clapping his hands together as if thrilled that the formalities were over. 'Shall we go in to lunch?'

The duke and duchess led the way into the private dining room which was a simple room by the standards of Amberley. It looked warm and inviting with its enormous raspberry-coloured rug and red and gold flocked wallpaper and, as everywhere else in the house - just as Richard had told her - there were a number of portraits gazing down at the room, as though the Bretton ancestors didn't like to miss a trick so made sure the whole house was covered between them.

The duke pulled out a chair for his wife and Richard mirrored his actions by pulling one out for Carys.

'Well,' Richard said awkwardly, as he sat down. 'This is nice, isn't it?'

The duchess gave a tight smile and the duke mumbled something that Carys didn't quite hear.

'Are the girls not coming?' Carys asked Richard quietly.

'No. They're eating with Nanny.'

'Oh,' Carys said, wondering if that was the norm. Not that she particularly fancied having the cool eyes of Cecily upon her whilst she ate her lunch but she instinctively felt that the sooner she made an effort to get to know Richard's daughters, the better.

She let her eyes glance around the room with its fine portraits and beautiful lamps and vases. And this was the least grand dining room at Amberley.

'It's a beautiful room,' she enthused.

The duke grunted a response and the duchess merely glanced to the side as if to look at it for the first time. Perhaps they had stopped seeing the great beauty of their surroundings after having lived there for so long. Yet Richard seemed so in love with the place - showing it off to her as if he'd just stumbled across it himself and was desperate to share his new discovery.

'I love all the portraits,' she continued enthusiastically. 'Who's he?' she asked, pointing to a gentleman above the fireplace. 'He's very handsome.'

The duke coughed and shifted in his seat and Carys noticed that the duchess was blushing. Oh, dear. Had she put her foot in it again?

She turned to Richard for help and saw that he was smirking.

'He's James, Marquess of Amberley. He became the seventh duke.'

'It's such a lovely portrait,' she said, looking at the pale, pensive face, the dark expressive eyes, and the proud way he held his head. 'Shouldn't it be in one of the public rooms?'

The duke's eyebrows rose in horror.

Richard cleared his throat. 'Bit of a naughty boy, the seventh duke. Had three mistresses that we know about - probably had a few more tucked away behind his wife's back, and disgraced himself by getting into a fight in the House of Lords over somebody else's wife.'

'Terrible business,' the duke said, jowls wobbling in consternation. 'Reprehensible fellow.'

'But the public *adore* that kind of story. You should definitely have his portrait in a prominent place. It would be of no end of interest to visitors. And get some postcards printed too. I'd buy one.'

The duchess gave a little smile.

'Wouldn't you?'

The duchess blinked at Carys's direct question.

'I mean, it would be a fine memento. You know - interesting.'

'What line of work are you in?' the duchess asked.

Carys wondered if it was to change the subject quickly or to find out if she was in marketing and really did know what she was talking about.

'I'm a PA at Gyland and Green.'

'Good company,' the duke announced.

'And do you enjoy your work?'

'Yes,' Carys said, wondering if the duchess was laying some kind of trap. 'They're good people.'

'And won't you miss it?'

Carys frowned. 'What do you mean?'

'When you marry Richard, won't you miss your job?'

'I don't understand-'

'Mother,' Richard cut in. 'Can't we talk about something else? I'm sure Carys doesn't want to talk about work.'

'It's all right, Richard. I don't mind.'

The duchess gave Richard a look that seemed to say, *mother knows best, dear.*

'Do you mean,' Carys began, turning to her future mother-in-law, 'that I should give up my job once I'm married?'

The duchess seemed surprised that she should be asked such a question. 'Why, of course. I think you'll find that Amberley Court is very much a full-time job in itself.'

'Mother-'

'And then there's Cecily and Evelyn, and-'

'MOTHER!'

Carys and the duchess both turned to face Richard.

'It's all right, Richard. She won't put me off, you know.'

'My dear,' the duchess said, but there was no warmth in her use of the phrase, 'that wasn't my intention at all. I was merely making you aware of the enormity of the position you're taking on. If only somebody had warned me about it, I might have been better prepared.'

The duke raised his eyebrows at his wife's assertion.

'I'm sure Carys will be absolutely fine - whatever decision she makes.'

It was then that lunch was served and the conversation turned to less provocative subjects. Carys, for the most part, sat listening and nodding politely, observing her future in-laws and wondering how on earth they'd managed to produce a son like Richard.

'This has been the most surprising day of my life,' Carys said as she and Richard took a pathway which led out of Amberley Court's main garden and straight up a hill.

'I'm sorry if things have been rather overwhelming.'

Carys's eyebrows rose a full inch. '*Rather*,' she repeated, beginning to realise that he was the master of understatement. 'I feel as if I've landed on a different planet.'

'Planet Amberley,' he said calmly. 'Now you see what I have to put up with all the time.'

She gave a little smile as they began climbing the hill.

'And now you see why I'm desperate for someone to share it with.'

'Desperate?' Carys said, stopping at his choice of word.

'That came out wrong,' he said. 'I sometimes feel desperate. It can be pretty lonely here. But I wouldn't take just anyone on, you know.' He took a step closer towards her and took her hands in his. 'Amberley might feel a little empty every now and then but it would be very foolish of me to grab the nearest girl and lock her away there for my entertainment.' He paused. 'It's been a long time since I felt this way about anyone and, more than anything, I want it to work.'

Carys looked up at him. His dark eyes looked full of hope.

'I want it to work too,' she said, tightening her fingers around his. For a moment, they just gazed at one another, their hands, their eyes, seeming to speak for them.

'I won't pretend I'm not terrified of your parents,' Carys said at last. 'And I won't pretend that taking on the role of mother doesn't scare me witless, but I'm willing to give it a go - for you.'

The smile he gave her filled her body with a wave of pure happiness and, suddenly, they were kissing.

The sun had found its way out of a cloudy morning and was pouring its blessing upon the perfect summer garden and making Amberley Court glow in golden hues, but Richard and Carys saw none of it. They didn't see the early summer roses or the swans upon the lake. They didn't notice the brilliant green of the freshly mown lawns. Nor did they see two little faces peering out of a bedroom window at the top of the house. Both were staring straight up the hill towards the kissing couple but only one of them was smiling.

CHAPTER 7

'WOW!' Louise screamed when she saw Carys's ring for the first time - a perfect oval sapphire whose blue depths seemed to speak of the sea. It was surrounded by five large diamonds which gave it the appearance of a flower.

She held Carys's hand up to the light for inspection. 'That's some jewel.'

'I know,' Carys said, almost feeling guilty for having the audacity to actually wear it.

'I thought you'd end up with some terrible hand-me-down or something. You know - one of those perfectly tiny Victorian rings which are so cute but don't really cut the mustard.'

'Me too.'

Louise sighed. 'Either it's true love or true lunacy.'

'Louise! How can you say that?'

'Because you love your job and your home and now, suddenly, you're giving both up.'

'But I'm getting married. I can't expect my life to stay the same. Anyway, I've been told there's a full-time job for me to walk into there. It's all rather exciting and I'm ready for a change and I really love Amberley. The thought of working there-'

'But it's monstrous!'

'It's beautiful and, anyway, I can hardly expect Richard to move into my house, can I? There's hardly any room for one person.'

Louise shook her head. 'This is all so strange. I feel like I'm losing you.'

'You're not losing me, silly.'

'The office won't be the same without you.'

Carys nodded, wondering if she'd be the same without the office. It had been a daunting decision to leave her job but Richard assured her that she'd have one at Amberley. But that was an unknown quantity. What if she didn't like it? What if she couldn't do it?

'I'm going to miss you lot too. But I'll be sure to visit,' Carys said. 'And you must visit me. I'm going to get lonely in that big old house

43

all day.'

'Rubbish,' Louise said, leaning back and wiping her tear-stained cheek. 'You'll be so busy, you won't have time to think about your old life or friends at all.'

'That's not true,' Carys protested.

But, as the wedding approached, she began to wonder if Louise was right. That was the trouble with weddings: they were so time consuming. Or, rather, family were. There were just so many Brettons to meet.

'Where shall I begin?' Richard said. 'It's going to be chaos. Everybody's in a different part of the globe at the moment. Phoebe's in France; Jamie's backpacking in Eastern Europe and Serena's in China.'

'What's she doing there?'

'God knows,' Richard said. 'Serena stuff, no doubt.'

Carys frowned, wondering what that entailed.

'You'll find out what I mean when you meet her.'

And Carys did. She tried very hard not to gawp at her first sighting of Serena Bretton but it wasn't easy. She had short hair cut pixie-style which glowed a dark purple and sported a tiny diamond stud in her nose. Her face was as pale as a Romantic poet's and her eyes were as large and dark as sloes. In fact, she was the spitting image of Francesca when she'd been young - apart from the choice of hair colour and the positioning of her diamond.

She was wearing a slouchy jumper big enough to camp out in and a tiny skirt which just peeped out from under it. Big biker boots completed the look.

'Carys, meet Serena, my littlest sister. Serena, this is Carys.'

'Hello,' Carys said warmly.

'Hi,' Serena said, stepping forward to shake her hand. She had tiny, child-like hands which were decorated with enormous silver rings. Carys couldn't help thinking how unlike a *Serena* she seemed. You imagined someone tall and elegant with a perfect chestnut bob and twin set, not this half waif, half biker chick.

Richard's younger brother, Jamie, was the next sibling whom Carys met. At twenty-four, he was slightly thinner than his brother, had the same dark hair and dark eyes that seemed to be the Bretton family trait but he didn't have that polish which Richard seemed to have. Richard was terribly old-fashioned in his dress: favouring the country tweed and wax look. In fact, Richard's clothes added a good ten-years to him but Carys didn't mind. She liked that look. It was somehow comforting. But there was no mistaking that Jamie was still a man in his early twenties: he wore the latest jeans and a T-shirt with some scary-looking band emblazoned across it.

Richard had told Carys that Serena and Jamie were as thick as thieves. Growing up, he'd said, it had been him and Phoebe, and Jamie and Serena who'd bonded, rather than the usual boy-girl split.

Carys couldn't wait to meet Phoebe. She'd heard so much about her from Richard. But, despite being the sibling in a country closest to England, Phoebe was the last to arrive home. Carys saw her taxi pull up at the front door and noticed the smile that suddenly sprang onto Richard's face.

'Phoebe!' Richard shouted, running out of the front door and clamping his arms around his sister.

Carys watched in amazement as they stood hugging one another, a happy tangle of limbs, their laughter bouncing off the golden stone of Amberley's porch.

'God, it's good to see you,' Richard laughed.

'It's good to be home. Honestly, Richie, I couldn't get away fast enough when I heard your news.'

'Phoebe,' Richard said, finally disengaging himself. 'Come and meet Carys.'

'Carys?' Phoebe all but yelled across the driveway. And Carys suddenly found herself the recipient of a bear hug.

'It's so good to meet you,' Phoebe said, leaning back so that Carys could get a good look at her. She had the same porcelain skin and dark eyes as her mother and sister and her hair was dark and left to spring around her shoulders in gentle waves. But she had the most wonderful expression. She positively glittered with enthusiasm and Carys found it completely infectious.

'I can't believe Richie's found someone brave enough to take him on,' Phoebe said, leaning in towards Carys and whispering conspiratorially. 'You do know what you're letting yourself in for, don't you?'

Carys smiled. 'I think so.'

'Well, anyway, I'm here now. So I'll make sure he looks after you.'

'You're staying?' Richard asked, carrying his sister's bags into the house.

'For a while. Until I decide what to do next.'

'That's my family for you,' he told Carys. 'They're like homing pigeons. They fly off into the world but, invariably, return to Amberley.'

'I don't see the point of a family owning a place like this if they can't make use of it,' Phoebe said.

'Me too,' Carys said. 'and I'll be glad to have your company.'

'Anyway, that's your role, big bro.'

'To stay at home and work like a dog whilst the rest of you swan off round the world?'

'Absolutely,' Phoebe laughed. 'It's only fair.'

'How on earth do you work that out?'

'Because you get to inherit all this one day. So, I figure, you've got to earn it.'

Richard shook his head as he led the way through the hallway into the family drawing room. Phoebe linked arms with Carys and sighed.

'It's so good to be back!' She craned her head back and grinned with delight. 'You know, it's the silly things you miss when you've been away.'

'You make it sound as if you've been to the moon,' Richard teased.

'France is far enough from Amberley for me, thank you very much.'

'What did you miss?' Carys asked, curious to know.

Phoebe smiled. 'The smell of old wellies in the hallway. The curve of the driveway and the first view of Amberley you get. The copies of *Cuthland Life* in the downstairs loo.'

Carys laughed.

'And DIZZY!' Phoebe suddenly shouted as the dog sprinted through the room, tail cork-spiralling out of control in excitement. And Carys could see now why she'd been given that name. She was full of life and warmth and enthusiasm - just like her owner.

Richard and Carys watched in delight as Phoebe cavorted with Dizzy on the floor. It was hard to tell who was the more excited.

'Now, I really feel as if I'm home,' Phoebe said, smiling up from the carpet, a wild tail whacking her in the face.

CHAPTER 8

For somebody who'd never envisioned being a bride, Carys hadn't done too badly: there were over six hundred guests in Carminster Cathedral, and a huge crowd of locals and tourists outside to see what was happening.

Arriving in an beautiful Rolls Royce Silver Ghost, her good friend, Duncan, the man who was giving her away, suddenly forgot his own nerves and became a pillar of strength, leading her to the great west door where she had no less than five bridesmaids: Richard's sisters, Phoebe and Serena, her best friend, Louise, and Richard's two daughters, Cecily and Evelyn, all wearing dresses the colour of bluebells in a floaty fabric which danced in the slightest breeze. Their bouquets were full of blush-pink summer roses and Cecily and Evie wore pretty halos of matching roses.

For five minutes, they all just stared, smiling and cooing at their collective beauty.

'Hey!' Duncan said at last. 'Shouldn't we be getting married?'

Dresses were quickly fluffed, trains and tiaras straightened and smiles were fixed into place. And then it began - the slow walk.

A bride, she'd read in one of the many magazines she'd leafed through over the past weeks, should have no misgivings when walking down the aisle towards her husband-to-be. Carys took a deep breath. How many had she counted the night before? She was worried about leaving her job, worried about becoming a second wife, worried about her new role as a step-mother, worried about her role as daughter-in-law to the formidable duke and duchess, worried about being able to fit in at Amberley, and worried about her future role as marchioness and duchess. How many was that? One, two, three, four, five, SIX! Oh, dear! Was that normal or should she turn and run? Surely it was too late now. There were over six hundred pairs of eyes watching her.

A comforting pat on the hand from Duncan restored a little of her faith. Had he felt her panic there for a moment?

Carys didn't dare look at anything but the few feet of aisle in front of her. She only knew a handful of people anyway as her family was so small. There'd be her mother and Aunt Josephine somewhere at the front and a handful of cousins she hadn't seen for years. There were plenty of people from the office, of course, but it was a bit of a poor turnout when you compared her guests to those who'd been on Richard's list. She'd never seen so many titles in her life. There were dukes and duchesses, earls and countesses, barons and honorables, lords and ladies. It was a whole level of society she had no knowledge of. Seeing them all now via periphery vision, she wondered how many Richard actually knew or, more to the point, how many he actually liked. Did they all get on or was there some unwritten code which stated that you couldn't have a wedding without them? She knew that only a select few of them would be coming back to Amberley for the reception and dinner but it seemed like an extraordinary waste of money to Carys. She would have been quite happy with a simple ceremony for their nearest and dearest but, apparently, that wasn't fitting for a future duke and duchess.

But it was a beautiful ceremony. It may have passed by in a blur of happiness but Carys would never forget the look of tenderness in Richard's eyes or the smell of the lilies by the altar. She'd never forget the gentle way he placed the slim gold ring on her finger or the way he kissed her so sweetly when they were pronounced husband and wife.

After that, it was back to Amberley where there was a reception in the Great Hall. The florist had created great billowing displays of pink and white roses and the cavernous space smelt heavenly.

Richard took her arm and led her upstairs to the Long Gallery. The room was alive with lilies and roses, and candles had been lit, their light reflecting in the crystal glasses. Carys had never seen anything so beautiful. She sat down with Richard and watched as the guests found their seats. Excited chatter filled the room and her eyes travelled the length of the table. She surprised herself by remembering quite a few of the faces that she'd greeted as they'd arrived. There was the gentleman who'd fondled her fingers. There was the woman who'd complimented her on her dress. And there was the little old lady in indigo. What was it she'd told Carys? She frowned. Think. It was something ridiculous. Something which had almost made her laugh out loud. Ah, yes, she remembered.

'You know why the last one left, don't you?'

Carys had responded with a look of puzzlement.

'She was scared off,' the old lady had said, a glint of mischief in her eyes.

Carys felt sure the old lady meant that Amanda hadn't been able to cope with being mistress of such a huge house. But she hadn't.

'She was *haunted out!*' the old lady had said. 'Amberley Court is haunted, you know.'

CHAPTER 9

Dear Diary

I've never kept a diary before in my life but, seeing as this was a wedding present from Francesca, I've decided to give it a go.

I still find it hard to believe that I'm a married woman. After a wedding night in the West Turret Bedroom at Amberley - another Bretton tradition - we journeyed up to the Highlands to Glentorran Lodge. It was wonderful if chilly. I was trying desperately not to think of girlfriends who've honeymooned in Barbados, the Seychelles and Hawaii, and content myself with miles of violet heather and a wind that did its best to skin me alive. And I tried not to think about scuba diving in crystal waters and sunbathing on sugared sand, and threw myself into ten-mile hikes.

When we got back to Amberley, we were greeted by Cecily and Evie. I say greeted, but I still haven't experienced anything approaching warmth with Cecily. Evie is an absolute sweetheart, though, and presented me with a beautiful bunch of flowers from the estate.

It's taken me a while to settle in because I'm still not sure how I'm to fit in at Amberley. Richard and I have our quarters and the duke and duchess have theirs but there doesn't seem to be any guidelines as to what to do about the space in between. It's not as though I'd wander around the house in my nightie, and I know it's best to avoid the public rooms when they're open but I don't feel entirely comfortable using the other rooms. The Yellow Drawing Room off the hallway is fine. I don't feel that I have to be on my best behaviour there, sitting ramrod straight in case Richard's mother walks in. I don't know what it is about her but she makes me feel slightly - maybe I shouldn't say. It might be wrong to write down my true feelings about her in a diary she bought for me. She might feel she has the right to read it and then I'll be discovered!!!

Carys closed the diary and stretched her arms and got up from the sofa where she'd been writing and walked over to the window which looked out towards the woods at the back of Amberley Court.

The house was curiously quiet and Carys wondered if it was always like this. The girls were with their tutor for their lessons and Richard's brother and sisters had also vanished, and she'd seen very little of Richard's parents too which was a shame because she'd really hoped that she'd bond with Francesca and that she'd give her some sort of informal induction into the business of being a new wife at Amberley. But it was clear that they were to lead separate lives under the same enormous roof.

Looking out of the window, the sun smiling down from a clear blue sky, Carys thought she'd do some exploring - outside. Richard had given her a quick tour of the estate after returning from Scotland but it wouldn't be quite the same as exploring it herself. He'd also told her she should spend her first few weeks redecorating their private apartments but she didn't feel like flicking through magazines and catalogues today. It was the sort of day that demanded you spent it outdoors and, venturing downstairs, she determined to do just that.

She was just wondering if she should put on a pair of boots when Mrs Travis, the housekeeper walked into the hallway.

'Good morning, Lady Amberley.'

Carys winced slightly at the use of her title. She still hadn't got used to it.

'Good morning,' she replied trying, at least, to sound like a lady even if she didn't yet feel like one.

'Lord Amberley thought, perhaps, you might like to take charge of the dog walking, my lady. If you were going outside?'

'Dog walking?' Carys exclaimed. She hadn't planned on that. She'd just wanted a nice little stroll around the estate.

'Yes,' Mrs Travis went on. 'There are five dogs and they like two or three good walks a day and-'

'*Five?*' Carys said, feeling very much like Maria in *The Sound of Music* when she's told how many Von Trapp children she'll be looking after. She'd heard about the great number of dogs the Brettons had but had conveniently forgotten about them. They were, she assumed, somebody else's responsibility.

'Lord Amberley thought it would be most enjoyable for you.'

'He did, did he?' she said. What a coward he was, she thought. He hadn't dared raise the subject with her directly because he'd known she'd have shot him down. 'But I don't have that many hands. How will I hold on to them all?' she asked, imagining a circus of crazy arms as she struggled to control five hounds.

'You don't need leads. Just take them out into the park. They'll follow wherever you take them but be sure they don't get into the deer park, especially Dolly. She likes to bolt every now and then. Here,' Mrs Travis said, digging into a voluminous pocket, 'take this whistle.'

Carys looked down at the tiny metal object which was her only means of controlling five unruly dogs.

'I've never owned a dog.'

'Don't worry, you'll be fine. It's a piece of cake.'

Carys gave a nervous smile, thinking she'd sooner stay indoors with a piece of cake.

'And Lord A thought it would be an excellent way to get to know the estate,' Mrs Travis added, seeing that Carys needed further encouragement. 'Badger, that's the black and white cocker, is getting on a bit now and might lag behind but he's fine. Just let him go at his own pace. Foxy, the golden cocker has a habit of trying to disappear down rabbit holes. Thinks she's a terrier. Drag her out by her collar. Dizzy's no bother - runs ahead and does her own spaniel thing, and Mungo, the Labrador, is an angel. He'd walk by your side if you took him over hot coals.'

Carys took a deep breath. 'So,' she said, 'where are they?'

Without any warning, Mrs Travis suddenly yelled, 'DOGGIES!' and the thunderous sound of paws across floorboards was heard. Where they'd all been, Carys could only guess but they knew Mrs Travis's voice when they heard it and were standing in the hallway at full attention in no time.

'Right,' Carys said. 'Dolly, Dizzy, Badger, Foxy and Mungo,' she said, pointing out to each of her new walking companions in turn. 'Sure there aren't any more?'

'Not at the moment but you never can tell. His grace has been thinking about getting a couple of pointers but-'

'Good heavens, I was joking!'

'And I hope his grace is too. He has no idea how much they all cost to keep. Oh, that reminds me,' she said, turning around to dig her hand into a metal container on a small console table by the door, 'you'd better take some of these.'

'What are they?'

'Treats - for the dogs. If you need to call them back.'

'What do I do with them?'

'Pop them in your pocket there,' she said, picking a weather-beaten jacket from the enormous coat rail by the door. 'You'd better wear this. It's going to rain later.'

Carys grimaced as she was handed the dog treats. Pockets were for crisp white tissues and an emergency lipstick, not smelly dog biscuits.

'What if I get lost?'

Mrs Travis smiled and gave a short laugh. 'You can see the house for miles. I don't think you'll get lost. But, just in case, you'd better take this.' She turned around and opened a drawer in the console table. 'Here,' she said, giving her one of the maps they sold in the gift shop. 'You can't go far wrong with this, my lady.'

Leaving Amberley far behind her, Carys's strides became longer and more confident and she breathed in the air as if it were made for her alone.

Mrs Travis was right: Amberley could be seen for miles and was beautiful from every angle. Carys couldn't stop looking at it, hardly daring to believe that this was her new home. She also couldn't stop looking at her watch. It was ten o'clock on a Tuesday morning. Just a few weeks ago, she would have been stuck in the office at Gyland and Green with no hope of a reprieve until lunchtime. Now, here she was, a mistress of her own time.

As soon as they were out of the house, the four spaniels had taken charge, bolting through the garden towards the hill that led to the wood above Amberley. Carys was happy to follow with Mungo, the black Labrador, for company.

'They seem to know where they're going,' she said to herself.

As she climbed, Amberley became smaller and smaller. She unfolded the map of the grounds and peered at the criss-cross of footpaths and then wended her way through the wood. The path was wide, soft and silent and the woods were filled with birdsong. She wished Richard was with her and, for a moment, wondered which part of the estate he was on. He always got up so early and yet there still didn't seem to be enough time in the day for them to be together. The relaxed husband she'd briefly been allowed to see on their honeymoon had vanished and had been replaced by a workaholic.

As she looked down from the woods, she saw the beautiful stretch of river which passed through the Amberley estate before wending its way down the valley into Carminster.

She walked on. The woods appeared to be never-ending and seemed to suck her deep within them until she forgot about everything but the rhythm of her feet and the sweetness of the air she breathed. She passed by a clearing where a great white statue of William, the ninth Duke of Cuthland, stood proudly surveying the view. At another clearing, there was a statue of Diana, the huntress, her arms laced with fungi as if she were trying, desperately, to melt away into the wood. And, every now and then, she caught a glimpse of Amberley through the trees. It was about the size of a doll's house now, but it wasn't until a full hour later that Carys stopped walking.

Standing perfectly still for a moment, gazing down at the river below which was a bright emerald with the reflections of the summer trees, she suddenly panicked. Where was she? She felt she'd been out for hours. Only Mungo remained by her side. She'd caught glimpses of the other dogs every so often. They were never very far away and she was relieved that they hadn't taken advantage of her inexperience to do a runner. Perhaps, though, she'd better gather them all together.

Feeling in her pocket for the little whistle, Carys held it to her lips and blew lightly. The result was very impressive. Dolly, the black and white springer, was the first to appear, her legs soaking wet and her belly splattered with mud. Dizzy, Phoebe's liver and white springer, was next, her ears and coat looking as if it had collected the remains of last year's autumn leaf fall.

'Where are the other two?' Carys asked them as if they might tell her.

Then, with a sudden crash from the undergrowth as if a wild boar were about to charge, Foxy surfaced, golden but dishevelled and, thankfully, Badger followed closely behind, looking thoroughly non-plussed by everything. Carys was thankful for small mercies. She would have hated to have lost one of Richard's precious dogs on her first walk but she didn't want to count her blessings too soon: they still had the walk back to go.

And she really did intend to go straight back to the house but, on the way down the hill, the sky darkened and great fat raindrops fell from the heavens. Was it worth running the rest of the way, risking a soaking? Carys decided it wasn't and sheltered as best as she could under the canopy of the oaks at the edge of the wood, the dogs happy to sniff and poke their noses into the foliage for a while. She didn't time the shower but, once it was over, she caught sight of a path which ran along the edge of the wood away from the house and couldn't resist finding out where it went.

'Come on, dogs,' she called and they instantly ran on ahead of her, delighted with their extended walk.

It wasn't long before Carys saw a tiny cottage. Built from the same mellow gold stone that Amberley was built from, it looked like something from a fairytale and Carys was instantly captivated. Even more exciting, it looked lived in. She saw a pair of candy-striped curtains in the window and the front door, painted a sunny yellow, was wide open.

Should she? This was, after all, private property. But, then again, wasn't it her role to find out about the estate and introduce herself? Or was that just a new excuse for her incurable nosiness? Louise had already teased her, saying she'd only married Richard so that she could have a good nose around the private quarters of Amberley Court.

She was just about to do the decent thing and head back when she heard the unmistakable crackle of a fire from behind the cottage. As she ventured around the back, the heat hit her and she smiled. Here was a chance to warm up a bit, maybe even dry off a little.

Branches snapped in the depths of the fire and ash butterflies floated down from the air, twisting and turning before disappearing into nothing on the ground. What was it about fires that was so mesmeric? Carys became so completely absorbed by the movement of the flames which seemed to have survived the recent downpour that the sudden interruption of a voice startled her.

'Can I help you?' a voice, filled with the softened syllables of the Cuthland countryside, asked.

Carys turned and came face to face with a stout man wearing green from head to foot.

'I'm sorry,' Carys said automatically, knowing that she had trespassed even though she was now part of the family that owned the estate.

'My lady?' the green man asked.

'Carys,' she said, 'please.' She stepped forward and extended her hand which was taken and shaken with alacrity.

'Begging your pardon, my lady, but I didn't recognise you.'

'I guess I do look a state, don't I?' Carys laughed.

'Not at all,' the man said, looking mortified that he might have offended her. 'It was the coat,' he explained.

'Oh, yes. It's a terrible coat, isn't it?' Carys smiled down at the coat which Mrs Travis had picked out for her.

'It was mine,' he said.

Carys instantly blushed. 'Oh, I'm sorry. I didn't mean-'

The man grinned. 'It's okay, my lady. I've owned many terrible coats in my time. It's an occupational hazard.'

Carys's eyebrows raised.

'I'm the head gardener.'

'Oh.'

'It's hard to keep things tidy when wrestling with rhododendrons or shifting compost.'

Carys smiled. There were some people in life that you knew you were going to like immediately and this head gardener was one of them.

'I'm Charles Brodie, my lady. But most people call me Ash.'

'Ash,' she repeated. 'Is that because you're always tending bonfires?'

'I reckon it could be. That or the fact that my hair's been grey since my early twenties.'

Carys blinked. He looked to be in his late forties now. 'Really?'

He nodded. 'Bad genes and a wife who left me after two weeks might've done it.'

'Oh, dear.'

'Still, mustn't grumble,' he said. 'I have this place and I'm happy here. No place in the world like Amberley. Expect you'll be feeling that way before long, my lady?'

She smiled. 'It's funny,' she said, 'but I already feel like I've been here forever.'

'Amberley worked its magic on you already? It gets under your skin and stays there.'

'That's what Richard says. Er - Lord Amberley.'

'Ay. He's an Amberley advocate through and through. Couldn't have a better boss than he. And his grace, of course. 'Though I reckon he could manage without the place sometimes.'

'You do?'

Ash nodded. 'Don't mean to speak out of term, like, but he's never seemed quite happy here.'

Carys thought about the bad-tempered old man who was now her father-in-law.

'I think you're right,' she said. 'I think his grace could easily be happier somewhere else but Rich- Lord Amberley - well, I don't think he'd know how to exist anywhere else. He was bad enough on our honeymoon,' she said, and then wondered if she should be confessing such things to a member of staff.

Ash nodded again as if he understood.

A sudden crack from the bonfire made Carys realise that time was passing. 'I suppose I'd better gather up the dogs and get back. It's been a pleasure meeting you.'

'You too, my lady.'

'*Carys*,' she laughed. 'Nobody will call me Carys anymore.'

Ash gave a little grin and then said, 'I think you should have something.'

'What?' Carys watched as he nipped into the cottage and came out carrying an old tweed cap.

'Here,' he said. 'It's a bit dusty, like, but it might help if it rains again, and I think it will before the hour's out.'

'Thank you,' Carys said, genuinely touched by his gesture. 'I'll bring it back.'

Ash shook his head. 'I've got dozens of them. It's all anyone ever buys me for Christmas.'

Carys tried not to laugh.

'Be nice to see you again, my lady.'

She looked at his kindly face and saw, at once, a man who was sweet and sincere, and desperately lonely.

Leaving Ash's cottage, the sun burst forth from the sky and Carys saw the lake in the distance, twinkling with diamonds of light. It looked so beautiful that she couldn't resist taking a closer look. The dogs, delighted with an extension of their extension, ran ahead, tails wagging wildly.

What a wonderful place Amberley was, Carys thought as she walked around the edge of the lake, watching the swallows skim over the water. In one morning, she'd walked up hills, through woods, crossed a river, seen statues and was now walking around a lake that was too beautiful for words. Time had evaporated and she was completely at ease with the world but all that was about to change.

Thinking it best she made her way back before she was reported a missing person, Carys headed back just as the skies decided to repeat their earlier shower. Cursing the fickleness of English summers, and placing Ash's cap on her head, Carys made a dash for it, the five dogs quickly catching on and sprinting like maniacs across the emerald lawn towards the house.

Once there, she fumbled for her key to the door at the back of the house. It was far away from the prying eyes of tourists but there would always be some cheeky visitor who thought the *private* signs didn't apply to them and would try their luck if a door was left ajar so it was always locked.

Taking off the cap and shaking her head, dog-like, as she entered the hallway, she closed the door behind her and carefully counted the dogs to make sure she hadn't lost any.

'Blimey,' she laughed. 'We'd better find some towels.'

Foxy's pale gold coat had turned to the colour of burnt butterscotch. Badger, Dolly and Dizzy's long fur was plastered to their bodies, their feathered legs and ears hanging long and limply, whilst Mungo's dark coat shone as if polished.

Carys dreaded to think what she looked like. There was no mirror in the hallway but she didn't have to wait long to find out because Richard strode towards her, his angry feet echoing around the enormous walls.

'Richard!' she called across to him. 'We've had the most amazing walk. You wouldn't believe-'

'Look at you!' he blurted.

'I know,' Carys said, beaming. 'We got caught in the rain - twice!'

'I didn't mean that,' he said.

Carys frowned.

'Your hair! It's all scraped back. You've got no make-up on. And look at your clothes.'

'What do you mean?'

He shook his head, his face a picture of utter bewilderment. 'There's been a change in you, Carys. You used to dress like a woman but now you look like a man.'

Carys felt herself blushing to the very roots of her being.

'And what the hell is this?' he asked, snatching the cap from her hand.

'Ash gave it to me.'

'Who?'

'Ash - the head gardener.'

'Brodie? Charles Brodie?'

Carys nodded. 'I got caught in the rain and didn't have a hood on so he gave it to me.'

Richard looked at it in distaste. 'It's disgusting. It should be incinerated.'

Carys dared to snatch it back from her husband. 'It's soft as new fleece and twice as warm,' she said quietly.

'It makes you look like a refuse collector.'

Carys's eyes shot an angry glance at Richard. 'I suppose you expect me to float around Amberley in designer clothes all day, do you?'

'It would make a pleasant change.'

She turned away from him. She'd never seen him so angry and wasn't sure how to respond.

'I've been worried sick about you, Carys. Where have you been?'

'What do you mean, where have I been? I've been out walking your dogs as per your instructions.'

'For four hours?'

'I kind of lost track of time. Anyway, they obviously needed the walk or else they'd have complained.'

'Those dogs are gundogs - they'd walk day and night for a week if you tried them. Which walk did you do?'

'What do you mean?'

'The lake? The woods? The ridge?'

'All of them. We did all of those.'

'Good grief! No wonder you've been out all day.'

'But you said I should try to get to know the estate.'

'Well, you must know every inch of every acre by now,' he said. 'And where was your mobile?'

'I don't have a mobile,' Carys said. 'My last one broke.'

'But I bought you a new one, don't you remember?'

Suddenly, she did.

'In a place this size, you've got to be contactable.'

She nodded. She felt like a naughty school girl who was on the verge of being expelled for very bad behaviour.

'I'm sorry,' she said, not because she felt particularly sorry but because she wanted an end to this conversation and thought, in his present mood, that apologising was the only way she was going to be able to do it.

It seemed to work because Richard nodded. 'You haven't

forgotten dinner at seven thirty? It's the representative from Cuthland Heritage.'

Great, Carys thought. Just what she was looking forward to: an evening with a stuffy suit talking about renovations.

'You might want to rethink your outfit,' Richard said, somewhat cruelly, Carys thought, but she didn't say anything as he left her standing in the hallway, her hair dripping down her back.

'Don't worry, dear,' Mrs Travis said to her as they shared a pot of tea later that day. 'He's just being territorial. I've seen it before with the Bretton men. They like to make their presence felt, you know? They like to show their new wives who's boss. It's all just noise and nonsense. Don't you let him worry you.'

But Carys couldn't help feeling worried. She felt as if she'd failed already.

CHAPTER 10

The honeymoon was well and truly over, wasn't it? Richard spent most of his time on some far flung corner of the estate, her new in-laws never spoke to her, Louise had been too busy to come up to Amberley over the last few weeks, and Cecily had been a complete nightmare. At first, Carys had been able to cope with the silent treatment she received at the breakfast table each morning. Richard hadn't even noticed it but, to Carys, Cecily's silence was thunderously loud.

'So,' Carys would begin at the breakfast table, her voice filled with an animation she didn't particularly feel. 'What are you girls up to today?'

'We have reading first,' Evie said. 'Then spelling - yuck! Then Geography then Maths.'

'And what are you reading?' Carys asked, directing the question at Cecily. Cecily looked up and, for a moment, Carys thought she was going to answer but her glance returned to her cornflakes which she stirred with melancholy precision.

'*Little Women*,' Evie chimed.

And that was the end of that conversation.

Carys hadn't expected it to be so heartbreakingly difficult to reach a child but she was determined not to give up. She'd vowed to spend the rest of her life with Richard, and Cecily was his daughter so there was no getting away from her.

As if that wasn't enough to be worrying about, there'd been the voice she'd heard in the night. It had been the first time she'd ventured further than the ensuite bathroom. Richard had told her to take a torch if she ever left the bedroom as a minimal number of lights were left on in an attempt to keep the hefty annual electricity bill down. Carys had cursed her raging thirst as her body became chilled to the bone in next to no time, goose bumps sprouting like a relief map of the Himalayas all over her body even though it was summer.

Life had been so simple in her Victorian terrace. It took only seconds to get from room to room but, in Amberley Court, it could take hours to find the right room or days if you were unlucky enough to take a wrong turning and found yourself in one of the wings you hadn't explored before; and there were plenty of them.

'Left, right, straight down the corridor with the china cabinets and it's the door with the dodgy handle,' Carys whispered to herself as her torch beam shone ahead of her. If only she could stop her torch from casually swinging upwards and picking out mounted deer heads or anxious ancestors hanging on the walls.

Never again, Carys thought as she recalled her expedition to the kitchen. After that, she'd make sure she never forgot to take a glass of water to bed with her.

It had been a night ripe for ghostly experiences, she thought: there'd been a rotund moon which had shone through the kitchen window and, in the distance, she'd heard a rumble of thunder.

She could just imagine telling her grandchildren. She'd be sat in the great winged chair she'd taken a fancy to in the Red Drawing Room. There'd be a full blazing fire and the room would be warm and cosy because they'd have sorted out all the draughty old windows by the time she was in her dotage. Her grandchildren would be angelic of face and crossed of leg, their wide eyes fixed on her creamy complexion - miraculously uncreased by time, and her hair retaining its golden sheen despite her advancing years.

But it wasn't her resilient beauty which would captivate them; it was her skills as a storyteller.

'There was a full moon that night,' she'd begin. 'It was hidden by clouds when I first ventured out of bed but, once in the kitchen, it fair blinded me!'

'Tell us about the storm, Nana.'

'Oh yes,' she'd say. 'When I looked out of the window, a fork of lightning cracked the sky in two and the thunder - well, when it rumbled, I could feel it in my very belly.'

'And then you heard the voice, didn't you?' their eager voices pressed.

'Indeed. That's when the lady first spoke to me.'

But it wasn't, was it, Carys thought now? She was positive she'd heard the voice before. The lady, for it was certainly a lady's voice, had spoken to her in broad daylight. There hadn't been a clouded moon or a ghostly night-time shadow in sight, and the only rumble she'd heard was her tummy as it made a protest for a lunch break.

Thinking about it now made her arms break out in goose bumps. She'd been in the Montella Room, attending one of the Amberley Enterprises' meetings which were held every week. The room, named after the eighteenth century Italian artist, Leo Montella, was full of gorgeous portraits of the Bretton family. Carys's eyes drifted across them. She hadn't quite learned all the names yet but she loved looking at them: all those haughty dukes and their beautiful duchesses, wearing their very finest robes and dresses and posing with graceful ease.

She wondered if she and Richard would ever pose for a portrait. It seemed rare, these days, to have one's portrait done but she found the idea rather romantic. What would she wear? Her ethnic dresses from her favourite boutique seemed wildly inappropriate unless she wanted to be known down the centuries as "the hippie marchioness".

'I don't see how you can possibly think the fountain is more important than the folly,' the duke said.

Carys blinked and tried to pay attention. It was so easy to get distracted by their beautiful surroundings and she pulled her mind back to the meeting. All the important people from the estate attended including dear Ash Brodie, the head gardener. Carys still felt that her role was a very passive one but she was eager to learn and tried her hardest to pay attention.

And that's when she'd heard the voice. They'd been talking about repairing the old stone fountain.

'It has to be made a priority,' the duchess insisted. 'It can't wait any longer.'

'It's waited a hundred years already. I think it can wait a couple more,' the duke retaliated.

'Silly old fool!'

Carys turned around. Who'd said that? Who'd dared to call the duke a silly old fool, even if he was one? It had definitely been a female voice and she and the duchess were the only women there. Well, there was Pearl Janson who was in charge of the shop but she wasn't the sort of woman to shout such things at dukes.

The voice, she thought, had come from behind her but there was nothing there but a large sash window which looked out over the lawn.

Hadn't anybody else heard it?

'I've received several letters about the fountain's state of disrepair,' the duchess complained.

'And I've received several letters of threats to sue if the folly collapses on top of unsuspecting visitors,' the duke replied.

Obviously not. Maybe Carys had imagined it.

'He's such a pompous old windbag!'

Carys almost leapt out of her seat.

'Are you all right,' Richard asked, looking at her with eyes full of annoyance rather than concern.

'Of course I'm all right,' Carys said.

Richard shook his head before returning his attention to his parents once again.

Carys looked around the room. It wasn't her imagination, was it? Perhaps it was Cecily or Evie playing games but, even if they had managed to escape the clutches of their tutor and had found a way into the Montella Room without being observed, surely everybody else would have heard them too?

'These meetings are nothing but a waste of time.'

Carys's eyes widened. The voice was definitely getting louder now.

'Look,' Richard said, 'we should take a vote on how this money is to be spent. It's obvious that you two aren't going to be able to agree,' he said, looking at his parents who sat, stony faced, at either end of the table.

'Those in favour of restoring the folly?'

Four hands shot into the air.

'Those in favour of restoring the fountain?'

Eight hands shot into the air.

'Right. The fountain is to be this year's project. I'll get the wheels turning.'

'About time too. That fountain is an eyesore.'

Carys felt the breath leave her body. Where was the voice coming from?

'Any other business?' Richard asked, the meeting obviously drawing to a close.

'Yes,' she said, suddenly finding her voice.

Eleven pairs of eyes focussed in her direction.

'I think it's time to increase the entrance fee.'

For a moment, the room filled with a stunned silence, as if nobody had dared to mention the ugly business of money before.

'Anyone have any thoughts?' Richard asked.

Again, silence filled the room from its beautifully carpeted floors to its ornate plaster ceiling.

'I agree,' Ash Brodie said at last, nodding from his place at the table. 'Keep in line with the recent increase at Barston.'

Barston Hall, Carys had learned, was Amberley's biggest rival. Just across the border in Eastmoreland, it was known as *Bastard Hall* because of the behaviour of its owner, Roland Buckley-Stewart, The Earl of Eastmoreland. Richard and he had been at boarding school together and, ever since, had been unofficial rivals.

'But Barston has so much more on offer than we do,' Pearl Janson chipped in, her voice squeaky clean like one of the tea towels she sold in the shop. 'Their shop is three times the size of ours and offers so many more quality goods.'

Carys, who had already been sent on a mission as undercover spy, remembered the beautifully wooden-floored shop with its gleaming counter and cute pots of jam, hand-crafted jewellery and exquisite pottery all stamped with the Earl's coat of arms.

'Our stock really should be updated,' Pearl went on hopefully.

'Has anybody else got any comments?' Richard asked, keen to move on.

'I think we should definitely put up the entrance fee,' Pearl said, misguidedly believing that her precious shop would see some more money if more profits were to be made by the Amberley Estate.

'Okay then,' Richard said. 'We'll carry that motion forward.'

Carys's eyes widened. She'd achieved something.

'Is there anything else?'

Eleven pairs of eyes cast down to their laps. Everyone was keen to venture back to their own particular corner of the estate and have a cup of tea.

'Right, see you next week,' Richard said, and everybody got up to leave.

Carys waited behind with Richard who was tidying up the stack of paperwork he'd brought into the meeting with him.

'Well?' she said.

He looked up, his face pale and tired. 'What?'

'Aren't you going to say, well done?'

'The entrance fee should have been increased years ago,' he said.

Carys frowned. He hadn't thought that when she'd mentioned it to him in the walled garden that first time she'd visited Amberley.

'I know,' she said, 'that's why I suggested it.'

He nodded. He was miles away. She had faded into the background once again.

'I'll see you later,' he said.

Would he, she wondered? Would he really see her? Or would it just be a peck on the cheek at bed time before he sunk beneath the duvet in a deep sleep. She watched him leave the room and sighed.

She'd been so angry with Richard that she'd completely forgotten about the strange disembodied voice until the next day.

She'd decided to return to the Montella Room with a copy of the Amberley Court guidebook. There was so much to learn: names, positions, dates of birth, and causes of death, who was related to whom, scandals …

'You can always ask me, you know.'

Carys instantly dropped the guidebook.

'Who said that?'

She looked around the room. She was completely alone. Or so she thought.

'You can't see me, can you?'

'Cecily?' Carys whispered. But she knew it wasn't Cecily. She wouldn't put it past her to play such tricks but the mysterious voice didn't belong to a child.

'Who are you?'

The room suddenly fell silent, broken only by the soft ticking of a clock on the mantelpiece above the fire.

'Where are you?' Carys whispered into the silence. But there was no reply. The voice, or whatever it was Carys had heard, had vanished.

The next time she'd heard it was during the storm in the night, but it hadn't been words that time - the voice had been singing - humming. Carys felt sure that it was the same voice she'd heard in the Montella Room, and she also felt sure that she had to discover exactly who it was.

CHAPTER 11

Who did you turn to when you started hearing voices? Should she tell Richard? Could husbands still have wives locked away for such things? Carys had been on the verge of telling him several times that evening.

'Sweetheart,' she'd begun and he'd looked up from his newspaper and smiled at her encouragingly. It was the first real smile he'd given her all day and she wanted to bathe in it for a while and not turn it into a frown, so she'd said, 'I wish you wouldn't work so hard,' instead of 'I think Amberley might be haunted.'

Later that evening, when they'd been snuggled up on the sofa together, she'd bitten her lip and begun again. 'I was in the Montella Room today and I heard the strangest-'

'*Daddy! Daddy!* Cecily's hidden my doll again,' Evie had shouted, running into the room and leaping onto her father's lap, demanding all his attention.

Then, when they'd gone to bed, she'd said, 'I think there might be a problem.' She'd waited anxiously for Richard's response before continuing.

'Tell me in the morning,' he'd said, kissing her cheek and falling into a deep sleep. Carys had immediately felt guilty. He'd had his share of problems for one day. What right did she have to burden him with another?

So she called Louise.

'But you don't believe in ghosts, Carys,' she said, walking into the grand hallway after work the next day. 'I distinctly remember you saying that all that sort of thing was *absolute twaddle* - to use your technical term.'

Carys blushed as she remembered how quick she'd been to write-off the whole of the spiritual world. 'Yes, but these things always are twaddle until you experience them for yourself.'

Louise considered this for a moment. 'You thought the same thing about the aristocracy, didn't you?'

'All right. Don't rub it in.'

Louise grinned. 'Come on, then, where's this ghost?'

Carys led the way to the Montella Room.

'Wow!' Louise exclaimed. 'Look at this. Look at the size of that table!'

'We have the estate meetings her each week. And this is where I first heard the voice.'

'The woman's voice?'

Carys nodded.

'And what did she say again?'

'That's the strange part. It was really odd things like: *'Silly old fool!'* and *'pompous old windbag!'* And then she said, *'These meetings are nothing but a waste of time.'*

'But nobody else heard the voice,' Louise said.

'I know. It was really strange. The other times I've heard it is when I've been alone so I can't really be sure, you know?'

Louise paced around the room as if looking for something that might prove the ghost existed.

'What's this?' she asked, pointing to a beautifully carved wooden box.

'A knife box,' Carys said without thinking.

'Who's she?' Louise asked, looking up at a painting.

'Georgiana,' Carys said. It was one of the portraits she had managed to commit to memory so far.

'She's very beautiful.'

'Yes, she is,' Carys said, staring at the porcelain pale face and the bewitching smile. The artist, Leo Montella, had definitely caught the sparkle of her eyes.

'Is that her too?' Louise asked.

'Yes,' Carys said. 'There are several portraits of her in the house. She was something of a society beauty.'

'I can see that.'

'Look,' Carys said, remembering that she'd asked Louise there for advice and not to stand around admiring paintings, 'do *you* feel anything peculiar in this room?'

Louise's face furrowed in a serious frown as she concentrated, her eyes surveying the room once again, sweeping over every surface and examining every shadowy corner. 'Nope,' she said at last. 'Absolutely nothing.'

Carys sighed.

'But I think somebody's overdone it with the furniture polish,' Louise added as if that might help.

'Yes,' Carys agreed. 'They're not meant to use it at all. I must get on to that.'

There was a pause.

'So, you don't feel anything out of the ordinary?'

'Only a bit chilly. These rooms are freezing.'

Carys rolled her eyes. She was wasting her time. She'd had such hopes for Louise too. She'd always been more in tune with those sorts of things. She was always the one to read out the horoscopes in the office; always the one to get her palm read if ever there was a passing gypsy.

'Come on, then,' Carys said. 'Let's have a quick tour and then a cup of tea.'

'I can't believe this is your home now,' Louise said as they walked through the Long Gallery. 'I mean just look at all these things: all these books and paintings and vases and stuff.' She let out a long, low whistle.

Carys nodded. 'It does seem unfair that one family gets to keep all this, doesn't it? But Richard explained it to me once. He said that it's because of the fact that one family - one line of that family: the male heirs - keep it, that it exists at all.'

'How do you mean?'

'Well, most of us don't keep what our family leaves us - not everything.'

'If most families are like mine then they don't have anything valuable to leave in the first place,' Louise pointed out.

'Exactly. But it's wonderful to have these houses with these great collections because, otherwise, all these things would have to be distributed: a set of chairs to one son, a cabinet to a daughter and a painting to another. Everything would get parted and lost down the centuries and there'd be no way of getting it all back together.'

Louise narrowed her eyes. 'You're defending the aristocracy.'

'Yes,' Carys said. 'I suppose I am. I didn't understand it all before,' Carys said in her defence.

'And now you do?'

'I *have* to. I'm part of it all now.'

'Gosh,' Louise whistled. 'Should I bow or curtsy?'

'Don't be silly,' Carys laughed. 'Just promise to visit me more often and I'll be happy.'

Leaving the Long Gallery, Carys opened a door which led into the Music Room. She hardly ever ventured into this part of the house and it still amazed her to see what each room held. But it wasn't the treasures of the room which held her spellbound today. It was the atmosphere. The Music Room was filled with the honeyed light of early evening and yet there was something vaguely shadowy about it too.

'Do you feel that?' Carys asked in a hushed, reverent tone.

'What?'

'Someone's just been in here.'

'Have they?'

Carys looked around the room. She felt strange. Her skin felt as if it were buzzing.

'The piano!'

'What about it?'

'Someone's been playing it.'

'But we would have heard it, surely?'

'The lid's up - look,' Carys said, pointing. 'The lid should never be kept up like that.' Carys walked across the room towards it. She had the strangest feeling that the piano had been played - very recently - yet there was nobody around. The lid was up but there wasn't any physical proof that it had been played: piano keys didn't stay pressed down, and yet the notes seemed to be hanging in the air like some strange aura. She could almost reach out and touch them.

'Carys?'

She turned around. Louise looked concerned.

'How's about that cup of tea you promised me?'

'Oh, right,' she said.

They left the room and Carys couldn't help feeling slightly disgruntled that she hadn't been able to stay longer but what would that have proved?

'You know,' Louise began a few minutes later once they'd sat down with a cup of tea, 'I think you need to get out more.'

'What do you mean?'

'I mean, I don't think it's healthy for you to be cooped up in this place all day long.'

'Cooped up? You can't be cooped up at Amberley - there are probably over twenty miles of corridors.'

'But it's not good for you. You need to get outside.'

'But I do!' Carys protested. 'I take the dogs out. You've no idea how far we walk each day.'

Louise didn't look convinced. 'I'm worried this place is getting to you. All these gloomy rooms with their dark panelling and moody curtains.'

Carys laughed. 'They're not gloomy or moody.'

'Well, I think they are, and I think they're affecting your brain.'

Carys put her cup down. 'You don't believe a word I've told you, do you?'

Louise's eyes suddenly flooded with sympathy. 'Of course I do-'

'But you don't really believe that the voices are real, do you? I saw the way you looked at me in the Music Room.'

'Carys! You're getting all worked up. Anyway, listen, I might be able to help you - if you'd just give me a chance.'

Carys instantly shut up.

'There's this woman,' Louise began, 'Lara something-or-other. She's got a reputation for being a bit mad but I once read this interview with her in *Cuthland Life* and she sounded as if she knew what she was talking about.'

'What was she talking about?'

'Ghosts,' Louise said matter-of-factly. 'The spirit world. That's her job.'

'You think I should employ some sort of ghost-buster?'

'Well, what else were you thinking of doing?'

Carys puffed out her cheeks. 'I hadn't really thought about it.'

'Well, you should,' Louise said. 'This is your home now and, if it's really haunted, I think you'd better do something about it.'

CHAPTER 12

After raiding the downstairs cloakroom for copies of *Cuthland Life*, Carys managed to track down the article Louise had mentioned. Not wanting to be caught reading it, she closed the cloakroom door and sat down on the loo seat.

"Who You Gonna Call? Ghost-buddy!"

Carys rolled her eyes but read on.

"Former socialite, Lara Claridge, is a ghost's best friend. Here, she tells of some of her most recent encounters with the spirit world."

Sitting on the toilet seat, Carys read about Ms Claridge's experience in a medieval manor house just across the border in Eastmoreland.

"She was a very friendly ghost. Just wanted somebody to talk to."

Then there was the disruptive spirit who obviously didn't agree with the renovations the new owners were doing to what he still considered his property.

"It can be very unsettling seeing such drastic changes being made. We have to consider the feelings of the dead as well as the living."

'Goodness,' Carys said. It was all incredibly fascinating but could this woman really help her?

Rolling up the magazine, Carys left the safety of the cloakroom and headed for the Yellow Drawing Room. It was usually quiet and she'd be able to make a phone call without being overheard. Luckily, Ms Claridge's number was in the telephone book and, when she answered the phone, Ms Claridge sounded very much like anybody else. Carys wasn't quite sure what she had been expecting but she was quickly put at ease and an appointment was made for the very next day.

'I don't like to keep a spirit waiting,' she told Carys. 'If they have something to say then it's best to listen.'

Of course, Carys found it impossible to sleep but, after several hours of tossing and turning, worrying about how she was going to keep this business from Richard, she fell asleep just as the sky was beginning to lighten and the first birdsong soared across the gardens.

As usual, Richard left for the estate office at the crack of dawn which came as a relief as Carys didn't relish the idea of explaining Ms Claridge's visit. She dressed quickly and splashed her face with water before tying her hair back into a ponytail and applying the lightest touches of make-up. She shared a quick breakfast with Cecily and Evie before packing them off to their tutor and beginning the long walk to the heart of the house.

Carys mused on the irony of her situation. A few months ago, she had been a sceptic who didn't believe in ghosts and didn't believe in the aristocracy. Now, she was a marchioness living in a haunted house. Somehow, she couldn't help thinking things had gone horribly wrong.

Reaching the Yellow Drawing Room, she looked out of the window. Facing south, the room was bathed in sunshine, its walls seeming to hum with colour. And it was from this room that Carys saw Lara Claridge arrive. Just as the French clock chimed nine, a small red Marlva Van bounced up the driveway, its suspension worthy of a museum.

'Punctuality is my middle name,' Lara Claridge had told Carys the day before. 'Well, actually, it's Lavinia, but nothing ever gets sorted out satisfactorily by someone who can't be bothered to be on time.'

Carys agreed but, as she watched the van coming to an abrupt halt on the gravel driveway, she wondered if she'd done the right thing. What if she'd made a huge mistake? What if it was all in her head? She'd hardly slept a wink all night for wondering. She'd even thought about venturing back into the Music Room but was too afraid to walk through the house at night.

But it was too late to change her mind now. She watched as the rainbow-clad ex-society hostess emerged from her Marlva Van, clutching a terrifyingly large tapestry holdall. The voice may have sounded perfectly normal on the phone, and the dimly-lit photograph of her in *Cuthland Life* had seemed perfectly ordinary but nothing could have prepared Carys for the vision that greeted her. Her eyes widened in wonder as she took in the bouffant hair which shone like moonshine, the lips painted poppy red, the face not so much dusted as detonated with powder, and the multi-coloured dress-coat depicting orchids, waterfalls, hummingbirds and beetles.

'So pleased to meet you,' she said as soon as Carys opened the door. 'Well, I say pleased but, of course, it's rather unfortunate for you to have to meet me, isn't it?'

'I suppose it is,' Carys said. 'Thank you so much for coming out straight away.'

'Have to, my dear. If there's one thing I've learned in this profession, it's that the spirit world does not appreciate being kept waiting.'

Carys wasn't sure how to respond to such a statement so nodded and kept quiet.

'Would you like a cup of tea before we begin?' Carys suggested.

'No, thank you, dear. Caffeine interrupts my field of perception. Now,' she said, clapping two tiny, perfectly manicured hands together, 'where have you been feeling the disturbances?'

'Follow me,' Carys said, taking her through the Yellow Drawing Room and along the snaking corridors to the Montella Room.

'Here is where I heard the voice,' she said.

'And only here?' Ms Claridge asked.

'So far. Is that normal?'

'Oh, yes,' Ms Claridge said. 'Spirits are just like us, you know: they have their favourite rooms. Yours is the Yellow Drawing Room, is it not?'

Carys nodded, the sceptic in her thinking that it wouldn't be hard to guess such a thing. It was virtually the only room in the house you could keep warm in.

'Yes,' Ms Claridge said thoughtfully, a finger pressed to her lips. 'It's certainly cold in here. I felt the temperature drop as soon as we came in.'

'Well, I wouldn't read too much into that,' Carys said. 'There are drafts everywhere in this house.'

'This isn't a draft, though. Oh, no!'

'It isn't?'

Ms Claridge shook her head. 'It's a presence. A woman, yes?'

'I think so.'

'The Blue Lady?'

'Who?'

'My dear, the whole of Cuthland knows about the Blue Lady: she's legendary.'

'Oh,' Carys said, wishing she didn't appear so out-of-touch with what was now her home.

'Not many people have seen her, of course. I think her appeal lies in her uncertainty. She doesn't appear before just anyone, you know. There have been experts and TV presenters and all sorts here hoping to catch a glimpse of her.'

'But why does she want to speak to me - if it is her?'

Lara Claridge took in a deep breath and then let it out very slowly. It was so cold in the room that Carys thought she'd be able to see it. 'I really have no idea,' she said at last.

Carys rolled her eyes. She was just as infuriating as Louise had been. Was she going to get any answers out of this old woman or was she wasting her time?

'What's in your bag?' Carys asked, deciding to try and move things forward as quickly as possible.

Ms Claridge placed it on the carpet and bent down over it, unzipping the metre-long zip. 'It's my mat,' she said, producing a rolled-up mat of gigantic proportions and eye-boggling colours. 'And cushions. I can't go anywhere without my cushions.' And, with a flourish, she'd unrolled the mat in front of them and quickly scattered three plump, purple cushions onto it. 'Care to join me?' she asked. 'I recommend that you do.'

Carys looked down at the swirling purples and rich oranges of the mat, shrugged her shoulders and went for it, sitting down and trying to make herself comfortable.

'Now, we'll have some deep breaths,' Ms Claridge said. 'Close your eyes and rest your mind.'

Carys tried to do as she was told. She could do this, she thought.

'I can feel your resistance.'

Carys blinked, opening her eyes and glaring at the colourful old lady sitting in front of her with her legs folded underneath her billowing coat dress of many colours. She really was a human rainbow.

'Close your eyes,' Ms Claridge said, shocking Carys. How had she known she'd opened them? Maybe she did have extra-sensory perception after all.

Carys closed her eyes again.

'Try not to think about anything,' Ms Claridge began again. 'Hard, I know, in this day and age but you must clear your mind of all your troubles if you are to be able to receive any new phenomenon.'

Carys frowned. New phenomenon? Was she referring to the spirit world? But hadn't The Blue Lady appeared to Carys without any preparation? Hadn't she just been worrying her head about the amount of work Richard was doing to say nothing of her on-going worry about Cecily and-

'Your mind is too full,' Ms Claridge suddenly bellowed.

Carys flinched.

'You must try not to be so preoccupied if this is going to work.'

'What, exactly, are you going to do?'

Ms Claridge sighed. 'Open your eyes,' she said and Carys opened them. 'I can see this isn't going to work - not like this.'

'I'm sorry,' Carys said and she really was. 'I don't mean to waste your time.'

Ms Claridge reached into her handbag which she'd placed alongside her enormous holdall. 'This should do the trick,' she said, producing a tiny glass bottle with a pretty stopper. It was filled with a luminous liquid the colour of bluebells.

'What's that?' Carys asked.

'It's a herbal relaxant,' she said.

Carys's eyes narrowed. She was as sceptical about herbs and their properties as she was about mediums and ghost hunters.

'Smell this,' Ms Claridge said. 'Go on.'

'What does it do?'

'Must you always question everything?' she asked.

'If I'm going to snort something, I want to know what it will do to me,' Carys responded.

'It will relax the mind and stimulate the senses - that's all. There are no side effects. Usually.'

'Usually?'

'Hurry up, now,' Ms Claridge urged, sticking the bottle under Carys's nose.

Carys took a wary look at the brilliant blue liquid. It really was very pretty, as if a piece of summer sky had been bottled up for a rainy day. Then, carefully, she wriggled her nose and sniffed.

'Inhale,' Ms Claridge said. '*Deeper.*'

Carys did. It smelled good. Rather like hyacinths but not quite as strong.

'Can you feel it?'

At first, Carys thought that Ms Claridge had got confused and had meant to ask if she could smell it but then she experienced a sudden wash of warmth flowing through her.

'Yes. YES! I can.'

'Good, good. Now, breathe. Don't forget to breathe. Feel the warmth from the liquid travelling through you. Let it work. Don't resist it.'

Carys wasn't resisting it. She closed her eyes, sinking into a velvety blueness of peace. 'I ... feel ... strange...'

'That's perfectly normal,' Ms Claridge assured her. 'You'll soon think that's normal. Can you feel it in your fingers yet?'

Carys concentrated her attention onto her hands.

'Give them a wriggle. Go on.'

Carys wriggled. 'They feel spongy.'

'Good. You're almost ready.'

'What for?'

'Don't ask so many questions. I told you; just feel.'

Carys nodded.

'Ready?'

'I think so,' Carys said. She could hear Ms Claridge's breathing: long, deep breaths which seemed to come from the very centre of her being. And Carys's breathing also became deeper. She hadn't felt so relaxed in ages. She wasn't sure if it was the mysterious blue liquid she'd inhaled or the fact that she'd allowed herself a moment to just sit and relax but it felt wonderful.

'You can open your eyes now,' a voice told her.

Carys shook her head and blinked as if coming round from a deep sleep which was silly, really, because they had only just begun, hadn't they?

'Is that it?'

Ms Claridge nodded. 'In record time too - only twenty-three minutes.'

'Twenty-three minutes?' Carys gasped. 'But I only closed my eyes a moment ago.

Ms Claridge smiled and nodded towards a small wooden clock on the mantelpiece She was right: it was twenty to ten.

'How did that happen?'

Ms Claridge stretched her arms above her head and then got up from her nest of cushions. 'So many questions,' she admonished with a chuckle. 'So much scepticism.'

'I'm not being sceptical,' Carys said. 'I'm just curious as to what happened.'

'I do believe,' Ms Claridge said with infuriating slowness, 'that-'

'What?'

'I'm ready for that cup of tea.'

Carys sighed, seeing that she was going to get no explanations just yet.

Rolling Ms Claridge's mat up and stuffing it and the cushions into her holdall, Carys led the way up a back staircase to one of the tiny rooms she'd had converted.

'I don't want to have to walk half a mile every time I want a cup of tea,' she'd told Richard shortly after moving in. 'And I want a private kitchen - not one I have to share with the butler and the cook.'

He'd given in to Carys's demand and let her have one of the rooms in the East Turret which had previously been used as yet another hoarding space for moth-eaten tapestries and chairs with dodgy legs. She'd got to work, stripping the wallpaper which was just plain old rather than being old and of national importance, and painting the walls a soft cream to make the most of the light. She'd also had a small sink built in and some cupboards and a worktop where she'd placed a microwave. Two comfy armchairs she'd found in one of the attics gave it a homely feel and the views over the parkland made the climb to the top of the turret worthwhile.

Carys thought it important to have a place like this where she could bring friends and visitors she didn't necessarily want the whole house talking about and Ms Claridge was certainly one of those.

'I hope you don't mind stairs,' Carys said as they reached the East Tower.

'Not at all,' she said but she decided to leave her holdall at the bottom all the same.

'You get very fit living in a place like this.'

'I remember your mother-in-law saying exactly the same thing.'

Carys turned around. 'You know Francesca?'

A cloud of hesitancy flitted across Ms Claridge's face before she answered. 'We were great friends for many years,' she said somewhat guardedly.

'You mean you aren't now?'

They had reached the top of the stairs before she answered. 'We sort of lost touch,' she said.

They entered the kitchen and Carys motioned to an armchair and

Ms Claridge sat down.

'What a delightful room,' she said. 'Did you do this?'

Carys nodded. 'I had to have somewhere to call my own. Somewhere normal, you know? A room that hasn't been slept in by a king.'

Carys got two floral mugs out of the cupboard and made the tea, handing a cup to Ms Claridge before sitting down in the armchair next to hers.

'I know exactly what you mean. You do have to put your own imprint on a house,' Ms Claridge said, 'but we're not here to talk about decorating, are we? We're here to talk about a duchess.'

'A duchess?'

Ms Claridge nodded. 'That's who's been causing you all this trouble. Amberley's *Blue Lady*, no less. Just as I thought. The wife of the fifth Duke of Cuthland. Georgiana Lacey.'

'Really? She spoke to you?' Carys's mouth was a perfect 'O' of amazement.

'She told me her name after much resistance but she wouldn't tell me why she was here which was most perplexing. Usually, the spirits I meet can't wait to unburden themselves.'

Carys's eyes were wide with astonishment. 'And all this happened whilst I was drugged? In those twenty-three minutes?'

'You weren't drugged, my dear. You were merely in a trance-like state of being. But, yes, I managed to contact the spirit who's been trying to reach you. She didn't seem too pleased with you, by the way. Says she's been trying to talk to you for weeks but you've been ignoring her.'

'I've been doing no such thing!'

'She told me you've walked right through her on several occasions. Most rude, you know.'

Carys flapped her arms in the air in annoyance. 'This is ridiculous. I've never even seen her!'

'Then you've not been looking hard enough.'

'I don't believe it. How can I be accused of doing things to somebody I can't even see?'

'But you knew something was going on, didn't you? Otherwise, why call me?'

For a moment, Carys closed her eyes, as if trying to shut the problem out completely. When she opened them, she said, 'I guess I knew something was wrong; I could feel that. But I didn't know what to do.'

'You were hoping I'd put your mind at rest, weren't you? You were hoping that I'd pat you on the head and call you a silly girl and tell you not to worry,' Ms Claridge said. 'That's what usually happens. People are more afraid of me confirming their fears than the fears themselves. I've lost count of the number of people who could live quite harmoniously with the spirits in their homes until I get involved.'

'Why do you make such a difference?' Carys asked.

'Because I make them *real*. What may just have been a few odd bangs and crashes turns out to be a very real visitor from another dimension.'

Carys's mouth dropped open. 'And you're saying that's what I've got - what Amberley's got?'

Ms Claridge nodded. 'Georgiana Lacey. The Blue Lady; call her what you will. She's not new to Amberley. In fact, since her death, she's probably never left. You'll have to ask her, of course. She wouldn't talk to me.'

Carys's eyebrows knitted together in consternation. 'What exactly am I meant to do?'

Ms Claridge put her empty mug on a table beside her chair. 'Don't panic. That's the last thing you must do. People don't realise it but we're surrounded by spirits all the time. As soon as you understand that, you can begin to communicate with them.'

'How?'

'Just as you would with a normal person. Spirits are just like you and me except in the fact that they have passed over,' she said with a little chuckle.

'And you can get rid of her, can you?'

For a moment, Ms Claridge's face dropped, her cheerful demeanour changing to one of frostiness. 'I don't really do that - not automatically, anyway and only in extreme cases. You must talk to her first. Find out what she wants. You can't just blitz her until you've done that.'

'*Blitz* her? Is that a technical term?'

Ms Claridge smiled. 'It's my belief,' she began, 'that spirits are as much a part of these houses as the antiques, if not more so. After all, it is they who made these houses what they are today.'

'I don't understand,' Carys confessed. 'I thought ghosts or spirits, or whatever you call them, belong somewhere else. I'm not at all sure I want one in my home. It's difficult enough for me thinking of Amberley as my home without it being haunted too.'

Ms Claridge simply smiled. 'I appreciate your concern. Perhaps it will help if you understand a bit more about spirits. Really, they're just like normal people. Some are nice and some are nasty. Like in life, you try and avoid the nasty ones - or blitz them back into their own dimensions,' she said with another little chuckle. 'But the nice ones can be a pleasure to have around. They really can be the making of a home, you know. Why not give her a chance? You might even become best friends. That's the wonderful thing about the spirit world: you never know what to expect.'

Carys shook her head. 'I can't quite see me making friends with a ghost.'

'You'd be surprised,' Ms Claridge said knowingly. 'I've lost count of the number of people who've called me in the hope that I'll be in and out in an hour, blitzing their spirits before they have time to make me a cup of tea only for me to tell them to try talking to them. It's only fair, isn't it? I mean, you wouldn't hire a hit man to rid you of new neighbours you haven't even met.'

Carys blinked in surprise at Ms Claridge's use of the term *hit man*.

'But ghosts - I mean spirits,' Carys said, 'they aren't neighbours, are they? They live in the same space as we do.'

'All I'm saying is give Georgiana a chance. She was meant to be very nice, you know.'

A sudden laugh escaped Carys. 'I can't believe we're having this conversation.'

'It will take a while to get used to the idea but the next time you walk through the Montella Room and feel a slight chill, pause and see what happens.'

'I always feel chilly in this house.'

'But pay special attention to that room: that's the one she seems to favour. I don't know why yet but I'm hoping you'll let me know when you find out.'

Carys bit her lip. 'You seem very sure that I will find out, don't you?'

'I have every faith in you, my dear.'

CHAPTER 13

Carys wanted to start immediately. When Ms Claridge left, she felt all fired up with energy and enthusiasm. She was going to talk to a ghost, and not just any ghost. This was one of Richard's ancestors. How bizarre was that? And it felt so naughty too because Richard didn't know anything about it.

Maybe now was the right time to tell him - before things went any further, she thought as she walked through the Yellow Drawing Room. Ms Claridge had said that the whole county knew about the Blue Lady so Richard would more than likely be aware of her already. Perhaps he'd even heard her himself and seen her floating around Amberley. Carys thought back to the estate meeting in the Montella Room. Richard hadn't given any indication that he'd heard the voice. He might have no idea about the Blue Lady or maybe he just didn't believe in ghosts.

Maybe, Carys thought, she should just go straight to the Montella Room and find out for herself first. Yes. That was it. There was no point in worrying Richard until she found out the truth.

The house was quiet that morning. Carys passed one of the cleaners who was working quietly with a duster in her hand. She nodded a good morning and she walked on through the house. In another half hour, it would be open to the public so she'd better get a move on if she wanted the Montella Room to herself.

When she arrived at the room, the doors were open in readiness for the public. Carys closed them quietly behind her and stood perfectly still for a moment. Did she feel a chill? It was hard to tell. She did feel odd, though, but perhaps that was psychological. Very few people had the time to just stand and be still, listening to their own heartbeat. It was a curious feeling to be alone in such a grand room and yet, at the same time, she didn't feel as if she was totally alone: there were the numerous portraits to keep her company.

'Which one are you?' Carys whispered, moving to view the paintings. But she knew. It was the painting Louise had shown an interest in. For a moment, Carys wondered if that had meant something. Louise had denied having any feelings and yet she'd been drawn to Georgiana's painting. Had Georgiana been trying to communicate with Louise?

Carys gazed up at the painting. There were at least three portraits of Georgiana in the room and several more throughout the house but this was the most beautiful. Not quite life-size, it was a full-length portrait of Georgiana wearing a pale blue dress which shimmered from out of the dark background. Was that why she was known as the Blue Lady? Did that mean that, when she made her rare appearances, she was still wearing this dress? After over two hundred years? It was all so confusing.

Carys noticed the delicate lace at the dress's neckline and the exquisite slippers peeping out from under the folds of the dress. And then she noticed something she hadn't seen before. Georgiana was also holding a single red rose - the famous scarlet Amberley Velvet - the rose with the astonishing scent. But it was the way she was holding it that was so curious. It was cradled in her arms as if it were a baby. Had her husband given her that rose and asked her to be painted holding it? Carys looked for clues in her face. She had a kind face: beautiful, vanilla-pale skin, her fair hair swept gently back. But there was something about the eyes that was bewitching: they were dark and mysteriously playful, as if she wanted to share a secret with you.

'What's your secret, Georgiana? Is that why you've come back - to tell me something?'

Carys sighed. As much as she wanted to, she just couldn't bring herself to talk out loud to an empty space. She tried to recall what Ms Claridge had said about ghosts.

They're just like normal people.

Right. That didn't seem very likely to Carys but, as she'd no prior experience of these matters, who was she to argue?

Give Georgiana a chance.

She wanted to, she really did, but she couldn't help feeling terribly sceptical about the whole thing. Somehow, her earlier buzz of enthusiasm had waned. Still, she couldn't not give things a try after coming so far already but what, exactly, should she do? Call her name again? That's what you'd do if you wanted to find a friend, wasn't it? And Ms Claridge had made it perfectly clear that ghosts were just like ordinary people.

'Georgiana?' Carys whispered, her voice, she felt, far too hesitant to reach anything from another dimension. 'Are you there?' she tried again, a little louder but sounding ridiculously clichéd.

There was nothing. No. Wait. She felt sure that buzzing sensation was returning. Her skin felt quite strange - just like the time in the Music Room. It was hard to explain. A certain frisson of the flesh. Or maybe it was Ms Claridge's strange blue liquid wearing off. Carys worried in case it might have some long-term effect which might send her into a trance at the most inappropriate moments such as estate meetings. Not that anybody would notice, she smiled.

'Concentrate,' she said to herself. Deep breaths, that was the way. She stood absolutely still and closed her eyes for a moment, trying to empty her mind just as Ms Claridge had instructed. A sudden calmness flooded her system and, for a moment, she thought she could smell - what? Was it the hyacinth smell of Ms Claridge's strange potion? No. It was roses. She could smell roses. And not just any rose: what she could smell was unmistakable. It was an Amberley Velvet.

'Georgiana?'

Carys felt her heartbeat accelerate. She didn't know what to do. Should she open her eyes? She was too afraid at what might greet her.

'Okay,' she whispered to herself. 'I can do this. I *must* do this.'

She opened her eyes.

'RICHARD!' she screamed. He was standing right in front of her. How long had he been there?

She waited for him to say something perceptive like, 'You look like you've seen a ghost,' but he didn't. In fact, it was he who looked like he'd seen a ghost.

'Richard? Whatever's the matter?' Carys leant forward and greeted him with a tender kiss. He was deathly pale. 'Are you ill?' Carys stroked his cheek. 'I've told you to slow down, haven't I? You're doing far too much and now you're paying the price.'

'No,' he said.

Carys sighed. 'There's no use arguing with me. You've got to take things easier.'

'No,' he said again. 'It's not me, Carys.'

She looked at him. 'What's wrong, then?'

He was silent for a moment, as if trying to work it out for himself.

Carys could feel her heart rate speeding again and, this time, it had nothing to do with ghosts.

'What is it, Richard?' she asked again. 'What's wrong?'

'It's father.' Richard said in a voice that was barely audible. 'He's had a heart attack.'

CHAPTER 14

The eleventh Duke of Cuthland had suffered a heart attack the year before and had refused to take the doctor's advice about taking things easy. He paid the price with his life shortly after reaching the hospital.

With the estate to run and the funeral to arrange, Richard had too much to do to find the time to grieve and Carys was deeply worried that he was heading the same way as his father.

'It's so awful,' Carys told Louise on the phone. 'I can't seem to reach him at all. I'm so worried about him.'

'It must be a huge responsibility. I mean, he's the new duke now, isn't he? And there'll be all those appalling death duties to worry about.'

Carys hadn't even thought of those. She'd heard the term mentioned before but wasn't quite sure what it entailed. All she knew was that it was the price the privileged paid for continuing to live at Amberley: each new duke would have to cough up the coffers if they wished to remain lord of the manor.

The funeral was to be held at St Mary's Church in the grounds of Amberley. It was where all the dukes were buried and, truth be told, was beginning to look a bit crowded. There was the option of cremation, of course, and a neat row of urns stood silently in a quiet corner of the Cuthland Chapel but Henry Bretton was not going to be extinguished quite so easily. He wanted a proper burial. Carys had an awful image of his likeness being chiselled onto his tomb like his ancestors, his faithful spaniels propping up his feet. But what made her sadder than anything was that she'd not really got to know the duke. Still, in a strange way, she knew that she was going to miss him. His bark, which boomed and echoed through the corridors of Amberley, was so much a part of the place that she couldn't imagine life without it.

There were a lot of people who wouldn't miss him, of course, like the errant walkers who dared to stray off the footpaths into the deer park and were chased away with irate shouts and menacing shakes of one of the duke's infamous walking sticks. But nobody would be left doubting that he'd been a larger than life character.

Richard's mother, now known as the 'dowager duchess', hadn't spoken a word to Carys since the death of her husband. That wasn't very surprising, though, seeing as they hardly spoke under normal circumstances. Carys tried, hopelessly, to think of something comforting to say. She so longed to have a good relationship with her mother-in-law and knew that she'd need her guidance more than ever now that she was about to take over the role of duchess herself.

Cecily and Evelyn spent most of their time in tears and, heartless as it may have seemed, Carys was pleased to see that Cecily was capable of some emotion after all. Of course, Carys was completely refused when it came to offering any comfort but there was one touching moment when, late at night, Carys had woken up to find Richard was not in bed. She'd slipped on her slippers and a dressing gown and followed the sound of whispered voices to the girls' room where, peeping through the door which had been left ever-so-slightly ajar, she saw Richard sitting on the edge of Cecily's bed, a warm arm around her shoulders.

'Grandpa knows you love him,' he whispered into the top of her head.

'But how?'

'Because families just know these things.'

There was a pause.

'Do you know I love you, Daddy?'

'Of course I do, sweetheart.'

'And does Grandma know I love her?'

'I'm sure she does.'

'But I should tell her, shouldn't I?'

'I think she'd like that very much.'

Cecily had nodded and Carys had watched as he'd tucked her back into bed, kissing her cheek and smoothing down her hair which was damp with tears.

With all the upset and upheaval of the duke's death, Carys had completely forgotten about Amanda, Richard's ex-wife and mother of Cecily and Evelyn and the role she would play. Incredibly enough, Carys had never met her. Every weekend, when she came to pick up the girls, Carys had been out walking the dogs. Richard had never offered an introduction and it didn't quite seem the right thing to ask him to do. But she had been a member of the Bretton family for twelve years and was, of course, invited to the funeral.

Carys had seen photographs of her but none of them did her justice. A statuesque five foot seven with rich brown hair and eyes the colour of jade, she was the kind of woman to give a newly-wed second wife the heebie-jeebies. She was also immaculate with a sharp suit, discreet gold earrings and perfect nails. She also owned a Marlva Panache in misty blue - a car Carys had been dreaming of owning for years.

'You must be Carys,' she said as they met in the Yellow Drawing Room on the morning of the funeral.

'Amanda?' Carys said, shaking the outstretched manicured hand which felt so much calmer and steadier than her own.

'My word,' Amanda said, glancing around the room. 'This place never changes, does it?' Her tone told of her relief to be shot of the place, her lofty glance finding every cobweb and forgotten patch of dust.

'That, I find, is part of its charm,' Carys countered.

'Yes, well, charm doesn't keep you warm in winter or pay the bills,' she said, making Carys feel incredibly naïve.

'Amberley usually finds a way.'

'It will need to with these death duties.'

Luckily for Carys, who didn't particularly want to spend any more time alone with Amanda, Phoebe, Serena and Jamie entered the room, their pale faces all the more stark because of their black clothing. Phoebe immediately crossed the room and hugged Carys.

'You okay?' Carys whispered.

Phoebe nodded but Carys could see that her eyes were red-rimmed. Still, Phoebe didn't forget her manners and greeted Amanda with a kiss on the cheek.

Richard entered the room with his mother who was wearing a pretty hat with a wisp of dark veil. She linked his arm and nodded to Amanda who came forward to kiss both her and Richard. Cecily and Evie followed, running over to greet their mother as if she might be able to make everything better.

And then, it was time to leave. It was damp and overcast which seemed to suit everybody's mood. Stepping out from the front porch, Carys saw the sombre black hearse and the dark wood coffin of the duke, piled high with white lilies and his favourite yellow roses from the estate gardens.

Carys travelled in the first car with Richard, his mother and Jamie. Phoebe and Serena followed with Amanda, Cecily and Evelyn. It was the saddest procession Carys had ever seen for standing in line along the driveway were all the estate workers in black, heads bowing as the duke's hearse drove by.

St Mary's Church was tiny and icy cold all year round. Carys shivered as they walked in behind the coffin. Following Richard and his mother to the front pew, she couldn't help thinking of her own future and how it was probably tied to this very church. She would more than likely end up there, wouldn't she - in a little urn on a stone ledge in the Cuthland Chapel? But what about her own family? Would she have to forget them? That was the thing when you married into these families: you went along with their traditions and forgot about your own history and heritage. She was a Bretton now and belonged here, and it was a position she'd take with her even beyond death.

The service was beautiful in its simplicity. *Immortal, invisible, God only wise*, was the first hymn but voices didn't want to be roused. Carys's own voice quavered somewhat when she heard Francesca's notes break off into a numbed silence, and Richard's voice was barely above a whisper. Would he be able to muster up the courage for his reading?

The hymn ended and Carys squeezed Richard's arm before he walked the few paces to the front of the church and faced the congregation. He read the moving words about Time from *Ecclesiastes* and his voice was low and calm and desperately sad and, when he finished, he lifted his eyes to the many familiar faces that had crowded into the tiny church.

'My father could never lay claim to being the easiest of men to live with,' he began, and his statement raised a few nervous chuckles from the pews, 'but he was a good man and much admired and, what is more, he loved Amberley and cared for it with the very fibre of his being.'

Richard paused and gazed into the empty space in front of him almost as if he could see his father standing there, listening to his words.

'And, I know,' he went on at last, 'that there will always be a part of him here with us and that it is now our responsibility to continue his extraordinary work.'

For a moment, he looked as if he were about to say something else but was waiting for the right words to form themselves. The church was silent with anticipation as everybody watched him, but his words never did materialise and he returned to his seat.

There were a few moments of silent contemplation. Carys picked Richard's hands up in hers and held them tightly. They felt like the hands of a little boy and she couldn't help feeling a little anxious for him, for it was into these hands that the Amberley estate had now fallen.

CHAPTER 15

It was one week after the duke's funeral and Carys walked into their private apartments to find Richard bent double over a packing box.

'What are you doing?' she asked him.

'Moving out,' he said simply.

Carys's eyes widened. 'What?'

For one awful moment, she thought that he'd cracked - that his job had finally got the better of him and he'd decided to leave Amberley for good.

'We're moving to the west wing,' he explained.

'But your mother's there.'

'She's moved out.'

'What? When?' Carys asked, not really surprised that nobody had told her what was going on - as usual.

'She's in Cuthland House. By the west gate.'

Carys knew of the property: a sturdy Victorian building with large windows and a pretty garden.

'Isn't this all rather sudden?'

'Not at all,' Richard said. 'It's perfectly normal.'

For a bleak moment, Carys saw herself in the future: an ancient lady of ninety being kicked out of her home by her own son. How heartless. How cruel! She was a lonely widow. She was-

'And, before you accuse me of being heartless, it was her own decision to go straight away'

'Oh,' Carys said. 'I guess I'll never understand how these houses and families work.'

'You will,' he said. 'You're the duchess now, you'll have to learn.'

Carys stood there feeling completely dumbfounded She was the duchess now - the Duchess of Cuthland. She hadn't even had time to get used to being the Marchioness of Amberley and now she was a duchess.

'But what's wrong with our apartments here?'

'Nothing,' Richard said. 'But it's usual for the duke and duchess to take up residence in the west wing. I'm sure you'll love it.'

'Don't you want to choose for yourself?' she dared to ask.

'What do you mean?'

'Where do *you* want to live?'

Richard frowned. 'The west wing.'

Carys shook her head. 'Don't you ever feel like rebelling a little bit? How about moving into a nice semi in Carminster? Or a little cottage out near the moors?'

'What are you talking about?'

'Choice,' Carys said.

'But we've got choice here - there are dozens of rooms.'

'So why the west wing?'

'Because it's convenient and comfortable,' he said. 'Carys, if you don't mind me saying, you're being rather perverse.'

She sighed. 'But I've only just grown to love it here.'

Richard smiled. 'I know we seem to spend our time moving around but it'll work out fine in no time. You'll see. Now, pass me that picture, darling,' he said, nodding to the old print of Amberley Court which was hanging on the wall. 'We'll take that one with us - make us feel more at home, eh?'

Moving rooms, in itself, didn't bother Carys. It was not being asked her opinion that irked. Nobody ever seemed to think she might have thoughts on a particular subject and that bothered her. She didn't want to become invisible. Her job at Gyland and Green had allowed her a certain level of responsibility that, although was not enviable in that it meant endless overtime, gave her a feeling of self-worth. That was important to her. She didn't want to be the unseen wife who worked quietly in the shadow of her husband.

Should have thought about that before marrying a duke, her inner voice told her as she walked around her new living room. It was beautiful, of course, with dark cream flocked wallpaper, a wine red carpet and ornate plaster ceiling. The views across the gardens were stunning too. She hated to admit it, but it was far lovelier than their previous apartments.

'All right?' Richard had asked her over breakfast on their first morning in their new quarters.

She'd nodded.

'Think you can make yourself at home here?'

It wasn't in Carys's nature to brood over such trifling things and so she'd beamed him a smile.

'Good,' he'd said before running out of the door to begin another frantic day of trying to make the estate pay for itself.

And that's when Carys decided to pay a visit.

She bolted down the rest of her breakfast and headed down the stairs, collecting Mungo and Badger on the way. The other dogs, it seemed, had already found somebody to take them out.

It was a bright summer's morning, the shadowed grass still drenched with dew. Casually glancing up at the sky to check for rain clouds, she saw that it was a peerless blue, dazzling the eyes and making you believe that grey days were but a myth. The air was soft and sweet and full of birdsong as Carys led the dogs down the driveway until they came to a footpath. It wasn't the most direct route, she knew, but it was the most picturesque, skirting the beech wood before crossing the open fields which afforded unrivalled views of the Cuthland countryside and Carminster Cathedral's proud spire in the distance. She could, if she looked hard enough, just make out where her old street was and liked to imagine her old house smiling back at her. It was rented now, to a young couple and no longer felt like her home at all which was just as it should be. Amberley was her home now and she couldn't imagine living anywhere else in the world.

She strode through the golden-green fields, her bare limbs warmed by the sun, her strides slicing boldly through the grass. The ground had been baked hard under the spell of sunny weather since the duke's funeral but the grass remained lush and felt cool against her legs. Badger ran on ahead, his tail wagging furiously like an overworked metronome, whilst Mungo strolled casually behind, stuffing his nose into various plants and holes in the hope of making some great doggy discovery.

'Come on, you two,' she called, climbing over a stile and taking another footpath which would take them to their destination.

There were many entrances to the Amberley Estate but the west gate was one of the most impressive. It consisted of one glorious arch topped by a bold relief crest of the dukes of Cuthland, with two smaller arches flanking its sides. It wasn't used very often so its gates remained closed and locked. But it wasn't the gate she'd come to look at and, seeing Cuthland House standing before her now, she wondered if it was such a good idea. What was she actually going to say? She didn't have anything planned. All she knew was that she had to speak to Francesca. She'd looked so pale and fragile at the funeral as if a great chunk of her heart had been chiselled out and carried away. As far as Carys was aware, Francesca hadn't spoken to Richard or to anyone. Carys wasn't sure how close she was to her daughters but suspected that they were all so isolated in their own grief that they hadn't thought to reach out and help each other.

But what made Carys think *she* could help? She'd never experienced the pain of loss. There was her father, of course, but that was a different story altogether.

'Mungo? Badger?' she called behind her and the they trotted towards her obediently.

There was a little gate which opened onto a path through a pretty garden. Ash had obviously been at work in time for Francesca's move and it sighed with delicate colour: palest pinks, mauves and silvery whites.

The front door was large and smart and very blue and Carys reached up for the dolphin-shaped brass knocker and rapped loudly.

Mungo and Badger were happily sniffing around the garden and a blackbird was singing in an old apple tree. It was rather lovely here, she thought, wondering how Francesca was settling into life away from the big house and if she welcomed the relative compactness of Cuthland House. It was still a large home by any standards. There must be at least five bedrooms over its three storeys, but it looked like a little doll's house when compared to Amberley Court.

Carys rapped again. Silence greeted her. She walked back from the door to look up at the dark windows. Pretty curtains had been drawn back to let the sunlight in but there didn't seem to be anyone at home.

With her footsteps crunching on the gravel path, Carys walked around the garden to the back of the house. Pots of scarlet begonias and geraniums greeted her and she felt both horrified and amused when Badger cocked his leg, splashing a particularly beautiful terracotta pot. Perhaps it was a blessing that Francesca wasn't at home.

But, as she walked away from the house, closing the gate behind her, she had the strangest feeling that she was being watched. She didn't see any curtains twitching or any faces peering out from the dark windows but she couldn't shake the feeling that the house wasn't empty after all.

'I thought you might like to see your office, your grace,' Mrs Travis said, leaping on Carys as soon as she returned.

'Office?'

'Yes, your grace. It was his grace's mother's and will now be yours.'

'I see.' Carys bit her lip as she remembered how wonderfully free she'd felt striding across the fields just moments before and thinking how lucky she was not to have an office.

'Perhaps now?' Mrs Travis said. 'It's just along here and I'm sure you'll be wanting to make a start on the paperwork.'

Carys tried not to flinch at the word paperwork. Nor did she want to show her ignorance in asking *what paperwork?*

They left the hallway and walked down a dark panelled corridor Carys hadn't explored before. She'd been aware that it comprised of offices of some description but she had been rather lax in finding out who did what in them. Several doors led off the corridor but it wasn't until they reached the end that Mrs Travis opened a door on the left.

'This is your office, your grace,'

Carys turned around to face Mrs Travis. 'Please, call me Carys,' she said.

'Oh, my lady, I couldn't do that.'

Carys bit her lip. She didn't feel comfortable being called *your grace* all the time: it sounded so dreadfully archaic, but it obviously made Mrs Travis uncomfortable to call her by her Christian name.

'How about a compromise?'

Mrs Travis gave a small smile of encouragement. 'Well, we were permitted to call her grace, Lady C before she became the duchess.'

'Lady C?'

'That's right, my lady.

'So I could be Lady C, could I? I think that will probably do nicely,' she agreed even though she was secretly thinking that it made her sound like a character from a James Bond movie. 'So, tell me about this office,' she said, peering in to the bright room which looked far too pretty to be a place of work.

Mrs Travis brightened. 'Well, it's known as the Old Sitting Room but nobody can remember who actually used it as a sitting room.'

Carys smiled. One more mystery of Amberley Court.

'It's been used as an annexe to the library too, which explains the shelves of books. We can have them moved if you need the space for your own things.'

'Oh, no. Please, leave them here,' Carys said. 'They look so at home and I'm sure I'll have fun reading them.'

'I think they're just old books on gardening and such. They should probably be given to the local scouts to sell but the Brettons do believe that once something finds a home here then it stays. I've lost count of the times that I've tried to persuade them to have a good sort out but they won't part with anything.'

'I'm the complete opposite,' Carys said. 'If something isn't earning its keep, out it goes.'

Mrs Travis nodded.

'This really is a lovely room,' Carys said walking over to the window and gazing down the driveway at the front of the house.

'I've always liked it too,' Mrs Travis said. 'It has that feminine touch which I often find lacking in some of the other rooms, if you don't mind me saying, Lady C.' Mrs Travis managed to control her blushing before continuing. 'I'm afraid the women of the house have very little say when it comes to décor. They make suggestions but it really isn't their place to make alterations on a grand scale. The private rooms are an exception, of course.'

'And is this classed as a private room?'

Mrs Travis's mouth tightened. 'Yes and no. The wallpaper is quite old and I believe his grace would not want that changed but you're welcome to hang your own pictures and place your own ornaments here, if you wish.'

Carys thought of the few decorative objects she'd had around her home and which hadn't yet been unpacked at Amberley. A pretty Victorian vase painted with flowers, a blue and white bowl in which she kept a handful of sherbet lemons, her collection of liberty photo frames and some bright glass figurines bought on a holiday in Venice. It wasn't much of a contribution to such a grand house but it would be enough to make the room feel like her own.

For a moment, she wondered what Francesca had placed on the shelves and mantelpiece. What had she taken with her on departing?

'You must try to make yourself at home here,' Mrs Travis said as if reading Carys's mind. 'One of the curses of belonging to a family like this is that each death brings a great shuffling of people and roles.

It's very unsettling. But this room belongs to the lady of the house so do make it your own, my lady. Her grace always spent her mornings here: writing letters and so forth,' she continued.

'Is there a lot of correspondence to handle?'

Mrs Travis nodded. 'Her grace dealt with a lot of the general enquiries about the house: film crews wanting to visit, historians asking questions, and charities getting in touch. You'd be surprised what gets sent our way. Her grace was also responsible for running the household staff and the collection, and took a great interest in overseeing the estate shop too. Then there was her charity work which, perhaps, you'd like to think about, and there will be the fund-raising events to take care of too.'

So, Carys thought, she might have some useful role in the running of Amberley after all. Her leisurely stay so far had been but an interlude. They had obviously been breaking her in gently.

'Sounds like a full time job,' she said.

'And then some,' Mrs Travis laughed. 'Mrs Franklin comes in for two mornings a week to help out. She was her grace's secretary and is happy to stay on if you need.'

Oh, *I need*, Carys said to herself, knowing, instinctively, that there was no manual for this job. She needed all the help and guidance she could get.

'The desk has been cleared for you,' Mrs Travis said. 'You'll find headed paper in the top drawer and there are always envelopes and stamps there too. There's an electronic typewriter in the cupboard.'

'And the computer?'

'Her grace never liked computers. She said they filled the room with an unnecessary hum.'

'I don't suppose it would look right either,' Carys said, looking towards the enormous mahogany desk. It was a piece of sturdy Victorian furniture that commanded respect rather than love. It gleamed darkly in the light from the large window, its many drawers set with decorative brass handles and its surface covered in a forest-green leather. A shapely wooden chair with balled feet stood close by. It looked very stately and very uncomfortable. That was the problem with these old houses, though. They were, invariably, built to impress rather than to comfort.

Carys turned back to her new old desk. There was no computer or printer; no in trays or out trays but there was a small mound of post waiting for somebody's attention. It was as far away from her work station in her old office as anything could be. But she loved the room. The bookshelves heaved with colourful spines and she couldn't wait to rifle through them.

Candy-striped chairs clustered around a tiny fireplace on which was perched a sweet wooden clock and two Staffordshire pottery spaniels. An enormous mirror hung above it, covered in bunches of thick gilded grapes. The walls were covered in a pretty wallpaper of cream with a burgundy print of roses and berries, and the carpet was a rich red like those in their private apartments which gave the room a cosy warmth.

Lamps were dotted around the room on occasional tables and there was a two-seater sofa resplendent in gold and pink and heaped with cushions. It was, Carys thought, the kind of room you could shut yourself away in and forget about the outside world. She could imagine curling up on the sofa, sinking back into the cushions, her feet tucked under her bottom, a hot cup of tea steaming on the table beside her and a good book to read and nothing to disturb her but the gentle chime of the clock on the fireplace.

'I think I'm going to be very happy here,' she said.

Mrs Travis smiled. 'Don't forget, there's the telephone. There's a list of extension numbers for the house if you need anything.'

Carys nodded. So ropes with bells on the end had lost favour, had they?

'Shall I bring you a cup of tea before you begin?'

'Oh, thank you,' Carys said.

As Mrs Travis left the room, Carys looked around, wondering if there was a socket and table where she could keep a secret kettle and supply of teabags. She so hated being reliant on staff for the most basic of things.

She walked around to the chair at the desk. It looked so austere as if it were daring her to sit on it. Carys trailed her fingers across the green leather top, wondering how many letters had been written there and how she was going to take over that role now. Could she do it?

She cleared her throat, pulled out the chair and sat down.

'There,' she said. 'That wasn't so hard.' And the chair didn't feel that hard either. Although she could probably do with a couple of cushions for reassurance.

She looked around the empty acres of desk. She would buy herself some nice desk stationery. Yes, that was it. A nice pot for her pens and a letter rack. A cheery coaster or two for the cups of tea she was going to need. Maybe even a mouse mat if she was daring enough to introduce a computer to the world of Amberley.

For a moment, she just sat, staring at the room around her. Then she cleared her throat again.

'How do you do? I'm the Duchess of Cuthland,' she said in a quiet voice. 'Do sit down. Now, how can I help you?' she said, her mouth suddenly full of plums and her eyebrows rising in a haughty manner. 'No, I'm sorry. I can't possibly agree to sell these books. You see, they've been in my husband's family for generations. They're heirlooms. Priceless, don't you know.'

She paused, her head cocked to one side as if listening to somebody. 'That's an extraordinarily generous offer. Yes, I'm quite aware we could replace the entire roof for that amount but, and I think I've said this before, the contents of Amberley remain at Amberley.'

She gave a coquettish laugh. 'My dear man. Flattery won't get you anywhere.'

Suddenly, the telephone rang, making Carys jump.

'God!'

What was she meant to do? Was that an internal call or not? If she picked it up, it might be a real person - from the outside world.

'Keep calm,' she said. Hang on a minute. It was an internal call, wasn't it?'

Her hand reached for the receiver and she picked it up. 'He-hello?' she said, not sounding like the over-confident, flirtatious duchess she'd portrayed so beautifully just a moment ago but more like an office junior on their first day.

'Lady C?'

'Mrs Travis?' she cried in delight.

'I'm so sorry, my lady, but did you want Earl Grey or camomile?'

'Earl Grey,' Carys almost laughed in relief.

Once her heart rate had returned to normal, she did as anyone who takes possession of a new desk does: checked the drawers. It was a pedestal desk with two columns of four drawers and a long horizontal drawer in the middle. Being right-handed, Carys began with the top drawer on her right-hand side. The ornate brass handle pulled the drawer away smoothly and it was so wonderful to observe its neat emptiness. In the past, when she'd inherited a desk, it would invariably be full of out-of-date memos, bent paper-clips and a bottle of congealed Tipp-Ex. No such tat in this desk. It had been loved and respected. Its owner had taken pride in its use. It wouldn't be a chore to sit at a desk like this, Carys thought, even though the job might seem strange to her at this moment, she felt that it must be made easier by being surrounded by beautiful objects. The aristocracy knew that, didn't they? They knew that the long passage through life was made all the sweeter by having lovely things around them. Not that a Queen Anne walnut chair could mend a broken heart, and a Chippendale bureau might not be able to chase the blues away, but they could make you feel a little happier by just looking at them.

Carys was enjoying this. She'd never been able to afford beautiful furniture before. Her pieces at her old home were cheap and functional and not many of them were made out of solid wood either. They had a *wooden veneer* or were made from the dreaded MDF. Was that her generation's gift to the world? Was this where the glorious timeline of wood end? Oak, walnut, mahogany, pine - and MDF? Somehow, she couldn't imagine the antique collectors of the future sweating with enthusiasm over a piece of MDF.

Ah, yes. That's a very early piece. Look at the craftsmanship.

MDF just wasn't the sort of thing to make record prices at auction houses, and she doubted very much that there would ever be books lining the shelves of Amberley's library entitled: *A History of MDF*.

There was a polite knock on the door and Mrs Travis came in, placing the cup of tea on Carys's new old desk.

'Everything in order, my lady?'

'Yes, I think so.'

'Just call if you need anything.'

'Thank you. I will,' Carys said.

No sooner had Mrs Travis left than the phone rang again. This time, it was definitely an outside caller.

'Hello,' Carys said tentatively.

'Is that Carys?'

'Yes,' Carys said, not recognising the lady's voice at the other end.

'Good. This is Valerie,' the lady said, pausing as if expecting

Carys to recognise the name. 'Valerie Buckley Stewart - the Countess of Eastmoreland.'

'Hello,' Carys said again, remembering that she and her husband, the earl, had been at their wedding but not actually remembering what they looked like.

'I was hoping to talk to you sometime. I thought you might like to come over - see the place - that sort of thing. I mean, we're practically neighbours.'

'Yes, I suppose we are.'

'Silly not to be friends, don't you think. What are you doing tomorrow? Would ten o'clock be all right?'

'Well, I-' Carys blinked.

'We could get to know each other - swap notes and stuff. No use listening to the rubbish our husbands come out with, is it?'

Carys frowned. She knew that there was some hostility between Richard and Roland Buckley-Stewart but she hadn't yet managed to get to the bottom of it.

'I'll be able to give you some advice on running that home of yours too,' Valerie added. 'I dare say you don't know where to start. Am I right?'

Carys couldn't help smiling. 'I could do with a few pointers, yes.'

'Then, that's settled. I'll see you tomorrow. Park outside the main entrance and explain who you are to old Tweedy on the door. She'll give you directions. Goodbye.' And she rang off.

Carys laughed. How extraordinary.

It wasn't until they were in bed that Carys broached the subject.

'Richard?'

'Hmmm?'

'What exactly is it between you and Roland Buckley-Stewart?'

'God! Do you have to mention his name in the sanctuary of our bedroom?'

'Sorry,' she said, thinking that wasn't the best of responses. 'I just want to try and understand. I was thinking of going over there-'

'I don't want you getting involved with them, Carys, okay? It's no coincidence that we nickname their place Bastard Hall. The only reason you have to go over there is to suss out how they're managing to stay afloat, okay?'

'And I've already done that,' she said, remembering the

embarrassing dark glasses and large hat she'd worn as she'd poked around their house, grounds and shop in order to steal ideas.

'We'll stay on our side of the border and they'll stay on theirs, okay?'

Carys nodded, deciding to keep quiet about her ten o'clock appointment the next day.

CHAPTER 16

Sliding into her Marlva Prima the next morning, Carys breathed a sigh of relief. It felt a long time since she'd driven her own car and just been herself. She started down the driveway, under the green corridor of summer trees which dappled the road, and left the estate, pulling out onto the main road which would take her over the moors and into Eastmoreland. She couldn't help feeling a little excited. She was rather looking forward to her trip to Barston Hall. Her last visit, which had also been her first, had been a disaster in her eyes. She'd been so self-conscious of her role as spy that she hadn't allowed herself the pleasure of actually enjoying her visit. But she wouldn't make that mistake today. As nervous as she was at meeting Valerie Buckley-Stewart, she wasn't going to let that get in the way of spoiling her trip.

The moors were a shocking purple under the early morning sun and Carys wound her window down to inhale the peaty air. It was glorious up here. She'd have to bring the dogs up on a walk one of these days now that she was quite sure that they wouldn't run away from her.

Her car bounced along the bumpy road across the border into Eastmoreland. It looked simply perfect under its brilliant blue sky; its moor stretching to the horizon and its forest blazing green.

Barston Hall was set deep in a valley not far from the border and Carys slowed her car to take the bends in the road. It was all well sign-posted - something Amberley could certainly benefit from, she thought, making a mental note to mention it at the next estate meeting - and she found the main entrance without any problems.

It wasn't long before she caught her first glimpse of the hall. Whilst Amberley was all golden turrets and mullioned windows, Barston Hall was white Georgian elegance: simple, uncluttered and symmetrical. It was beautiful - the kind of grand house that one expected to host a Viennese ball or a romantic masquerade. It was a long sleek building with enormous sash windows and great columns at the main entrance.

Carys parked her car as per instructions and headed for the front door which was also the main route into the house for the tourists who were already up and about. Amberley Court didn't open its doors until eleven o'clock and Carys was beginning to wonder if they were missing out to Barston on that score too.

Seeing an elderly lady on the door with a clipper at the ready for her ticket, Carys thought it best to introduce herself. 'Mrs Tweedy?'

'I beg your pardon?'

'You're Mrs Tweedy?' Carys tried again.

'My name is Ursula Carstairs,' the lady said somewhat indignantly.

'Oh, my mistake, do forgive me,' Carys said, at once noticing that she was dressed head to toe in tweed - despite the warm weather.

Carys cleared her throat and tried again, telling herself that a duchess would never get flustered. 'I'm Carys Cuthland - here to see the countess.'

'I see,' Mrs Tweedy said, weighing her up with obvious disapproval. 'Then you'll be wanting the office. Follow the main route and then turn left at the end of the dining room. It's the first door on the right.'

'Thank you,' Carys said and she was no sooner in the dining room than a booming voice greeted her.

'Carys? Darling. Welcome.'

Several tourists turned around and watched as Valerie Buckley-Stewart danced across the room in stiletto heels to air kiss her special visitor.

'Perfect timing, my dear,' she enthused and Carys smiled into a pair of bright eyes, taking in the immaculately golden coiffured hair which looked like something out of *Dynasty*. She was wearing a stunning suit in lavender - the sort that could only be from London . as no boutique in Carminster sold anything quite so beautifully tailored. Her whole look, in fact, was that of a very stylish headmistress and yet she only looked to be in her mid-forties.

Carys suddenly felt very under-dressed in her white blouse and floral print skirt.

'Did old Tweedy give you the once-over?'

Carys grinned. 'Yes, rather.'

'Never misses a trick that one,' Valerie said, leading Carys out of the dining room and unhooking a rope which blocked off a corridor from the tourists.

Carys took one last look at the room. 'The flowers are so lovely,' she said, nodding towards the grand display on the dining room table.

'All from our own gardens,' Valerie said. 'It's all in the details, you see. Flowers breathe life into a room. Photographs too. People love to see family photographs. Doesn't matter if the kids are ugly as sin, they love to look at people's private things. I always make sure I dot a few silly holiday snaps around the house. People think they come to these houses to see the famous paintings and the antiques but, really, they come to see if they can spot a half-eaten sandwich left on a plate or a dented cushion that makes it look like the chair's occupant has only just left the room. They need to know it's a home.'

Carys nodded. It was all so fascinating. She hadn't been at Barston for more than five minutes and she was already learning so much.

'This way,' Valerie said, opening a door into a gorgeous sitting room in dazzling white. 'My room. No public allowed in here. And no children and no dogs.'

'What about husbands?' Carys smiled.

'If I ever saw mine, it would be a miracle,' she said, motioning to a chair.

Carys sat down. 'I know what you mean. I sometimes wonder if I really got married at all.'

'These men are married to their houses. You'd better learn that early on or you'll end up being much aggrieved. Us wives come in a very poor second, I'm afraid. No use griping about it, though. There are a lot of benefits, it has to be said. I remember visiting this place when I was a teenager on a school trip. We had to write a report about it for homework but I wrote an account of what it would be like to live in a house like this.' Valerie glanced around the room with a wry little smile on her face. 'Thought it would be floating round the rooms all day in long gowns, carrying armfuls of lilies and drinking tea from china cups.'

Carys nodded. 'I was introduced to my office yesterday.'

'Poor girl. They've sprung that on you early. I had a good couple of years before Roly took over the running of this place. Needed it too to find my way around.'

'I got lost on the way to the kitchen on my first day,' Carys confided. 'But I did find the most glorious rooms en route.'

'Ah, yes, you'll never stop discovering things. Amberley's much larger than this place. It will take you years to get to know all the rooms and discover each one's personality.'

Carys smiled. She knew that and yet it was a comfort to hear somebody else tell her.

'I love your coat of arms,' she said, nodding towards the ornate fireplace and the crest above it. 'What's the motto?'

'Nil illegitimi carborundum.'

Carys frowned. It sounded familiar.

'Don't let the bastards grind you down!' Valerie explained.

'No!'

Valerie laughed and clapped her hands in delight at Carys's gullibility. 'No. But it should be. The *bastards* being the ancestors, of course. It should be every family motto, don't you think? Unfortunately, ours is some tosh about lighting the way for the future! Who on earth comes up with such extraordinary rubbish? What's yours?'

'Something about guarding the earth.'

'How dreary.'

The door to the living room opened and a young woman entered carrying a tray of tea and biscuits.

'Lovely. Thank you, Charlotte. Quick drink and dunk and then I'll give you a tour, all right?'

Carys had assumed correctly. Barston Hall was as beautiful and as elegantly put together on the inside as it was on the outside. Each room was a neat symphony of sophistication. There were no tatty curtains or threadbare rugs like at Amberley. Barston had obviously had a lot of money thrown at it because it positively gleamed and glowed with health and vitality.

'Of course, it was all a terrible mess when we first moved in,' Valerie assured her as if aware of Carys's thoughts. 'Taken years and years to restore it but worthwhile, don't you think?'

'Oh, yes,' Carys enthused.

Valerie led the way through the rooms at a great pace. 'And now,' she said, 'the crème de la crème.'

Carys's mouth dropped open as they entered the Great Hall. It was a perfect fondant of a room with ice-pink walls, great plaster friezes and enormous chandeliers hanging from a ceiling that was wedding-cake white. It was full of tourists who were gaping at its splendours and little girls demanding that their bedrooms at home be decorated just like it. It was a perfect Cinderella ballroom.

'Amberley doesn't have anything like this,' Carys confessed.

'Nonsense. This is all show. I think it's quite gaudy myself. I much prefer your wonderful long gallery.'

'You do?'

Valerie nodded. 'But don't tell darling Roly. He'd shoot me for being so disloyal. So,' Valerie said, clapping her hands together and giving Carys an eyeful of her plum-coloured nails, 'that's the house.'

'It's magnificent,' Carys sighed.

They walked across the room and Valerie opened a door on which hung a notice that read, Do not open this door. This led into a dark corridor at the end of which was another door. Valerie produced a large key and opened it and they were at once greeted by birdsong and the prettiest walled garden Carys had ever seen. It was filled with honeysuckle and roses and the smell was heavenly. There was a beautifully romantic white swing with lacy cushions and white metal seats and a small round table.

'This is my other secret hideaway,' Valerie confessed. 'I only show very special guests my garden.'

Carys felt sure that she must use that line on every single one of her guests but she smiled and blushed politely.

'It's lovely,' Carys didn't know what else to say. Her whole visit to Barston Hall had her in raptures and she seemed only capable of the most inane words of praise.

'Now,' she said as they sat down at the round table, 'tell me how you're settling into life at Amberley.'

'Well,' Carys said, puffing out her cheeks and wondering where to begin. 'I'm just beginning to realise how big a job it is.'

Valerie smiled. 'Nobody warns you, do they? It's most wicked.'

'And nobody seems to be there to tell me what to do either.'

'You have to find that out for yourself, I'm afraid. It's a role that no two people ever do the same but I'm sure you'll fall into a routine sooner or later. Let's hope it's sooner. But, tell me, do you really have a ghost?'

Carys felt the colour draining away from her face. Had Valerie heard of Lara Claridge's visit?

'What do you mean?'

'This Blue Lady I keep hearing about. Don't be coy!' Valerie said, leaning forward, her eyes sparkling with mischief. 'You've been living there for some time now. Have you seen her at all?'

Carys felt flustered. She didn't know what to say. 'Well, no,' she said at last because that was the truth - she hadn't seen her.

'Oh, what a shame,' Valerie said with a frown. 'We have Albertine, of course.'

'A ghost? You have a ghost?'

Valerie looked shifty for a moment, 'Well, between you and me - no - not really. But saying you do really brings in the public in droves. Nothing they like better. I'd think about getting one if I were you.'

Carys bit her lip. This was a very odd conversation. 'And - er - how long have you had this ghost?'

Valerie smiled a small, secretive smile. 'Ever since we found out the cost of the roof repairs.'

Carys gazed at her in wide-eyed wonder for a moment until Valerie burst out laughing and Carys could do nothing but join in.

'Seriously,' she said, 'I'd think of doing something daft - something really crazy. It's the only way for these old houses to survive. And always make a habit of walking through your house carrying something homely like a cup of tea or a ball of wool and knitting needles. Tourists love that. They love being able to identify the owners, and don't be a bit surprised if they ask you to sign their guidebooks. You'll find you become quite a celebrity. It's all marvellous fun.'

'I'm not sure I've got what it takes,' Carys said, thinking about the time she'd played angel number two in her primary school nativity play and had walked onto the stage and fallen flat on her face, squashing her halo and showing a pair of floral knickers to an hysterical audience.

'You'll get used to it,' Valerie said. 'No, really - you will. You'll be serving in the gift shop and giving guided tours before you know it.'

'Richard's already said I should give tours.'

'And he's quite right. It's the best way to get to know the house.'

'But that's what I'm worried about. I don't really know the house yet.'

'Well, who's to know that?'

'The public,' Carys said.

'Rot! They won't know if a chair is walnut or mahogany and nobody really gives a damn about dates. All they'll be interested in is what you're wearing, how you survive winter and whom, down the centuries, squandered the family money. And affairs. You must find out about affairs and the like. You know the sort of thing: illegitimate children, mistresses dying in poverty. Dear Roly thinks it's terribly immoral to recount such things but he hasn't once told any of the staff to stop. There was even an article in last week's *Vive!*. Did you see it? The Bastards of Barston Hall!'

Carys smiled.

'Not very original. I think half the county refer to us that way but our head count soared that weekend and we've taken several bookings for private parties too. Can't beat a bit of negative publicity.'

Just then, the secret door into the garden opened and a portly gentleman strode in sporting a startling red and white polka-dotted eye-patch.

'Roly, darling. What on earth are you doing here?'

'Nice to see you too,' he grumbled, his dark moustache twitching miserably as he bent to kiss his wife on the cheek.

Carys had been warned about the appearance of Roland Buckley-Stewart. He had, it was reported, got a little too friendly with one of his Amazonian parrots which he kept and bred in a huge aviary at Barston. Ever since, he'd sported an assortment of gaudy eye-patches.

'Darling, this is Carys Cuthland. Richard's wife.'

'Yes,' Roland said, extending a hand. 'We were at your wedding,' he said. 'You didn't say hello to us.'

'I'm so dreadfully sorry,' Carys said, somewhat taken aback by his honesty.

'Darling, don't be a bore. You know how busy brides are and she's saying hello now.'

'Sent you to spy on us, has he?'

Carys flushed from head to toe.

'Roly, what an accusation!'

But the look he gave Carys with his one eye seemed to betray his knowledge. Did he know? Had they caught her in disguise on a security camera?

'I wouldn't put it past that husband of yours.'

'Don't be silly, Roly. What an idea.'

'Anyway,' Roland said, dismissing his previous accusation, 'need your advice on a matter.'

'Can't it wait?' Valerie asked.

'No, not unless you want a disaster on your hands.'

'Oh,' Valerie looked apologetically at Carys.

'Please, don't worry. I've got to get back, anyway.'

'You're such a sweetie,' Valerie said, leaning forward and squeezing Carys's arm. 'We'll do this another time, though?'

Carys nodded. 'And you must come to Amberley - er - both of you.'

Roland guffawed loudly. 'That'll be the day.'

Leaving Barston, Carys couldn't help dwelling on Valerie's words of advice about acquiring a ghost. She'd been deadly serious, Carys thought, smiling at her own pun. It had made her feel terribly guilty too because she'd completely put the Amberley ghost to the back of her mind since the old duke's death and funeral. It was strange but she'd never felt more guilty about anything in her life. She felt as if she'd abandoned the mysterious 'Blue Lady' which was ridiculous because she didn't really believe she existed, did she?

Driving across the moors and crossing back into Cuthland, Carys thought back to that moment - that precise moment - when Richard had interrupted her in the Montella Room. The smell of roses had been quite overpowering and she'd known it wasn't any aftershave of Richard's.

The imagination was a powerful thing, she told herself, but could it really conjure up such scents and sensations?

As she reached the driveway of Amberley Court, she knew what she had to do. She had to go back to the Montella Room - as soon as it was closed for the day - and find out the truth. And she mustn't let anything stop her this time.

CHAPTER 17

Carys tried to pass the hours away in her office but her mind wasn't really on paperwork. The little clock above the fireplace seemed to have sticky hands for it wasn't moving quickly enough.

'Concentrate,' she said, picking up a lilac coloured envelope and opening it. It contained a single sheet of paper neatly folded around a cheque for two hundred pounds. *Cheque enclosed*, it said, the writing in blue ink in a scrawling hand. *Make sure you cash this one. Aunt Vi.* Who was Aunt Vi? She laid the cheque and note to one side and decided to ask Richard later on.

Ten to five, the little clock told her. The house closed at half-past five. Last admission was at five o'clock and meant that tourists should be out of the Montella Room by twenty past five at the very latest. That was still half an hour away.

Carys absent-mindedly opened a desk drawer hoping she'd find something to tidy and thus take her mind off the time. As she did so, she realised that she hadn't really been in possession of the desk long enough for it to get into a mess in the first place but she opened the top drawer on the left-hand side anyway. And that's when she found it.

Frowning, she took out what appeared to be a large notebook. That, she thought, certainly hadn't been in there before. She had, very carefully, gone through the desk and was quite sure she would have noticed it. Perhaps Mrs Travis had placed it there thinking it might be of use to her.

Carys ran a hand over the bright chestnut cover. It was certainly a lovely item. She opened it to discover creamy-white pages with feint lines but, what was even more of a surprise was that it had been written in.

She flicked through the notebook. Every single page had been written in and there were dates too. It was a diary. She'd found a diary in her desk.

Turning back to the first page, she read.
July 5th 1970

Will I ever be able to think of Amberley as my home? It seems far too big and cold and I can't ever imagine being cosy here.

Carys bit her lip. The words echoed her own initial thoughts on moving into Amberley. She read on.

H doesn't seem to understand. Keeps telling me that I can leave if I want but he's staying here. Not much of a compromise, is it? And there doesn't seem to be anyone I can talk to who'd understand. Feel like I'm going out of my mind.

My goodness, Carys thought. There was only one person who could have written this: Francesca. And 'H' must surely be Henry, her late father-in-law.

Carys closed the book. She felt as if she was trespassing and, as much as she wanted to, didn't think she had a right to read on. She'd have to return it. She'd have to go back to Cuthland House.

The clock struck a quarter past five. Carys placed the diary back in the drawer and got up to leave her office. It would take her a good five minutes to walk to the Montella Room and she couldn't wait any longer.

Her heart was racing as she walked through the house but she tried to calm herself. She was sure to see and hear nothing if she worked herself into a state. Breathe. *Breeeeeaaathe.* But her heart was still racing as she entered the Montella Room.

'Oh, Mrs Percival.'

'Your grace.'

'I'm sorry. I didn't mean to disturb you,' Carys said, surprised to find the room steward still present.

'Not at all, your grace,' she smiled. 'I was just getting my things together.'

'Has it been a very busy day?'

Mrs Percival looked pensive for a moment which meant she was trying to think of a tactful way of telling her that only a dozen people had passed through Amberley's rooms.

'Average for the time of year, I'd say,' she said, taking her glasses off and folding them into a conker-coloured case.

Bless her, Carys thought, watching as she left. And then she had the room to herself. She closed the door Mrs Percival had left by and then crossed the room to close the other one and, almost immediately, silence floated through her. That was one of the things about living at Amberley - you could guarantee silence. Not like her little house in Carminster which had wafer-thin walls through which you could hear your neighbours sneeze - and worse. No, Amberley was a haven of quietness and, standing there in the Montella Room, the only sound Carys could hear was the delicate ticking of an old clock and her own breathing.

She looked around the room, taking in the long scarlet and gold drapes which fell in beautiful pools on the floor, the golden chandelier hanging from the ornate plastered ceiling, and the long dining table which sparkled with fine crystal and silver cutlery. Only then did she look at the portraits. The faces were starting to become familiar to her now. She was even beginning to recognise features that were still discernible in the Brettons today. Large dark eyes. Thick dark hair. Alabaster skin. She wondered if her own pale genes would be able to compete. Pale was recessive, wasn't it? So her blonde hair and blue eyes wouldn't disrupt the Bretton lineage. Georgiana had been fair-haired and that hadn't been passed down through the centuries, had it?

She studied the beautiful face in the painting once again, and waited, as if she expected it to slowly come to life and speak to her.

'What am I waiting for?' she whispered to herself, looking around the room as the low tick of the clock reminded her of the passing of time. Would she hear the voice again? Or would she actually see something this time?

She walked across to the window and looked out across the expanse of garden towards the lake which was a brilliant silver in the early evening light. She closed her eyes and tried to relax but nothing seemed to be happening.

No, she thought. Nothing was going to happen, was it? It was just as she'd thought: the voices had been a figment of her imagination and Lara Claridge had cashed in on that.

Yet, as she left the room to return to her office, she couldn't stop the disappointment from coursing through her. She hadn't realised how much anticipation she'd been storing up but now she realised it was all a big bogus and that she'd been stupid to believe in it. It was just a good job Richard hadn't found out about any of it.

It was curiously quiet when she returned to her office. Not that it was ever anything but quiet in there but it felt strange - different - as if there was a texture you could almost reach out and touch.

Carys shook her head, determining to bring a small CD player into the room so that she could banish any unwanted silences, or introduce a computer so that she'd be greeted by its comforting hum every time she came in.

She sat back down at her desk and wondered if she should plug in the old-fashioned electronic typewriter sleeping on the floor behind her and make a start on the letters that were waiting but she didn't feel like working. She felt strangely mellow as if she could fall asleep at any moment, and yet her mind felt incredibly alert. She probably needed to get outside and stride out across the estate with the dogs. She'd just type one letter-

'I'm not always in the Montella Room, you know.'

Carys span around in her chair, her heart immediately kicked into overdrive.

'Who said that?'

There was a light laughter that reminded Carys of warm sunshine and bright summer leaves.

'Who do you *think* said that?' the voice asked in obvious amusement and Carys saw the strangest thing for there, right in the middle of the room, was something that looked like a bright blue mist. Carys looked in utter bewilderment as it descended slowly and gracefully - in the shape of a woman.

'Aren't you going to welcome me?' the woman said, her face and her figure becoming fully visible as the blue mist cleared. 'I think I'm all here now, aren't I?' she asked, her long pale fingers smoothing down the folds of her silvery blue dress. 'Oh, yes. That's better. I feel quite complete now and not a single side-effect. Such a relief. You don't know what it's like sometimes. It can be quite, quite horrid. Sometimes, only my head will appear or sometimes the head will remain behind and I am just a body. Most disconcerting and not just for me, as you can imagine.'

Carys stared, her mouth wide and gaping.

'You do look a picture. You know who I am, don't you?' the woman said. 'I'm Georgiana - from the painting you've been admiring.' She smiled encouragingly, seemingly waiting for Carys to say something. 'Wife of the fifth Duke of Cuthland?' she added. 'Sometimes known as *The Blue Lady*?'

'Yes,' Carys said. It was all she could manage.

'Good. And you're Carys, wife of the twelfth duke, yes?'

'Yes.'

'I have a feeling we're going to be great friends. Got lots and lots

in common, you and I. I've been watching you, you know.'

'You have?'

'Of course. Not much else to do round here, is there? Thought I would come and make you welcome. Amberley can be rather daunting, do you not agree?'

Carys nodded.

'Look,' Georgiana said, 'if you're just going to stare, would you mind if I sat down?'

'Of course not,' Carys said, clearing her throat which suddenly seemed very dry.

'Thank you. Oh, what a lovely chair. I do like these big comfortable armchairs. We never had anything like these. Upholstery wasn't the norm. You know,' she said, looking around the room, 'this was once my sitting room.'

'Really?' Carys said. 'I've been told it was a sitting room but nobody was able to tell me whose it was or when.'

'Well, now you know.' Georgiana smiled again and her whole face lit up the room. She really was exceptionally beautiful.

There was a moment's silence when the two of them just stared at each other.

'You look as if you want to ask me some questions,' Georgiana said in a quiet voice.

Carys nodded. 'I - I can't quite take all this in. You're really a ghost?'

Georgiana nodded. 'I really am.'

'And it was you I heard - in the meeting that day? And that night in the storm?'

'It was. I hope you didn't mind me not putting in an appearance, though. The storm would have made it difficult. I think you would refer to it as a technical hitch. And the meeting - well - I never could stand meetings.'

'Georgiana.'

'That's me.'

'Why have you come back?' Carys dared to ask. 'Lara Claridge said-'

'Oh, she is such an awful busybody. I wouldn't listen to her. One of life's great meddlers.'

'But she said you'd have something to tell me.'

Georgiana's eyes widened and Carys saw that they were the colour of new beech leaves and yet they'd looked so dark in the painting - sparkling with mischief.

'I have a lot of things to tell you.'

'Like what?'

'Patience,' Georgiana told her. 'All in good time. Now,' she said, 'tell me how you are settling in.'

And Carys did. She told Georgiana how strange it had been to move from her tiny town house into the sprawling acres of Amberley Court. She confessed how isolated she felt sometimes and how Richard's parents had never really shown any interest in her. She admitted, for the first time, how much she resented the time Richard spent away from her and how nobody had ever sat down and explained what her role was.

Carys felt incredibly relaxed when she came to the end of what had turned out to be a rather long tirade. And Georgiana had proved the most excellent of listeners. Not once had she interrupted and, what was most refreshing, she didn't come out with banal and predictable comments like, *well, what did you expect?*

'But you love it, do you not?' Georgiana asked once she was quite sure Carys had finished.

'Amberley?' Carys said with a smile. 'Oh, yes. I love it. I love it like I've loved no other place. People warned me about it but I didn't really believe them, but it gets a hold of you, it really does, and I can't imagine life anywhere else now.'

Georgiana nodded, recognising the sentiment. 'Ah! How many times have I heard that?'

'Does it look any different to you?' Carys asked.

Georgiana looked around. 'I have been here longer than you think. You know, keeping an eye on the place. I have never really left. But, I don't suppose it has really changed that much.'

'I don't think the Brettons like change, do they?' Carys said. 'I once complained to Richard about the appalling draft under our bedroom door and he told me that the wind had been howling under there for three hundred years and we couldn't stop it now.'

'How very Bretton,' Georgiana said, making Carys laugh. 'The Brettons are a unique family,'

'I've never met one like them,' Carys agreed. 'I mean, there's Phoebe - Richard's sister - she's so warm, so lovely - would do anything for you but then there's Francesca, Richard's mother, whom

I can't make out at all. It's as if I've done her some great wrong in a previous life, only I can't work out how to make amends.'

'I noticed you have been having problems with her,' Georgiana said.

'I don't suppose you've any suggestions,' Carys asked hopefully, wondering if Georgiana's purpose was as advisor.

'I think she still misses Amanda,' Georgiana said. 'They got on famously and I think she still cannot believe things didn't work out.'

'Great,' Carys nodded as if she'd expected as much. 'Then there's nothing I can do?'

'Allow time to weave its magic.'

Carys sighed. 'Always time. Seems to be the answer to everything.' It was then that Carys noticed something. 'You're wearing that dress from the portrait.'

Georgiana laughed. 'Of course. It's my favourite. I do believe that if you find something that works for you then you should stick to it.'

Carys smiled but, at the same time, couldn't help wondering if it wasn't a bit worse for wear by now. Did she dare ask if ghosts perspired?

A knock on the door made Carys's heart skip a beat.

'Your grace?' Mrs Travis's head popped around the door.

'Mrs Travis?' Carys tried to sound perfectly normal but couldn't help being aware of the ghost sitting in her armchair right in front of Mrs Travis.

'I wondered if there was anything I could get you, my lady.'

'Oh,' Carys said, suddenly realising that it was after six o'clock. 'No, I'm fine. Just - er - finishing off some letters.'

Mrs Travis looked over Carys's desk, noticing, no doubt, that the typewriter was still on the floor. But she was too polite to say anything.

'Are you all right, my lady?'

'Yes,' Carys said, keen to get rid of her as soon as possible before she noticed Georgiana.

'Only, you look a bit pale.'

'I'm always pale. That's normal.'

'No,' Mrs Travis said, shaking her head. 'This is a different pale.'

Carys bit her lip. What on earth did she mean, *a different pale*? How ridiculous. She swallowed. 'Now you come to mention it, I do feel a bit strange.'

'Nauseous?' Mrs Travis suggested.

Carys nodded, surprised, indeed, to find she really did feel 'pale'. 'Yes. How could you tell?'

'You've gone exactly the same shade as her grace used to go when she-'

'When she what?'

'When she was expecting,' Mrs Travis finished, and there was an awkward silence.

'Well, I'm not,' Carys said quickly.

Mrs Travis blushed. 'I beg your pardon, my lady. I spoke too hastily. It wasn't my place.'

'No need to apologise,' Carys assured her, noticing her flame-red cheeks.

'I'll be going then.'

'Goodnight, Mrs Travis,' Carys said and watched, with relief, as she left.

Georgiana immediately burst out laughing.

'Oh, my goodness!' Carys exclaimed. 'Didn't she see you?'

Georgiana shook her head. 'People only see what they expect to see. Mrs Travis does not believe in ghosts.'

Carys frowned. 'But *I* didn't believe in ghosts.'

Georgiana's eyes narrowed. 'Are you quite sure?'

'Yes!'

'It takes a brave person to admit they believe in the supernatural, I know.'

'But I didn't - I mean, *I don't.*'

'Then, why are you having this conversation with me?'

Carys sighed in exasperation but had to admit that the question had her stumped. She leant back on the edge of her desk and drummed her nails on the polished wood.

'Does anybody else know you're here?' Carys asked and watched as Georgiana got up from the chair and walked across the room. There was a beautiful fluidity about the way she moved and Carys was completely mesmerised.

'I am quite a private person,' Georgiana said, selecting a copy of *Fruit Gardening for the Faint-hearted* from one of the bookcases. 'I don't like fanfares whenever I want to make an appearance. Not like some ghosts who buy chains to rattle at the poor mortals of their choice.'

Carys could have pursued this comment but decided not to. 'But does Richard know you're here?'

Georgiana laughed. 'What do you think?'

'He barely has time to notice *I'm* here let alone a ghost.'

'Exactly,' Georgiana said, replacing the fruit book and pulling out *Pruning for the Panicky*. 'What extraordinary titles.'

For a few quiet moments, Georgiana pulled out title after title, frowning and laughing whilst Carys watched, fascinated by her new friend and her astonishing, ethereal beauty. It was strange. She wasn't *solid* like a normal person. Her skin wasn't opaque - it was kind of translucent - not so much that you could see right through her but more like a hologram or a reflection in water.

'Georgiana's such a pretty name,' Carys said, suddenly feeling quite mellow about having a ghost in her office.

'Everyone was called Georgiana back then; it was so hard to be original. I tried being called 'Georgie' for a while but my husband went quite mad. At least yours is original.'

'A bit too original,' Carys pointed out. 'People can never get it right and I always end up being Carrie or Clarice.'

'But now you're *your grace*,' Georgiana said with a conspiratorial wink.

'That's what they say. But, quite frankly, I'm not quite sure who I am any more'

'You think *that* is a problem. My problem is, I don't know *when* I am half the time.'

'I beg your pardon?'

'I know *where* I am, because I've never really left Amberley, but I do not know, for sure, *when* I am.'

'Oh, I see,' Carys said. 'Well, you're in 2007.'

Georgiana frowned. 'Means absolutely nothing to me. Decades come and decades go. I always think it is rather difficult to remember what day it is when it changes every day, and it is even more difficult to keep a track of time when you are dead. Days, months - whole centuries - merge into one another.'

'I suppose they must,' Carys said because she'd never really given it much thought before.

'Anyway,' Georgiana said, replacing *Onions for the Uninitiated*, 'I didn't come here to talk about the vagaries of time. I came to find out how you are getting on. When a woman moves into a house like this, it can be a bit unsettling. It is not her home. Normal couples choose a home together, do they not? But Amberley is inflicted upon us - we do not get a choice.' Georgiana looked across at Carys, her delicate eyebrows raised ever-so-slightly, as if she was wondering if she'd hit the mark.

Carys nodded. 'You're right. You're absolutely right.'

'I know I am. I've been thinking about this for two hundred years.'

Carys smiled. She was warming to this woman very quickly.

'The Bretton men have their whole history to keep them warm: twelve generations to be precise. There are portraits and photographs, treasures and trophies. You know what I brought when I came to Amberley, other than the Bridedale estate in Yorkshire? Four trunks of clothes. That was it.'

Carys nodded again, thinking of all the little knickknacks she'd packed away or left in her old attic whilst she decided what to do with them.

'When I first came here,' Carys said, 'I thought I'd be able to put my things wherever I wanted to but I was soon put right on that point. But I don't suppose my collection of pottery owls would look right in the Red Drawing Room.'

'This is exactly the point I am trying to make,' Georgiana said huffily. 'This place has hundreds of rooms but we are not allowed to fill any of them with our own things, are we?'

'Well, I've been told I can pretty much use this one as I want.'

'Oh, you mean you can get rid of all these useless books? And roll up that horrid rug and burn it? And move that terrible portrait and hang up a poster of - er - what's his name? Johnny Depp?'

Carys laughed. 'No. No. I can't do that, I'm afraid.'

Georgiana sighed. 'I always longed to rebel whilst I was mistress here,' she said with a naughty little giggle.

'What, like paint the rooms in lime and magenta?' Carys suggested.

'Wonderful. And not so outrageous when you think of the terrible scarlets and turquoises they used to favour.'

'How about ripping out the library and installing a cinema? You do know what a cinema is?' Carys added, remembering that Georgiana was from the eighteenth century.

'Of course. We do manage to keep up with the times in the afterworld, you know. How else would I know about gorgeous Johnny Depp? And I think a cinema would be a fabulous idea. It might actually make some money too.'

'And that old stable block that's never used - we could turn that into a luxury health spa with swimming pool and sauna...'

'You know, we might be joking but I think we're actually making a lot of sense.'

Carys looked thoughtful. 'I don't think Richard would be very happy if I suggested-'

'You keep saying that, don't you?'

'What do you mean?'

'I've been reading your mind a lot lately, and it is always, Richard wouldn't like this. Richard wouldn't approve so I won't do that.'

'It is his house.'

'But you have to share it. Surely you should have some say?'

'Did *you*?' Carys challenged and, for a moment, Georgiana looked angry - as if she'd been caught out.

'Of course I didn't but it didn't stop me from voicing my opinions. I've heard what you have to say in those boring old meetings and your ideas are good. You should just say them a bit louder and make sure they are followed up and that you get the credit for them. Too often, I've seen the women of this house being taken advantage of. These Bretton men have a habit of stealing their wives' ideas and passing them off as their own. It is sly and it is brutish and you must not stand for it.'

Carys gave a little smile. She had the feeling that this was a pet topic of Georgiana's and wondered if she'd given that particular speech before.

'Yes, I have,' Georgiana said.

'What?'

'I have given this speech before.'

Carys looked dumbfounded and then remembered that Georgiana had said that she could read her mind. It was a most unsettling thought.

'I am sorry if you find it intrusive but it does save a lot of time,' she said, sitting down again in the armchair. 'You see, there have been a lot of unhappy wives at Amberley and I came to the conclusion that I could be a sort of welcoming committee: an unofficial family if you like. Us women must stick together. We are the ones who provide the male heir and continue the great dynasty, are we not?'

Carys nodded vehemently.

'Without us, the real history of these houses would be lost because it is the details - it is the *stories* - that make these houses what they are and men are too busy to remember any of these things, do you not agree?'

Carys felt that, if she nodded any more, her head might fall off.

'To men, these houses are a business. They love them, of course, and are deeply proud of them but not in the same way as a woman. They take pride in them the same way they would any expensive item. It is a symbol to the outside world of who they are. But, to a woman, these places mean family - a handing on from generation to generation.'

'Yes,' Carys said. It seemed quite inadequate because she truly believed that Georgiana was right, but it was all she could think of to say in reply.

'I mean, I bet Richard doesn't know who was married to the third duke.'

'No, Richard's really good with the family tree.'

'Are you sure?'

'Yes.'

Georgiana didn't look convinced. 'You just try him - next time he's-'

There was a knock on the door.

'Carys? You in?'

It was Richard, as if he'd heard his cue.

'Yes. Come on in.' Carys looked pleadingly at Georgiana.

'Do not worry,' she said. 'I will make myself scarce.'

'Will I see you again?'

'Of course you will,' Georgiana said, her voice softer as she slowly began to dissolve into a beautiful blue mist before fading away into nothing.

'Extraordinary,' Carys whispered just as Richard entered the room.

'What is?' he asked.

'Oh, nothing. Just thinking about something.'

He frowned for a moment but let it pass. 'Listen,' he said, crossing the room quickly and kissing her on the cheek. 'There's been a crisis up at Joe Bempton's farm and it's got to be sorted.'

'What kind of crisis? Anything I can help with?'

'I have to go straight back there so I won't be around this

evening.'

'But you said–'

'I'm sorry, sweetheart. It'll have to wait. You have a nice meal.'

'On my own–'

'And I'll see you later,' he said, turning to leave. She watched him cross the room.

'Richard?'

'Yes?'

She bit her lip. Did she dare? Yes. She did. 'Do you know who was married to third duke?'

He looked puzzled for a moment as if wondering whether she was testing him. 'I don't know,' he said, 'Catherine somebody or other.' And, with that, he rushed out of the room as if the very devil was at his heels.

Carys sighed in disappointment because she knew Richard was wrong and Georgiana had been right.

'It was Caroline,' Georgiana's disembodied voice came from the shadows by the bookcase. 'Caroline Percy.'

CHAPTER 18

The next few days passed by in a blur of activity. Carys had never been so busy in her life. Her personal correspondence seemed to have quadrupled, she'd appointed herself manager of the shop as there wasn't one already and everything was a mess, there was the day-to-day running of the house and staff to cope with, and she'd set herself the task of raising an obscene amount of money for Amberley as a surprise for Richard but still had to work out how she was going to go about it. For the first time since her arrival at Amberley, she was looking forward to the weekly estate meeting. It would give her an opportunity to have a rest.

Francesca no longer attended the meetings although Richard had encouraged her to do so.

'She said it's over to us now,' he told Carys. And Carys had truly felt as if the baton had been handed on to her when she was given Francesca's chair at the first estate meeting since the old duke's funeral. Richard, of course, sat in the chair that had been his father's but, for the time being, that still left two empty chairs.

And that's when Carys remembered the diary. She had to return Francesca's diary. It had obviously been placed in her desk by mistake. It also made Carys realise how easy it was to get into her office and whether she should have the lock fixed on her door. Richard, however, frowned on internal locks apart from on the most important rooms of the house and none of the keys were ever kept in them. Even their private bathroom door didn't have a lock which Carys found deeply unsettling. With so many staff, anyone might interrupt her as she lay in the bathtub. Carys often worried that the bits of slack rope, and Private signs weren't enough to deter a particularly nosy tourist.

'Well, say something about it, then.'

Carys started. It was Georgiana.

'If you feel that strongly, say something. That's what these boring old meetings are for. Tell them you had to stop a young man sneaking into the private apartments last week.'

Carys blushed. And then dared to speak.

A stunned silence greeted her as she finished.

'Why didn't you tell me?' Richard asked, frowning at her from his end of the table.

'I - forgot,' Carys said, feeling her blush deepen. 'And I didn't want to worry you.'

'But this does worry me.'

'And concerns us all,' Pamela Church, Amberley's curator piped. 'Think of the dangers this could impose on the collection. He might have stolen any number of things. I've always been concerned about the lack of security here.'

Richard still looked hesitant.

'And then I saw a woman wondering along the corridor towards my office,' Carys said.

'When?' Richard's face had completely dropped in horror.

'Yesterday,' Carys lied.

'How on earth did she get there?'

'Well, it isn't hard,' Carys said. 'Not if you really want to.'

'*And she really wanted to,*' Georgiana's voice said.

'And she really wanted to,' Carys echoed.

'This is terrible,' Richard raked a hand through his hair which was beginning to look stressed like the rest of him.

'I've said it all along...' Pamela Church went on but nobody was really listening to her. Everybody was talking over each other.

'...fire risk...'

'...clippings from the garden. It'll be objects from the house next.'

'No room is safe...'

'...not enough room stewards either.'

'Private isn't enough these days.'

'...have to keep things under lock and key.'

'QUIET!' Richard bellowed and gave a huge sigh. 'Clearly, something has to be done. I hadn't realised the extent of the problem.'

Carys's heart was racing. She'd been listened to - again. It was a small triumph but a triumph nonetheless.

As the meeting ended, Carys sprinted across the room to grab Richard before he could lose himself on the estate again.

'Richard? Can I have a word?'

'Can it wait?'

Carys desperately wanted to say, *Until when?* But thought better of it. 'It's your Aunt Violet. She's sent another cheque.'

'Tear it up.'

'What?'

'She doesn't really have money to throw around like that. I don't know why she keeps posting us these cheques. Just bin it. With that, he was gone.

'She means well,' Pearl Janson said.

'I beg your pardon?' Carys didn't like her private conversations with her husband being listened to but she hadn't had much choice in the matter if she'd wanted to speak to him.

'Dear old Vi. She means well but, between you and me, she's not all there.'

Carys frowned. Who was this poor old relative who'd been so cruelly dismissed by, it seemed, everyone at Amberley?

Mrs Travis was quick to provide Carys with the information she needed. 'She doesn't get out much, poor lady.'

'She wasn't at our wedding, was she?' Carys asked, feeling awful that she couldn't remember.

'She was at the ceremony as she lives in the Cathedral Close but she doesn't come to Amberley any more'

'All the more reason that we should visit her,' Carys said, thinking it terrible that an elderly relative had been left out in the cold as it were.

Mrs Travis scribbled the address and phone number down on the back of an old envelope and, putting everything else on hold, Carys made a quick call and left at once, driving into town and parking in her old road which was only a quarter of a mile from the cathedral.

Great Aunt Violet lived in one of the tall thin Georgian houses in Carminster's Cathedral Close. It was one of the many properties dotted around the city that belonged to the Brettons. Most of them were rented out but there were still relatives of the family inhabiting a few and Great Aunt Violet had the most handsome of them all.

Immediately banishing her picture of a formidable matriarch with a heaving bosom and a stern demeanour, Carys thought of the friendly voice which had greeted her on the phone when she'd been asked over.

'The door will be open so come on in. I'll be in the living room on the first floor,' a jovial voice told her and, when Carys arrived, she followed the instructions, walking up a red carpeted stairway where a plethora of black and white family photographs were hung. Were they all Brettons, Carys wondered?

'Aunt Violet?' Carys called.

'In here, dear.'

Carys turned left at the top of the stairs and entered a gloriously light room with a huge picture window overlooking the cathedral.

'Hello,' she said, walking over to the great winged chair and bending to kiss the old lady's powdered and rather scarlet cheek.

'Hello, dear. How lovely to meet you at last.'

'I can't believe nobody's told me about you before. You must think me awfully rude.'

'Not at all. Not at all. There are rather a lot of us to cope with.'

Carys smiled and sat down in the chair opposite which Violet motioned to.

'Now, let me see if I've got this right. You're Henry Bretton's aunt and Richard's Great Aunt?'

'That's right,' she said with a warm smile. 'It's all so complicated, isn't it? Other people's family trees. One's own is bad enough but other people's!'

'I'm just about keeping up.'

'I'm sure you are.'

'I'd love to know more about everybody, though. They're just names at the moment, you see. I've spent hours poring over books and such but it's always nice to get a proper feel for people.'

'Well, I'm not sure if my memory will serve me when it comes to the history of the Brettons,' she said, her dark eyes gazing upwards. 'But I can tell you about my own little branch of the family.'

Carys nodded and smiled.

'It all began quite simply with my son, Robert. He married Antonia - a lovely girl but she did insist on moving to Canada where her family are from. I was very put out, of course, because I detest travelling, in any form, but most of all by aeroplane. And I hardly ever get to see my grandchildren.'

'You have four, yes?' Carys said, remembering her study of the family tree.

'That's right: Adam, Teresa, Madeleine and Alice. All grown up now. Adam and Alice have families of their own so I'm now a great-grandmother.'

'That's wonderful.'

'Not so wonderful when they live on the other side of the Atlantic Ocean.'

'But they visit, don't they?'

Violet sighed. 'They have their own lives to lead. Why would they want to spend half a day on a plane to visit an old woman in England? I don't blame them and I don't make a fuss about it. That's the way life is. I was the same at their age: busy with me and mine, and that's the way it should be. But I could do with some company now and again,' Violet confessed. 'One of those old-fashioned companions,' she added with a little laugh. 'To read to me.'

Carys looked across at her and then noticed all the books in the room as if for the first time. 'You like reading?'

'Used to,' she said. 'Can't read a blessed thing now.'

Carys frowned and then an idea occurred. 'I could read to you.'

Violet looked across the room in surprise. 'You? Read to me?'

'Why not? It would be my pleasure.'

'Are you sure? I mean, I couldn't afford to pay you and I'm sure you're far too busy already.'

Carys's mouth dropped. 'I don't expect payment. Oh, Aunt Violet, it would be a pleasure to read to you.'

'Well,' the old lady said, 'I'm not sure what to say.'

'How about yes?'

Violet's mouth turned up into a cute smile and her cheeks glowed cherry-red with excitement.

'We could start now,' Carys said, leaping up from her chair in excitement. 'You have so many books to discover, right here.'

'Oh, no! These are all so old and dull. They have even less life in them than I do.'

'Well, what if I raid the library at Amberley?'

Violet shook her head. 'Dull, dull, dull. You really wouldn't want to read *The Complete Works of William Bretton*, would you?'

Carys laughed. She'd seen the self-published collection of novels in the fading covers and had dared to peep inside only to find page after page of self-pitying prose.

'Or,' Violet continued, '*The Keen Discoveries of-*'

'*a Reluctant Duke*,' Carys finished and they both erupted with laughter. 'Yes, I found that one.'

'I dare say it didn't appeal.'

'Not really bedtime reading.'

'No, the ninth duke was something else entirely.'

'Then I should raid the local library?'

Violet nodded. 'Good idea.'

'What sort of books do you like? Fiction? Non-fiction?'

'Fiction,' she said without a moment's hesitation.

'Me too. Any particular genre?'

'Romance.'

'Me too,' Carys said.

'I think we're going to have a lot of fun,' Violet said, her cheeks still glowing in anticipation of a very merry future indeed.

'There's just one thing,' Carys said.

'What's that, my dear?'

'I've been asked to return this to you.' Carys dug in her pocket for the cheque and handed it to Violet.

'Oh, my gracious.'

Carys watched as her expression of merriment was replaced by one of consternation. 'There's no need, really.'

'No need? What absolute rot. Don't forget, I was brought up a Bretton. I know what it's like. It's all very well living in a sprawling mansion but there's never enough money in the kitty.'

'But you must look after your own needs.'

'I've got enough, don't you worry.'

Carys didn't say anything but she saw a definite twinkle in the old lady's eyes which seemed to hint at hidden secrets.

After tea which was served in huge mugs with *ARS* printed across them which Violet explained stood for Amberley Rural Show until somebody commented on the unfortunate acronym and it was changed to ACS: Amberley Country Show, Carys left, kissing the powdery red cheek of Aunt Violet.

'I'll come and see you soon,' she said, 'with some books.'

'Romance. Nothing but romance will do at my age,' Aunt Vi said.

'I'll see what I can find.'

'And, Carys,' she said, her eyes suddenly filled with concern.

'Yes?'

'Don't let everyone at the big house get you down, will you? You're too sweet for that.'

Carys nodded and gave a weak smile. They hadn't talked about

Amberley at all. So how had Violet known?

Mrs Franklin was working her way through a pile of correspondence when Carys returned to her office.

'Mr Morris called, your grace, wondering if you got his letter about the Montella exhibition.'

'Thank you, Mrs Franklin, I'll call him back later.'

Mr Morris was the curator of Carminster's Castle Museum - a grand Victorian Gothic building housing one of the best art collections in the country. They were arranging an exhibition on Leo Montella and, naturally, were interested in featuring some of Amberley's paintings. This was one of the many new responsibilities which now fell to Carys. She had to check everything with Richard first, of course. She couldn't just decide to ship his family portraits out all over the country whenever somebody requested, and there were all manners of thing to arrange from safe removal to transportation and insurance.

'And Mrs Travis wanted to know if you'd be around for lunch.'

Carys looked at the clock. It was after midday already.

'I'll grab a sandwich a bit later,' she said. She had something she felt she must tackle first. She wouldn't be able to concentrate on anything else until it was done. 'I'm just popping out to Cuthland House,' she told Mrs Franklin. 'I won't be long.'

Carys opened the drawer of her desk and removed the diary.

There was only one dog hanging around the house and that was Mungo, the black Labrador.

'Come on, boy,' Carys said, opening the door into a bright garden, the early afternoon sun burning out of a brilliant blue sky. With her pale colouring and her face's tendency to give way to freckles, she really should've worn a hat but her mind was fixed on getting out as quickly as possible.

Heading out across the fields, she slowed her pace to accommodate the leisurely tread of Mungo who didn't even want to break into a trot. She didn't blame him; it was so hot. Carys tried fanning herself with the diary but it was too big and cumbersome to afford any relief. Instantly, a wave of temptation overcome her.

No. She shouldn't.

Apart from those first few pages when she'd first discovered it, she'd managed to resist but, away from the house with no eyes to watch her, she felt an irresistible urge to delve into the cream pages. She bit her lip. What harm could it do? She sat down on a patch of sun-warmed grass and read.

October 1979

I am becoming more and more convinced that these houses aren't family homes. I actually lost Richie yesterday! What a horrible feeling that was. Phoebe and I searched for hours. I was so worried he'd got up to some mischief in the attics and we'd never be able to find him. Phoebe was convinced that the ghost had got him. I must tell the staff not to encourage her with such nonsense as ghosts. The only thing that haunts Amberley is the perpetual cold.

Carys grinned in instant recognition. It didn't say where they found Richard or when for that matter which was rather a shame so she flipped some pages and read another entry.

April 1981

Came downstairs this morning to find nanny in an awful state. 'It's Lady Phoebe!' she kept shouting and I didn't find out what the fuss was about until I went through to the hallway and saw Phoebe sitting, in full riding regalia, on her pony, Minstrel. She looked quite unapologetic and demanded to know why dogs were allowed into the house but not ponies. 'He's wiped his hooves,' she said. I didn't really have a suitable answer to that.

Carys flicked through the pages, pausing to read a few more entries before turning to the final page.

December 1984

I can't believe this is the last page already. So much has happened since I began this diary over seven years ago. I haven't been a very good diarist. Sometimes, many months can pass without a single entry. I have three children now: my handsome sons and my beautiful daughter, and I have the feeling I may be expecting again.

I feel a little more contented here now than I was when I first moved in. It's taken all this time for me to think of Amberley as a home. It has its faults: I will never get used to having the public walking around the house, and I'm still not a huge fan of Chippendale, but I'm learning to live with Amberley's quirks.

Carys closed the book and got up from the rock-hard ground, rubbing her numbed bottom. Her limbs would probably be red-raw from the sun now and she was beginning to feel a little dehydrated. She hadn't meant to read so much but, as soon as she'd opened the diary, time had been swallowed up as curiosity had taken over. She could have read for hours, dipping in and out of the years like a nosy yo-yo, but time had marched on and she had to be on her way.

She slowed her pace as she approached the large Victorian house. Mungo edged up beside her and looked up expectantly. She could see that an upstairs window was open and a pretty flutter of curtain was trying to escape. Francesca, Carys thought, must be in.

She knocked on the door and waited.

And waited.

And knocked again.

'Francesca?' she called. Mungo gazed up at the house, his tail wagging in mild excitement before he lost interest and went to nose around the plants in the garden.

'It's Carys. Are you there?'

Carys stepped back from the door and looked up at the windows before shrugging and sighing. Once again, she had the feeling that the house wasn't empty. She also had the feeling that Francesca wasn't washing her hair or tied up in the kitchen. She didn't want to see her, did she?

Stepping back into the tiny porch, Carys laid the book down on the slatted seat underneath a hanging basket. She hoped it would be safe there.

'Come on, Mungo,' she said, and he followed her out of the garden and back towards Amberley.

'Long time, no see,' a cheery voice greeted her as soon as she stepped into the hallway. It was Phoebe, closely followed by an ever-attentive Dizzy the spaniel.

'Phoebe!' Carys said, and they embraced. It felt an age since they'd had a chat - long before the old duke's funeral. Phoebe had been a little distant since then, finding a job in the nearby town of Pennington Bridge and living quietly.

For a moment, Carys just smiled at her. 'How are you?' she asked, trying to banish the image of the dark-haired youngster in the hallway on her pony, Minstrel.

'Okay,' she said, her smile warm and genuine. 'Moving on,' she added.

Carys nodded. 'It takes time,' she said, realising, too late, that she'd used the very phrase that she hated to hear herself.

'And how are you?'

Carys shrugged. 'Fine.'

Phoebe's eyes narrowed. 'Yeah?'

'Yes.'

'Sure? You look tired.'

Carys nodded. 'A little.'

'They're treating you okay - everybody?'

'Yes, fine.'

Phoebe didn't look convinced. 'Including Richard?'

Carys blinked. There was no hiding from Phoebe. She was a woman who couldn't be fooled and she always managed to isolate a problem immediately.

'To be honest, I don't see much of him.'

Phoebe frowned. 'I thought as much. Rotten man.'

'No. No, he's not.'

'He jolly well is. He doesn't deserve you. Expecting you to run his house for him all day every day whilst he goes off and-'

'He's got so much to cope with.'

Phoebe placed her tiny hands on her tiny hips. 'When was the last time you two went out for a nice meal?'

Carys blinked even harder. 'Well, he's always so busy-'

'When?'

Carys's mind span back through the months since their wedding. They hadn't, had they? They didn't even have time for a proper sit-at-a-table meal alone together any more It was always grab-a-sandwich or else a stifling meal with local dignitaries in the State Dining Room where conversation was invariably mundane and impersonal.

'Just after we got engaged,' she said at last.

'I thought as much. It's not good enough.'

'But, Phoebe-'

'Stop making excuses for him. It's outrageous!'

'Not really-'

'We need to discuss this,' Phoebe continued. She was off now and there was no stopping her. 'We need a meeting.'

'I don't really think-'

'There's only one thing to do at a time like this.'

For a moment, Carys was silent with wonder. 'What?'

'Get the YBG's together, of course.'

CHAPTER 19

'So, are you going to tell me what the YBG's are?' Carys asked. It was later that evening and she was sat in the Yellow Drawing Room with Phoebe and Serena who were looking at each other with sisterly intimacy. Phoebe had kicked off her shoes and was resting her feet on Dizzy who had rolled over to expose a fluffy white belly which demanded much rubbing, and Serena was curled up in a winged chair, her feet tucked under her bottom, making her look like a contented cat.

Finally, Serena nodded.

'The Yew Bower Girls,' Phoebe explained quietly.

Carys tried not to giggle. 'What on *earth* is that?'

'You've not been to the yew bower?'

Carys shook her head.

'It's a part of the wood above Amberley. It's mostly beeches but there's this spooky little corner of yew trees.'

'Not spooky,' Serena said, 'magical.'

'Oh, yes,' Phoebe corrected. 'I forgot. You used to practice all your spells up there.'

Serena gave Phoebe a glare which could easily have become the Medusa.

'We used to hide out there as kids,' Phoebe explained. 'It's very important to have a place to call your own when you're a kid, even when growing up in a house the size of Amberley. It's vital to have a little hideaway where nobody can find you.'

'Away from the house,' Serena added.

'Most important,' Phoebe stressed.

'And one the boys could never find out about.'

'And we only ever went there at dusk,' Phoebe said.

Serena gave a little smile. 'We used to sneak out and run across the lawn in our nightgowns.'

'But it's miles away,' Carys pointed out.

'That was all part of the fun,' Phoebe said. 'Cupboards and wardrobes were no good to us. Where's the adventure in that? But a secluded part of the wood when evening is drawing in - now that's exciting!'

'I'm not sure I like the sound of that,' Carys confessed.

'Town girl,' Serena admonished.

'I have just as much country running through my veins as you.'

'Prove it then.'

'Okay,' Carys said. 'We'll go.'

'Great.' Phoebe clapped her hands.

'We'll have to tell Penny,' Serena said.

'Of course. We couldn't go without Pen.'

'Who's Pen?'

'A founder member of the YBG's. We can't think of holding a meeting without her,' Phoebe said.

'It would be unlucky. And Natasha too.'

'Of course,' Serena said.

'Another founder member?' Carys asked, becoming more and more intrigued by this secret society. 'Anyone else?'

'Anyone you'd like to invite?' Phoebe asked.

Carys thought. Who could she think of who'd enjoy traipsing through the undergrowth at night?

'Louise - my best-friend,' Carys said at last, thinking she couldn't possibly let her friend miss out on such an adventure.

'She'll have to be initiated,' Serena pointed out.

'So will Carys, but that won't take long.'

'Initiated?' Again, Carys sounded a little unsure.

'Initiation by Bailey's,' Phoebe explained. 'Simply delightful.'

Carys smiled. 'When do we go?'

After a few phone calls, they left the house when the sky's burning apricot light was mellowing and fading. Carys had told Richard that she was going to meet Louise in the local pub and he'd simply nodded before tumbling onto the sofa with a glass of whisky.

Louise had parked down the driveway, away from the house, and had waited for Carys behind a big rhododendron bush.

'This is rather fun,' she giggled, nodding to Phoebe and Serena. 'What do we do now?'

'We're meeting Pen and Nat by the stile,' Phoebe said. 'Less suspicious that way.'

Carys frowned. 'Who are we hiding from?'

'The men, of course,' Serena said.

'They mustn't know.'

Carys decided that this must be some sort of hang-up from childhood and that they weren't willing to reveal their secret hideaway even now.

'They had their secret dens and so did we,' Phoebe explained.

'Do they still use theirs?' Carys asked, trying to imagine Richard and Jamie sneaking off to some secluded spot on the estate.

Phoebe shrugged. 'I wouldn't put it past them. Come on.'

They ran across the lawn like naughty school girls. Then, it was up the bank and into the beech trees and along to the stile where Penny and Natasha were. Penny was as tiny as a church mouse but had a huge smile. Natasha looked more serious, her dark eyebrows hovering over a pair of stern, inquisitive eyes.

Once over the stile, they slowed their pace to a fast walk.

'What's the hurry?' Louise asked.

'I think it's the thought of a plastic cup of Bailey's,' Penny said. 'If memory serves me correctly.'

'It does,' Phoebe called back.

'So, Carys,' Natasha began. 'How are you enjoying life at Amberley?'

'Gosh!' Phoebe laughed. 'Can't you say anything without sounding like you're interviewing someone?'

Serena grinned back at Natasha and Carys.

'You're a reporter?' Carys said, somewhat startled.

'Don't worry,' Serena said, 'she's one of us.'

'A true YBG,' Phoebe added.

'Okay,' Carys said. 'Well, I didn't think it would be quite so much work,' she confided to Natasha. 'Everything's so big after my little terrace in town.'

'I bet you don't know what half the rooms are for,' Natasha laughed.

'I think I'll get there eventually but I do tend to get a bit lost every now and again.'

'Nobody can be expected to feel at home straight away,' Louise said in defence of her friend. 'Whether it's a huge stately home or a tiny bungalow.'

They walked on through the silent wood. They'd passed through the beeches now and everything suddenly seemed much darker.

Large smooth trunks gave way to dark, gnarled, knuckly trees with sharp-looking foliage.

'This is it,' Phoebe said in tones that were hushed and rather reverential. 'We're nearly there.'

Louise looked at Carys and her eyes widened as if to say, what are we doing here? But Carys was rather taken with the place, deciding that both Phoebe and Serena were right: the yew tree bower was both magical and spooky. The thick, twisted trunks and dark emerald fronds were quite bewitching to behold in the fading light and everything was so quiet. Carys believed that she'd never heard a silence like it before.

She reached out and touched one of the yew trees, surprised that the fronds felt so soft. The ground was carpet-soft too and swallowed the sound of their footsteps. Then, all of a sudden, there was a small break in the woodland where you could see out over the rolling fields beyond.

'What's that?' Louise asked, pointing to a white bird flying low.

'A barn owl,' Penny said. 'Out looking for mice.'

Louise pulled a face. She didn't like being anywhere where there might be mice.

'This way,' said Phoebe unnecessarily: there was only one pathway after all.

Carys felt a hush of excitement and half wanted to scream out in delight at their little adventure.

'Just up ahead.'

And then they were there. The path seemed to end in a secluded bower - a little cathedral of trees.

'It's completely weather-proof,' Phoebe said. 'We've been here when it's pouring with rain and you stay wonderfully dry.'

Serena spread a large red tartan blanket on the ground and Phoebe quickly placed a bottle of Bailey's in the middle.

'I hereby declare this YBG meeting open,' she said in an ever-so-serious voice.

They all sat down and plastic cups were handed around.

'Anyone for Baileys?' Phoebe asked, her dark eyes sparkling with joy.

'Come on,' Penny said. 'I'm dying for a drink.'

Phoebe unscrewed the lid of the bottle and poured a generous amount into each cup. 'Save time later if we have trebles now,' she said with a little laugh.

'What about the initiation?' Natasha said.

'Oh, yes. Carys and Louise haven't done this before.'

Louise gave Carys an anxious glance in fear of what might be about to take place. 'Don't look so worried. It's just a few words.'

'And you've got to hold your cups out, like this,' Serena said, holding her cup high in the air in demonstration.

Carys and Louise held their cups aloft.

'I solemnly declare,' Phoebe began.

'I solemnly declare,' Carys and Louise repeated in unison.

'That all said and done in the privacy of this bower ...'

'That all said and done in the privacy of this bower ...' they chanted, trying hard not to giggle.

'Will be repeated to no-one.'

'Will be repeated to no-one.'

'Now drink,' Phoebe ordered and Carys and Louise lowered their cups to their lips and drank deeply, the creamy liquid turning to fire as they swallowed.

For a few moments, there was the complete silence of appreciation.

'This is good,' Penny sighed.

'Mother's best,' Serena said.

'She left a good collection in the drawing room,' Phoebe nodded. 'We thought it wouldn't do to waste it.'

'Quite right,' Natasha said. 'I hate waste.'

'And I can't stand a drink without something to nibble,' Penny said, unzipping her jacket and taking out a carrier bag hitherto hidden. 'Cheese straw, anyone?'

'Oh, Pen!' Serena laughed.

'Penny, you are priceless!' Phoebe said. 'Penny can't go anywhere without bringing some home baking along,' Phoebe explained to Carys and Louise as she took a perfect, golden straw.

'These are delicious.'

'Always the best.'

All six of them munched happily, little waterfalls of golden crumbs spilling onto the dark forest floor.

'Right, then,' Phoebe said. 'We're not here just to drink, eat and be merry.'

'More's the pity,' Serena said.

'The YBG's serve a purpose.'

'Listen to her. She sounds like a politician. And she had the nerve to reprove me for sounding like a journalist,' Natasha tutted before taking another sip of Bailey's.

'We're here,' Phoebe continued undeterred, 'to discuss Carys.'

Louise looked at Carys and frowned. 'What wrong with Carys?' she asked quietly.

'Nothing. Nothing's wrong with me,' Carys said blushing and obviously not looking forward to being the centre of attention.

'It's Richard,' Phoebe said. 'He's being absolutely beastly and it's got to stop.'

'Is he? Is he being beastly?' Louise asked. 'I can't really imagine that.'

'He leaves her alone all day, doesn't he, Carys?' Phoebe said.

Five pairs of eyes turned to her for confirmation.

At last, Carys spoke. 'Well, I have often thought about opening a missing person's file on him.'

Penny giggled and Phoebe and Serena nodded in sympathy.

'It's always been the same with the Bretton men,' Serena said. 'Poor Mummy used to say that she'd forgotten what Daddy looked like.'

'So what makes you think you can do anything to stop it?' Natasha asked.

'Because, if we don't, then-' Phoebe paused, her brow crinkled in anxiety.

'I may have to run away,' Carys said.

Phoebe turned sad eyes on Carys. 'I do hope you're joking.'

'Of course I am but I don't know how much more of this I can take. Anyone would think I was married to his secretary. I speak to her more often than him.'

'And I bet he doesn't really listen to you when you do speak to him' said Natasha.

'Yes!' Carys agreed. 'His mind is always somewhere else, you can tell it is.'

'I wouldn't allow my husband to treat me like that,' Serena said quietly, and everyone turned to look at her. 'What? Well, I wouldn't! I mean, if I was married.'

'We believe you,' Penny said, passing her another cheese straw.

'But what are we going to do about Richard?'

The six women were silent. Perhaps for longer than was healthy.

'Come *on*,' Phoebe encouraged. 'This is Carys and Richard's marriage we're talking about here. Hasn't anybody got any suggestions?'

'Other than a divorce?' Serena said.

Phoebe glared at her.

'Only joking.'

'I don't think there's any point trying to change a man,' Penny said, handing out another course of cheese straws. 'I tried to with my Ewan.'

'Didn't it work?'

'Only for about a fortnight.'

'What was wrong with him?' Natasha asked.

Penny rolled her eyes. 'He's the complete opposite of me. I'm neat; he's messy. I plan; he's spontaneous. I squeeze the toothpaste from the bottom; he squeezes it from the top. You name it and we're poles apart.'

'So why did you marry him?' Serena asked.

Penny looked a little sheepish for a moment. 'Because,' she said in a whisper, even though there was nobody else around for miles, 'the sex is fabulous.'

The yew bower was filled with sudden laughter.

'But couldn't you have the sex but not the marriage?' Natasha asked. 'I mean - live apart but come together - if you get my meaning.'

Penny grinned. 'I'm not like that. It's all or nothing. So I've got a lifetime's supply of great sex as well as a house that will always look as if it's hosting the world's biggest jumble sale.'

'A small price to pay,' Serena said. 'I wish I could get some great sex.'

'Serena!' Phoebe chided, her mouth dropping open at her little sister's declaration.

'What? What have I said now?'

'I don't think we wish to hear about-'

'I do,' Natasha said.

'Well, you would,' Phoebe said. 'Wouldn't be surprised if you wrote up our confessions in tomorrow's papers.'

Natasha rolled her eyes. 'Lighten up, Pheebs. We're only joking around.'

'But we're not meant to be joking around. We're meant to be finding a solution for Carys.'

They were silent for a moment.

'I don't think there is one,' Carys said at last.

'Don't say that,' Phoebe said.

'But she's right,' Serena said. 'Some problems don't have a solution.'

Phoebe frowned. 'But there must be one.'

'Have you talked to him?' Penny asked. 'Told him how you feel?'

Carys gave a small smile. 'He's not around to talk to. That's the problem.'

'Well, he'll have to make time. Slot you in to his busy routine. You're his wife, for goodness sake. It seems to me that he's treating you worse than one of his precious family antiques,' Penny said.

'Yes, you must try and talk to him,' Phoebe agreed, greatly relieved that somebody had made a sensible suggestion at last.

Carys nodded in agreement. She couldn't quite see how that would work but it was easier to agree with everyone.

'Now,' Serena said, 'who's for another drop of Baileys?'

Over an hour later, when the cheese straws and Baileys were but a distant memory, the secret six stumbled out of the yew bower following Phoebe's solitary torch beam.

'What was that?' Louise asked.

'What was what?' Serena answered.

'I heard something - some sort of snuffling.'

'Snuffling?'

'Something was snuffling behind me.'

'Oh, that will be the bear,' Serena said, nonchalantly.

'Bear! Are you joking?'

'Shush! Of course she's joking,' Phoebe said.

'Or else the wolf of Amberley.'

'Don't talk about wolves at a time like this,' Louise said. She'd never been very good with animals. She was even afraid of her nan's old budgerigar.

'I have heard tell,' Serena began in a dark whisper, 'of a wolf the size of a small horse seen prowling in these woods late at night.'

'What utter rubbish,' Phoebe chided.

'It is not. Just because *you've* not seen it.'

'It probably *was* a small horse,' Phoebe said. 'Or else you'd drunk too much,' Phoebe said, tripping over the roots of an old beech tree.

'Look who's talking.'

'Shusssssh!' Penny giggled. 'Someone will hear us.'

'There's nobody around for miles,' Serena said. 'We could be screaming for our lives and nobody would hear us. That reminds me, did I tell you the story about the young couple walking through the woods at night when there was a mad man was on the loose?'

'Shut up. *Shut up!*' Louise yelled. She was beginning to get seriously spooked now.

As luck would have it, they were nearly out of the woods and the grounds of Amberley opened up before them.

'I'll never go in a wood again - ever,' Louise said, her face as pale as a daisy.

They trooped down the footpath towards the gardens and walked across the dark lawn.

'I'll give you a call next week,' Penny told Phoebe once they'd reached the house. 'Lovely to meet you, Carys. And you, Louise.'

'You couldn't drop me off at my car, could you?' Louise dared to ask. 'It's parked half way down the drive and I really don't want to walk passed all those trees.'

'No problem,' Penny said, laughing.

'Night everyone,' Louise said. 'Bye, sweetheart. Give me a ring soon, won't you?'

Carys nodded. 'I will. Promise.'

Natasha, who wasn't afraid of anything, had parked her mountain bike by the side of the house.

'Are you sure you wouldn't rather wait until morning?' Phoebe asked. 'It's awfully late.'

'Don't fuss. I've got lights.'

'I'd be much happier if you stayed.'

'No can do. I've got an early start.' She kissed Phoebe on the cheek and then Serena. 'All the best, Carys. I hope things work out.'

'Thank you.'

The three of them watched as Natasha placed her helmet on her head, switched her lights on and swung herself onto her bike before peddling down the driveway into the dark.

'Completely mad,' Serena said.

'Bonkers,' Phoebe added.

Entering the house and quickly punching in the code for the new alarm system Richard had had installed, they walked up the staircase towards the private quarters. Both Phoebe and Serena were staying at Amberley although Phoebe was hoping to buy her first home in nearby Pennington Bridge soon and Serena was planning to live in Florence for a year and find work.

The house was eerily silent as they headed towards their rooms, and the shadows were deep and dark in the minimal lighting.

'I love Amberley at night,' Serena whispered. 'Don't you?'

Carys smiled. 'I haven't made up my mind yet.'

'And have you made up your mind about tonight?'

'What do you mean?'

'About Richard?' Serena pressed.

'You will talk to him, won't you?' Phoebe asked.

They reached their parting of the ways before Carys spoke. 'I'll try,' she said. 'I promise I'll try.'

'Good,' Phoebe said with a sigh of relief.

And then they all said goodnight and went their separate ways and Carys suddenly felt desperately alone after the evening's camaraderie. She wanted to shout out, *Wait! Let's have a drink in the drawing room*, and so delay the end of the evening. But, when she turned around, Phoebe and Serena had vanished as quickly and quietly as Georgiana might have.

Georgiana. She'd forgotten all about Georgiana. Not that she would have discussed her new friend at the YBG's meeting. It might have proved too tempting for Natasha and would've appeared in the newspapers the very next day. And what would the others have made of it all? She dreaded to think what Louise would say if she confessed to her. She'd probably demand Carys's immediate departure from Amberley on grounds of mental health. And Phoebe and Serena? What would they have made of her confession? Serena would have probably shrugged and said something like, 'Well, of course there's a ghost. What do you expect from a house that's so old?' She didn't expect Phoebe would be quite so nonchalant about the business, though. 'That's it,' she'd probably have said. 'You can't go on living here. Something's got to be done.'

Dear Phoebe. So kind and caring and constantly worried for other people's well-being. Carys did feel lucky to have her as a sister-in-law.

Opening the door to their private apartments and tiptoeing

through the living room to their bedroom, Carys saw the sleeping figure of Richard mummified in the duvet. She got undressed, had a quick wash and sneaked into bed beside him. He didn't even stir. He probably hadn't even realised she'd been absent for half the night.

CHAPTER 20

'Morning, darling,' Richard murmured somewhere above Carys's left ear.

'Morning?'

'Quarter to eight.'

Carys groaned. She felt as if she'd only just fallen asleep.

'I'll see you later.'

Suddenly, Carys was bolt upright in bed. 'Richard?'

'Yes?' He turned to look at her from the door.

'We've got to talk.'

His eyes squinted quizzically.

'About us,' Carys said. 'I hardly see you, Richard. I think we should be spending-'

Richard shook his head. 'Can we do this another time, sweetheart? It's just that I'm rushing to the estate office. There's a man from the council due and I really have to be there to oversee this.'

Carys suppressed a desire to scream like a banshee and fling the pillows across the room at him. Instead, she waited until he'd shut the door and then hurled her pillow across the room.

A long, warm shower managed to calm her only a little. By the time she was dressed, she felt the sort of numbed annoyance that she was getting used to. The she- wasn't-going-to-change-things-so-why-bother attitude.

She wandered through their living room into the kitchen where Cecily and Evelyn were sitting at the breakfast table and nanny was hovering over the sink.

'Aren't you girls going to be late for class?'

Evie gave a little smile. 'It's Saturday, silly!'

Carys frowned. It was Saturday. She'd completely forgotten. That meant that, officially, she didn't have to report for duty in her office. She should, of course. There was stacks to do but she refused to turn into a slave to her job like Richard. And what was Richard doing seeing someone from the council on a Saturday? It didn't seem very likely. Then again, Amberley did have a timetable all of its own.

'Oh, yes. Just testing,' she said, sitting down and pouring some cereal into her bowl. They all munched in silence; only the sounds of spoons hitting bowls and molars crunching flakes could be heard.

'So,' Carys began hopefully, 'what are you two up to today?' She addressed the question to both of them but her eyes were fixed on Cecily trying to discover signs of life.

'We're going riding.' Predictably, it was Evie who answered.

'Oh, right,' Carys said, trying not to sound disappointed. Nobody, it seemed, wanted to spend any time with her. She was even being denied the pleasure of Cecily's miserable face.

'Mummy's away this weekend so we thought we'd go riding. You can come too,' Evie suggested.

Carys shook her head. There were few thoughts more terrifying than getting up on a horse. As much as she wanted to bond with these girls, she wasn't going to overcome her fear of riding to do it. 'I think you're better off without me.'

'Are you scared of horses?'

Carys blinked. The question had come from Cecily. Okay, so she hadn't looked up at Carys to ask her, but she had made contact.

'I think I'm more scared of actually sitting on one.'

'It's easy,' Cecily said. 'Anyone can do it.'

'I don't think they can. I think you must be very brave and talented to do it.'

Cecily shrugged.

'We'll teach you,' Evie said, full of enthusiasm and the boundless belief of the young.

Carys chewed her lip. 'Another time.'

Evie's forehead wrinkled. 'Okay.'

'No, *really*. I'll come another time,' Carys said. She knew the implications of the phrase, *another time*.

'What will you do, then?' Evie asked.

Carys chewed thoughtfully on her last spoonful of cereal. She could look over her correspondence. She could make some headway with the removal of the Montella portraits for the exhibition. She could put on her glad rags and tackle the storage room at the end of the east wing.

'I'm going to the library,' she said.

'Boring,' Cecily announced.

'Not at all. I'm going to find the most wonderful books for a very special person.'

Carminster Library was heaving with people. Young mothers were running after screaming toddlers, a group of elderly men sat around a table reading the newspapers and a queue was forming for the free internet access.

Carys scanned the shelves, trying to remember Aunt Vi's requests.

'Nothing historical,' she'd said. 'I grew up surrounded by history. And nothing with police in it. I can't be doing with all those dull interviews with suspects.'

Carys chose a few books: a magical romance by Deborah Wright, a sparkling comedy by Raffaella Barker and a lyrical novel by Linda Gillard. Then she saw a small display of books with a notice above them, 'Go on - be tempted!'

Would Aunt Vi like to be tempted?

She reached out and picked up a book with a white cover. *Places of Passion* by Marissa Dahling. The name rang a bell. She read the blurb. Exotic locations, a strong heroine fighting the odds. No police and nothing whatsoever to do with history. And the cover was so beautiful: completely white but for an embossed red rose.

It was only when Carys was half-way through Chapter 1 of *Places of Passion* that she remembered why she knew the name Marissa Dahling. There'd been a radio interview with her a few weeks ago. She'd only caught the end but there'd been an irate caller talking to the author, or rather shouting at her about her book.

'Filth. Utter filth,' Carys had heard before the woman had been cut off. Marissa Dahling had laughed it off, saying she wasn't ashamed of what she wrote and that people shouldn't be ashamed to read it.

Now, sitting in Great Aunt Vi's living room, Carys realised that you could, indeed, be ashamed of reading a book.

'You know,' she said, breaking off from her reading, 'I'm not sure this is the sort of book we should be-'

'What do you mean?' Aunt Vi interrupted. 'Go on - go on. I was just getting interested there.'

Carys bit her lip as her eyes scanned the page. This really was most unsuitable. They'd only reached page eight and, already, Rosa Cavallini, the heroine, was reaching orgasm.

'I'm not sure I can read this,' Carys whispered.

'Why not?'

'Because -' Carys stopped, her eyes scanning the explicit vocabulary. 'It's - it's-'

'Sexy?' Aunt Vi asked. 'Is it sexy? Is that the problem?'

'I'm afraid it is.'

'Why afraid? What's to be afraid of?'

'The language - it's rather explicit.'

For a moment, Aunt Vi's tiny eyes squinted hard and she pursed her mouth into a narrow line.

Carys sat waiting, nervously chewing her lip. Why, oh why had she picked up Marissa Dahling's book? Why hadn't she skimmed it for content? She should have thought. Or she should have played safe and picked up something a little tamer. A nice warm and cuddly Rosamunde Pilcher, for instance.

'Carys,' Aunt Vi began. 'I have had sex, you know.'

Carys felt herself blushing.

'And I'm sure you have too. So why make a fuss about it? We both know what happens between men and women. And, very often between women and women, and men and men.'

Carys's mouth dropped open. She couldn't quite believe what she was hearing.

'So why worry about a few printed words?'

'Well,' Carys said, 'when you put it like that.'

'And it can be our little secret, can't it?'

Carys felt a naughty giggle building up inside her. 'Yes,' she said.

'But I don't want you to feel embarrassed. Promise me you won't feel embarrassed.'

Carys took a deep breath. 'I promise I'll do my best.'

'Wonderful,' Aunt Vi said with a smile. 'Now, do read on. I can't wait to find out if young Johnny is going to give Rosa a good seeing-to!'

It was a pleasure to read to Aunt Violet. It was also thirsty work and they got through gallons of tea. Carys also popped out to buy a loaf of bread and some fresh salad and made a light lunch for them both, finishing off with a very red raspberry tart. Carys didn't want to leave. She felt she could quite easily move into the narrow town house. At least she'd always have somebody to chat to.

'You look thoughtful,' Aunt Vi observed as they sat back after their lunch. 'Everything all right up at the house?'

Carys nodded.

'Are you sure?'

She looked up into the old lady's gentle eyes. 'I get a bit lonely sometimes,' she confessed. 'I seem to be constantly surrounded by people but everyone's got a job to do and they don't seem to have time to stop and chat. There's always someone to call or something to mend.'

Aunt Violet nodded. 'But you and Richard have to make time for each other. In every marriage, there has to be private time.'

'That's what my friends have been saying too but I can't even make him slow down for a moment in order to *arrange* some private time.'

Aunt Violet clucked. 'That's a bad business. And you'll have to find a way around it if you want your marriage to succeed.'

The dogs were waiting for her in the sitting room and rushed into the hallway to greet her when she arrived back. At least they could spare some time for her.

Changing her footwear quickly, she decided on a walk around the gardens. It was overcast with huge banks of angry-looking clouds rolling across a bruised sky. Carys grimaced but the dogs didn't seem to notice. There were always fine smells to smell and corners to explore whatever the weather.

Carys looked across the garden at the beautiful borders. Ash and his tiny team of part-time gardeners did a good job. The roses were particularly beautiful at this time of year, their rich perfume enveloping and intoxicating, fat and blowsy and looking like pink clouds which had settled and fallen asleep in the borders.

Not for the first time since arriving at Amberley did she realise that the earth was something to treasure and bless. It was the very essence of life and it had to be cherished above all other things. She smiled as she thought about the walled garden where she'd met Richard on her first visit to Amberley. She had plans to turn it around one day and make it something very special indeed. That would be her gift to her husband.

As she was admiring some lilies at the back of one of the borders, something caught her eye from the trees in the distance. It was a glint of glass in a brief break of sunshine. Carys was immediately on guard.

Although Amberley was open to the public on Saturdays, this was the private garden.

She walked over to where she'd seen what she guessed to be a camera and no sooner was she across the lawn than she saw a man dressed head to toe in navy.

'Can I help you?' Carys asked, deciding that it was always best to handle these things in a polite manner and, with all five dogs behind her, she didn't feel afraid to confront anyone.

'No, thank you,' the man said with a nervous smile.

'I'm afraid this part of Amberley isn't open to the public but there are some gardens near the car park and there are miles of footpaths to explore.'

The man nodded. 'I'm sorry to disturb you. I was trying to get a photograph of the house.'

'Oh, I see,' Carys said, turning around to see his chosen vantage point. 'Yes, it does look lovely from here.'

There was an awkward silence as Carys looked down at the man's camera. It had the biggest zoom lens she'd ever seen. It looked more like some kind of musical instrument than a camera.

'We'll, I'd best be off,' he said, clearing his throat and turning to go.

Carys watched him through narrowed eyes and then shrugged and walked back to the hall, the dogs following close behind.

'It's useless to even try. We can't compete with that.'

As Carys walked into the hallway, she heard Richard's voice from the living room.

'Hey!' Carys said, walking towards the sofa where he was sitting. Phoebe was on a chair opposite him. 'Didn't your meeting go okay?'

'Oh, that was fine.'

'So, what's the problem?' she asked, kissing him on the cheek.

'This!' he threw down a leaflet on the coffee table. Carys picked it up. It was a leaflet for Barston Hall. *Barston Hall - £10 for all!* Read the caption in big bold scarlet letters.

'Oh, dear,' Carys said.

'Barston's offering a family ticket for £10. That includes two adults and up to three children. We can't compete with that.' Richard massaged his temples.

'It's as if they're goading us,' Phoebe sighed.

'I'm sure they're not,' Carys said, remembering how kind Valerie Buckley-Stewart had been to her.

'They get twice as many visitors as we do, and now this. And they've even installed an *olde worlde* English pub in their courtyard with Sky TV.'

Carys's eyes widened. She remembered seeing a lot of workmen and scaffolding on her visit to Barston but they'd kept their new olde pub well under wraps.

'Maybe,' Carys began, 'we could fight back with a leaflet of our own? *Amberley Court - with no Sky Sport?*

Richard frowned but, luckily, Phoebe burst into a fit giggles.

'Yes, yes!' she said excitedly. 'Or, Amberley Court - Pay More and Get Less!'

Carys laughed but Richard wasn't joining in.

'This isn't helping,' he said, getting to his feet.

'Oh, Richard, we're only joking around,' Carys said. She was of the belief that, the grimmer the situation, the more one should search to find the humour in it.

'This is important. There isn't a funny side to it,' he said, leaving the room and slamming the door behind him.

'Oh, dear,' Phoebe said. 'That went well.'

'See what I mean?' Carys said. 'I can't seem to say anything right at the moment.'

Phoebe sighed. 'I guess it's just not an easy time. He's got so much on his mind.'

'You haven't said anything to him, have you?'

'God, no. He'd bite my head off. But I did tell him he should take more time off - with you.'

'What did he say?'

'He showed me that bloody leaflet and started ranting.'

'Right.'

'Listen, Carys. I hate to love you and leave you but I'm meant to be looking at flats in Pennington Bridge this afternoon.'

'Anything nice?'

'I hope so. A new apartment on the outskirts, an old mill conversion by the river and the top floor of a Victorian building. Keep your fingers crossed for me or I'll be begging for my old room back here.'

Carys smiled. She wouldn't mind. She adored Phoebe and it would be nice to have her smiling face and infectious giggles to hand whenever she was feeling down.

Once Phoebe had left, Carys retreated to her office. There was no point in following Richard. He wouldn't be in the right frame of mind to talk about spending time together let alone having a whole day off.

She closed her office door behind her, the silence of the room enveloping her with just the comforting tick of the clock on the mantelpiece as company.

'Are you all right?' a voice suddenly said.

Carys spun around and saw sparkly blue mist forming into Georgiana.

'You look surprised to see me,' she said, her features shaping and taking on a more solid appearance. 'Did you forget about me? Or perhaps you thought you had merely imagined me,' Georgiana said, in a mocking tone.

Carys smiled. What with Richard, Aunt Violet, the girls and now the Barston Hall wars, she had actually managed to forget about Amberley's resident ghost.

'I'm so sorry, Georgiana.'

'It's quite all right. I'm used to being forgotten. It's a bit of an occupational hazard being dead.'

Carys watched as she glided across the room and sat in what was fast becoming her favourite chair. 'So, tell me how things are going?'

Carys perched on the edge of her desk and sighed. Why did people keep having to ask her that? She knew they meant well but it was becoming very wearisome.

'I do wish there was something I could do to help,' Georgiana said a few minutes later.

Carys shrugged. 'I wish there was too.' She drummed her fingers on the desk behind her. 'What we need is something different. Something that Barston Hall doesn't have. They've done everything, you see. Car rallies, concerts, craft fairs.'

Georgiana nodded. 'But Amberley is so much more beautiful.'

'I know.'

'It is older, has more historical interest–'

'I *know!* But people aren't interested in those things any more. Historic houses have crossed over into the leisure industry and people won't come unless you have playgrounds and boats on the lake and ice-cream. Now, don't get me wrong. I don't think there's anything wrong with these things, and Amberley really is moving into the future with our gift shop and tea room and plans for a nature trail and weddings. But we need something bigger if we're really going to compete.'

Georgiana looked thoughtful. 'Something different,' she mused. 'Something big.'

'Yes.'

The two women sat quietly for a moment, the clock measuring the passing of time.

'You need to have something that Barston doesn't have?'

Carys nodded. 'I think that would be the best option.'

Georgiana's pale face suddenly lit up. 'I have it!'

'You do?'

'The answer is staring you right in the face.'

'It is?'

'Yes. *Me!*'

'You?' Carys said.

'Yes. No need to look so surprised. I really do not know why we didn't think of it before. It's a wonderful idea.'

'What, exactly, do you mean?'

'I mean, I am a ghost, am I not?'

Carys nodded. So far, so good.

'And Barston Hall doesn't have a ghost, does it?'

Carys frowned. 'Well, the countess told me that they did - kind of.'

'You mean, as far as tourists were concerned?'

'Yes.'

'They tell the tourists what they want to hear and reap the rewards?' Georgiana asked.

'I think that's it, more or less.'

'You see? That is where I come in. I am *real*.'

'I'm not quite sure I under-'

Georgiana got up from the chair. 'I could be your main attraction.'

'You would help Amberley?'

'Of *course* I would. It is still my home, is it not? And it would do me good to have a job. I do not believe I have ever had a job before.'

'It would be the first real ghost tour in the country. We'll really put Amberley on the map,' Carys said suddenly very excited.

'They will come from miles around.'

'We can charge them a fortune. An absolute fortune.'

'They will want to film here. I may become a film star,' Georgiana gasped.

Carys flapped her hands. 'Now, let's not get too carried away. How, exactly, is this going to work?'

They both sat down again. Carys could feel her heart racing in unison with her mind.

'I mean, are we going to do this? You know, deliberately stage when you're going to appear and how?'

Georgiana pursed her lips together. 'I rather imagine myself floating through the long gallery, don't you? I would have to have a *new* dress, of course. I couldn't possibly keep wearing this old thing.'

'Oh,' Carys exclaimed. 'But you're known as the Blue Lady. Everyone would expect you to wear your dress. It's your thing.'

Georgiana sighed. 'I never get to wear anything new. It really is most unfair.'

Carys suddenly felt rather sorry for Georgiana, knowing how much she enjoyed the sensation of new clothes herself. 'Perhaps you could wear a new blue dress?'

'You really do have no idea how hard it is trying to get new clothes on the other side,' she said. 'Honestly, Carys. If I have one piece of advice to give you, it is this: make sure that you die in your favourite outfit because you will be stuck in it for eternity.'

Carys smiled. 'I'll try and remember.'

They sat and thought some more.

'I once went on a ghost tour in Edinburgh where they had jumper-ooters,' Carys said. 'They were people planted along the route through the Old Town who would suddenly jump out on the poor unsuspecting tourists. It was quite funny really.'

'Oh, I'm not sure that sounds very dignified,' Georgiana said. 'I cannot see myself doing that. I thought, perhaps, that I could waft through a few doors and maybe give a regal wave and a silvery laugh.'

'That could work,' Carys said. 'But wouldn't it be a bit obvious?'

'How do you mean?'

'People would get a good look at you if you did that. They'd know you were a ghost.'

'Isn't that the whole point?'

Carys frowned. 'I'm not sure. It might really freak people out. You know - give someone a heart-attack or something.'

'Oh, I see what you mean. We're talking law suits and what not.'

'Exactly,' Carys said. 'This is meant to be raising money, not costing us.'

'Maybe we should go for something a little more low key, then?'

'Yes. Something more ambiguous. Where we keep the tourists guessing if you're real or not. Maybe have you walking out of a door some way ahead of the tour - so that some people see you and others don't but you're too far away to prove anything.'

Georgiana nodded. 'I could still laugh, couldn't I?'

'I don't see why not. I'm sure a little laugh could work.'

'Don't worry. I wasn't going to cackle or anything.'

Carys could feel her face flushing with excitement. 'This is such a great idea. I can't believe we didn't think of it sooner.'

'If I'd known you were in trouble, I would have come along much earlier.'

Carys was touched by this. 'Would you? Would you really?'

'Of course,' Georgiana said. 'There really is not much else for me to do. But I did want to give you time to settle in. I think it's important that the women of this house have time to find their own space - their own way with things.'

'But I don't feel settled at all,' Carys confessed. 'It's very strange. In some respects, I feel as if I've been here forever. When I'm outside, walking through the gardens and the woods or around the lake, I can't imagine being anywhere else, and yet this new role of mine seems very strange still. I'm still discovering all sorts of things about the house and my duties.'

'And that will never stop.'

Carys smiled. 'You're probably right.'

'But this ghost tour idea will be such a great success for you, I can just feel it!' Georgiana's face was alight with wonder.

'You think so?'

Georgiana nodded enthusiastically and, at once, reminded Carys of Phoebe.

Carys smiled. 'I'm so glad you came,' she said. 'I think we're going to have such fun together.'

CHAPTER 21

Carys and Georgiana spent most of Sunday shut away in the privacy of Carys's office, plotting and planning their ghost tour.

'We should make it rather exclusive, don't you think?' Carys asked.

'Most definitely. If it is available to everyone at any time, it will be much less attractive.'

'One a week, then?'

Georgiana frowned. 'Two. We want to make some money, don't forget.'

'How could I possibly forget about making money whilst living at Amberley?'

Sitting at her desk, Carys jotted down some notes on a pad whilst Georgiana paced up and down the room in a restless way. Well, not exactly paced. She floated. She was a ghost, after all, and pacing was far too solid a pastime.

'Five pounds per person?'

'*Five pounds!*' Georgiana shouted. '*Five?* I do believe five pounds does not get you very much nowadays.'

'But ten pounds sounds so much,' Carys said.

'But you charge £7.50 for a tour of the house, anyway.'

'That includes the garden,' Carys pointed out, pleased that the new entry fee to Amberley had been increased at long last.

'But a ghost tour, think about it. This is a personal tour around rooms not normally open to the public. It's special. It's a rare experience.'

Carys smiled. 'All right, then. Nine pounds. Doesn't sound quite so off-putting.'

'Believe me,' Georgiana said, 'if it sounds expensive, people will think it's worth paying because they will expect something special. It is when things are too cheap that they start to become suspicious. I would suggest no less than fifteen pounds per person.'

Carys nodded. 'Okay, if you're sure,' Carys said, tapping her pen against her jaw. 'Now, we need to decide a route through the house and what I'm actually going to say.'

Georgiana looked at Carys in surprise. 'So, you have decided to conduct the tours yourself?'

'Well, not all of them, obviously, but Richard thinks I should start. It's the best way to get to know the house and at least we can stage your appearances precisely.'

'Yes. Do let us discuss that. Where do you want me?' Georgiana asked, excitement bubbling inside her like an overfed cauldron.

'I think we should start in the main entrance hall so we don't need to worry about security issues with other entrances being used. We'll probably do it in groups of twelve and move through to the drawing room and the tapestry room. Then -'

'The corridor leading to the kitchens downstairs. We must have plenty of corridors and spooky, unused rooms.'

'Wouldn't that be rather dull?'

'The duller the better. They will be more inclined to think that those places are haunted rather than the beautiful state rooms.'

'And are they? I mean, do you prefer them to the more beautiful rooms?'

Georgiana looked horrified. 'Gracious, no. I wouldn't be caught dead in those places. But people always love corridors. I think it must be that feeling of anticipation,' Georgiana added.

'I think you're right. We could take them along that one that leads to the cloakroom full of old chairs. That always gives me the creeps.'

'Oh, this really is so exciting! When do you think we can start?'

Carys looked up from her notes. 'Well, we'll have to get some sort of souvenir guide book, I suppose.'

'Absolutely. Tourists love to take something away with them. But keep it cheap. With a few photographs of the house and my portrait, of course.'

Carys wondered if she could really keep such a venture cheap. 'I guess it will make us more money in the long run. We'll have to advertise too. It's going to take such a long time. Do you think we can cram it all into a month to cash in on the summer tourists?'

Georgiana nodded. 'I have every faith in you. And a month should give me time to get a new dress sorted out.'

For a moment, Carys looked startled. 'A new *old* dress?'

'There is no need to be alarmed. I won't turn up wearing Versace if that is what you're worried about.'

Carys smiled, trying to imagine Georgiana in a sexy black number with plunging neckline and diamante straps.

They spent the rest of the day discussing their ghost tour.

'Are we going to allow people to take photographs?'

'Certainly not. We want that element of doubt, don't we?'

'What do we do if they actually ask if you're real or not?'

'We tell them the truth, of course.'

And then they explored the house together, searching for spooky passageways and rooms that looked as if they might be haunted.

'I can't believe Amberley's kitchens have never been open to the public before,' Carys said as they descended to the very bowels of the house. 'These rooms are amazing.' Carys's shoes echoed across the great expanse of stone flags. 'Look at this fireplace. It's enormous.'

'My goodness!' Georgiana exclaimed. 'Is that old table still here?'

Carys looked across at a gigantic slab of wood which stood in the centre of the room. 'How old is it?'

'Older than me,' Georgiana said. 'I cannot be sure of its date but it was here when I was alive.'

Carys ran her hand over the rough surface. 'Imagine baking on this. Imagine the meals that must have been prepared here.'

'Imagine the hours you would have worked. It was no fun living downstairs, let me tell you.'

'No, I don't suppose it was.'

'You may sometimes complain about being the lady of the manor but it is far better a position than scullery maid.'

Carys smiled. 'The kitchen we have now seems so different - space-aged compared to this.'

'Everything hums.'

'What?'

'All those bits of equipment. Have you not noticed? Everything hums. It is very noisy.'

'I hadn't really noticed, no.'

'Awful interference when one is trying to materialize. Computers are the same. I do hope you are not really considering placing a computer in my sitting room,' Georgiana said.

'You sound just like Francesca. She never wanted one either but it's the way forward, I'm afraid. I'll try and find a quiet one, though' Carys assured her. 'Now, how can we use this room?'

'Well, you could tell tourists that strange noises have been reported from this part of the house and that it is not often used.'

Carys nodded. 'We can tidy it up a bit but still leave that air of neglect. It's so wonderfully echoey in here. It's going to be easy to believe in ghosts in this part of the house.'

'But *you* believe in ghosts now, surely?' Georgiana gave Carys a mocking little smile which made Carys frown.

'I believe in *you*,' she said slowly, smiling at the shimmering blue form of Georgiana.

'But nobody else? You don't believe in ghosts in general?'

All of a sudden, Carys felt very confused. She was getting so used to Georgiana's presence that she'd stopped thinking of her as a ghost. She was a friend. 'I - really don't know...'

'Would you like me to introduce you to some of my friends?'

'Oh, gracious - no,' Carys panicked.

Georgiana laughed heartily. 'You should see your face. Oh, what a picture!'

'You won't, will you?'

'What?'

'Bring anyone else here. You know - dead people.'

'My dear sweet Carys. Amberley is *my* haunt. I would never allow another ghost here so there is no need to worry. Although, I have to say that it would make the ghost tour rather wonderful, do you not think?'

'NO!' Carys wailed. 'I do not think. I mean, *don't!*'

'We could have Old Tilly banging windows in the passageway, Lord Brumley floating up and down the stairs, and the Countess of Stalford could send a shiver down the tourists' spines by tickling them when they are not looking. What a scream it would be.' Georgiana looked absolutely delighted with her idea.

'I think it would be dreadful. One ghost is all I can handle so let's leave things as they are. Now, let's get back upstairs,' Carys said shivering. 'It's so cold down here, it's like standing at the bottom of the ocean.'

'Makes absolutely no difference to me,' Georgiana said.

'Really?'

'Temperature means very little when you pass over which is rather glorious really because you can wear anything you want to. It's probably the reason ghosts frequent old houses so often - they don't feel the cold like you mortals.'

Carys shook her head. She never ceased to be amazed by what she could learn from Georgiana.

There was no need to mention Georgiana's involvement, of course, but Carys still asked Richard's permission.

'A ghost tour? What do you want to do that for? I'm not sure I like the idea of that at all.'

'But it will bring in the tourists. I was thinking of fifteen pounds a head.'

He pursed his lips together. 'Good idea,' he said.

It all came down to money. If money could be made, bad taste could be conveniently forgotten.

Everything, it seemed, was going swimmingly. Carys had a worthy job to do, she was making the most of living in a haunted house - in fact, she kept thinking that she must ring Lara Claridge to tell her that she'd been right all along and that ghosts could make the most marvellous of friends - and Richard actually seemed to be proud of her. He even made time for her on Sunday evening and, after a light dinner with the girls, they took a stroll around the garden with the dogs. The evening light gave everything an amber glow and the scent of roses perfumed the air. It was the kind of evening you dreamt of in deepest winter when dampness and darkness were merciless jailers.

For a while, they walked arm in arm, happy to follow the haphazard route of the dogs and then Carys had an idea.

'Let's go to the walled garden,' she said. Richard nodded.

Entering the archway covered in the yellow roses which had been Henry Bretton's favourite, they looked around at the bare borders and empty beds.

'It's not much to look at, I'm afraid,' Richard said.

'But it could be. It could be the loveliest garden.'

Richard said nothing.

'I think we should throw some money at it, don't you?' Carys said in a quiet voice, immediately regretting using the word, *throw*, knowing Richard would pick up on it.

'*Throw!* It would be throwing money away at the moment.'

Damn, Carys thought. 'But it wouldn't. It would bring the tourists in. A walled garden is always special. We could feature it in our advertising. We could even sell the produce grown here.'

Richard's eyebrows rose. 'Produce?'

'Yes. Ash and I have been talking about what we could grow here.

We could have apples and pears and plums, great fat cabbages and beans and peas for the kitchen and herbs too. Just imagine.' She sighed, dreaming of borders of fresh chives, fennel and rosemary. 'It wouldn't take much more work - another part-time gardener perhaps-'

'Another salary to pay.'

Carys sighed. 'You always look on the negative side.'

'The realistic side,' Richard countered.

Carys realised this wasn't going well. 'But this garden is special. It's where we met,' she said, stopping and squeezing his hand, determined that she was going to work her magic on him.

He smiled. 'Yes,' he said. 'I hadn't forgotten, you know.'

'Well,' Carys said, 'I sometimes wonder.'

Richard brought her hand to his mouth and gave it the most tender of kisses. 'I remember walking into the garden and hearing Dizzy being greeted by the happiest of voices - a voice I didn't dare hope to recognise. I remember seeing you standing there, looking so shy, your cheeks burning scarlet as I approached. And I remember wanting to kiss you.'

Carys's eyes widened.

'Oh, yes,' he said. 'I wanted to kiss you there and then and I knew that I would ask you to marry me.'

'You did?'

Richard nodded. 'What else could I do? I'd fallen madly in love with you the moment I saw you.'

Carys laughed.

'What?' Richard frowned. 'You don't believe me?'

'I'm not sure what to believe.'

'You've never driven a man crazy with desire before?'

'I didn't say that.'

'Then what is it?' he asked. 'You've gone all shy on me.'

And she had. She could feel herself blushing. She'd barely seen her husband even to speak to over the last few months and his undivided and amorous attention now was deliciously embarrassing. So she did what any self-respecting wanton wife would do. She kissed him.

'That was nice,' he whispered when they surfaced some moments later.

Carys nodded. And, as much as she'd have liked it to continue, she couldn't shake the subject of the walled garden out of her mind. She was truly turning into a Bretton, she thought. She was putting Amberley before the people who lived there. But, she reasoned with herself, she might not get another chance to raise this subject with Richard for months.

'I think we really should do something about this garden,' she dared to say in a voice barely above a whisper.

At first, Richard didn't say anything. 'I suppose you're right,' he said at last and, for one wonderful moment, Carys thought she'd won. 'But not for the next three or four years at least.'

Her smile vanished and was quickly replaced with a frown. Three to four *years*! That seemed a lifetime away. 'But I thought the money from the new ghost tour-'

'If you make any money at all from that then, by all means, spend it on this garden.'

'You mean it?'

He nodded. 'But don't build your hopes up. I don't think anybody will be interested.'

CHAPTER 22

Despite Richard having no faith whatsoever in the success of Carys's ghost tour, they spent the rest of the evening together without so much as a glance at a clock which was nigh on impossible in Amberley because there were more clocks than residents. Instead, they shared a long hot bath and had an early night. Richard even let Carys light a few candles in the bedroom.

'Not many now. I'm not setting my own house on fire.'

'But they're just little tea-lights - look!' Carys had pleaded with him.

They looked so pretty now, winking and twinkling in their cranberry red glasses, turning the room into a magical place. And so they dismissed the very slight possibility of turning Amberley into a pyre, they forgot about the piles of papers in their offices, and they forgot about death duties. They even managed to forget to close their curtains before getting undressed but it really didn't matter. They were on the second floor of a house surrounded by fields and trees. It would take one seriously devoted Peeping Tom to catch them.

They'd also left the window open and the cool summer night breeze whispered into the bedroom, sending goose pimples dancing across their skin but they kept each other warm with their kisses and, when they finally closed their eyes, much, much later that night, they slept the sleep of the sated.

It was a typical Monday morning in the kitchen in their apartment. Nanny was making breakfast for the girls who were arguing over whose turn it was to claim the plastic finger puppet from the cereal packet. They'd succeeded in sending a shower of cereal over the tablecloth and were making such a noise that nanny actually shouted at them. But nothing could upset Carys that morning. Or so she thought. She felt she was glowing from the roots of her hair to the tips of her toes. The evening walk and early night of pampering and passion had done her the world of good. Richard too. He'd left for the estate office with a smile on his face instead of a frown.

'Will you two stop fighting - *this instant!*' Nanny shouted, grabbing hold of the plastic finger puppet and placing it in the pocket of her apron.

'That's not fair!' Cecily whined. 'See what you've done now, stupid!'

'I'm not stupid. You're stupid. And you're too old for finger puppets, anyway. You're always telling me you're a grown-up!' Evie retorted.

Carys couldn't help but smile at Evie's logic. Buttering two slices of toast, she munched happily, thinking of the day ahead. The ghost tour! She'd get to work on the advertising and the guide. And she had to ring Mr Morris about the Montella exhibition. He wanted to come over this week to discuss the paintings he wanted on loan.

Washing her breakfast down with a glass of cold apple juice, Carys danced down the stairs and almost skipped along the corridor to her office where she saw that the door was ajar.

'Mrs Franklin?' Carys called. It was early still but Mrs Franklin might have turned up early knowing how much work there was to get through.

Entering the office, she saw that it wasn't Mrs Franklin at all. It was Richard.

'Darling! What a nice surprise,' she said, delighted to see him again so soon. 'I thought you'd disappeared for the day and I wouldn't see you for at least -'

'What the HELL is this?' he asked, throwing a newspaper down on her desk.

'What?' Carys asked, alarmed by his anger. 'Is it that Barston Hall again? Don't tell me, they've-'

'It's not bloody Barston Hall.'

Carys picked up the copy of *The Cuthland News* and immediately felt all the blood draining from her face. It was her! There was a photograph of her on the front cover of *The Cuthland News*. She was wearing Ash's old tweed cap, her hair scraped away from her face in a ponytail. It had been whilst she was walking the dogs - taken at the precise moment when she'd been frowning up at the clouds.

'Duchess deep in thought' the caption read.

Deep in thought! Like every other Englishman, she was doing no more than berating the weather.

Her mind reeled back. The photographer. That man hiding in the trees with his outrageously elongated camera.

'He said he wanted some pictures of the house,' Carys said.

'Who did?'

'The man who took this photograph.'

'And what about this?' Richard pointed to the headline.

Carys swallowed hard as she read the words *Duchess in Distress over Marriage*. 'Oh my God,' she whispered. 'Why have they written that?'

'You tell me!' Richard thundered.

The telephone rang. Richard, without asking, picked it up. 'No she bloody isn't available for comment.' And he slammed the phone down.

'Who was that?'

'One of the bloody nationals has picked up on this now. Carys, how could you?'

'But I haven't done anything!'

'Then how do you account for this?'

Carys shook her head. 'I really don't know,' she said. Or did she?

'What? What is it? Because you'd better tell me if you know something.'

'I think somebody *has* been asking me questions,' she said in a very quiet voice. 'But I had no idea...' her voice petered out as she picked up the newspaper and skimmed the story. It was awful.

'I don't know what half the rooms are for,' the duchess said, eyes glazed.

'I didn't say that!' Carys protested as she read. '*She* said that!'

'Who?'

'The reporter!'

'But you agreed?'

'Well, I-' Carys read on.

The new duchess complained that she never sees her husband and said that she had even thought about running away.

'This is the trouble when the aristocracy marries outside its own circle,' Lady Bleasingdale of Haver Abbey said. 'They don't understand what they are taking on.'

Carys's mouth dropped open at the thought of somebody she didn't know passing judgement on her marriage in such a damning and knowledgeable manner.

'Who on earth is Lady Bleasingdale?'

'That's of very little consequence,' Richard said. 'God, Carys! Do you realise what damage this could do to us? Do you realise how we come across in this piece? What's everyone going to think?'

'It's not my fault!'

'Then whose fault is it?'

'Natasha's! The reporter,' Carys said, her face burning scarlet as she remembered talking to her - trusting her. What a fool she'd been.

'She was only doing her job.'

'But I wasn't to know that. I didn't know she was interviewing me.'

'Whenever you speak to a reporter, you're being interviewed. You really are very naïve.'

The words hung between them like a barrier. Carys could feel tears pricking her eyes at the harshness of Richard's gaze and the sharpness of his words. How could he talk to her like that? How could this have happened after their wonderful, golden evening together?

Quickly, she blinked her tears back and took a deep breath. 'I thought you said Amberley could use some extra publicity.' She was grasping at straws, she knew, but she didn't know what else to say.

'That's not the kind of publicity I had in mind,' Richard said dismissively.

'But Valerie Buckley-Stewart told me even bad publicity is good.'

Richard's frown deepened. 'You've been talking to the Buckley-Stewarts?'

Carys bit her lip. She could do no right at the moment; that much was obvious.

'Look,' he said at last, 'I've got things to do. I could be doing without this at the moment. For God's sake-'

She'd never heard him swear and blaspheme so much before.

'-For God's sake, don't go talking to anyone else.'

'I won't,' she said, frowning, and watched as he left the room. He didn't take the paper with him.

Carys picked it up and opened it. The story continued on page three and there was another unflattering photograph of her striding across the lawn. She looked like a farmer in her cap and wellies. There was even an editor's comment on page twelve. *What have the aristocracy to complain about?* No doubt that would spawn a deluge of letters in the next few days' papers.

What really annoyed Carys was the fact that, underneath the headline were the words, *Exclusive by Natasha Bryant*. The cheek! The absolute effrontery of the woman. Carys could picture her running into the office the day after the YBG meeting.

'Listen to this, everyone! You won't believe the scoop I've got. That naïve Carys Cuthland - the new duchess - well ...'

Carys winced. It was just too much. She sank down onto her chair, her shoulders slumped in defeat.

There was a light knock on the door.

'What is it?' Carys asked, half expecting it to be some impudent reporter.

'My lady?'

'Oh, Mrs Travis. What is it?'

'I thought you might like a cup of tea,' she said, crossing the room and placing a china mug on her desk.

'Thank you,' Carys said, hoping Mrs Travis wasn't going to be too kind. Kindness, she thought, might just burst the dam of tears she was doing her best to hold back. 'I suppose you've seen the paper?'

'Oh! I do hope you're not worried about that, my lady.'

'It's terrible. Just terrible!'

'You should've seen what they used to print about Lord C's mother during her time as duchess.'

Carys blinked. Francesca! She hadn't even thought of her. She was going to see the paper, wasn't she? What was she going to make of her new daughter-in-law now?

'What did they used to say?'

'Dreadful rubbish. All made up to sell a few extra copies. If they can't dish the dirt on actors, they go after aristocrats.'

Carys gave a faint smile. 'And I was a sitting duck.'

'It isn't your fault.'

'Can you tell Lord C that for me, please?'

'Oh, is he worried? He should know better than that. And it's all publicity for Amberley.'

'That's what I told him.'

'You'll have people queuing round the block to catch a glimpse of you now.'

Carys started. 'You think so?'

'Absolutely. I've seen it before.'

'But I looked so horrendous in those photos.'

'Doesn't matter. People know you're not. We all have our cap and welly moments,' Mrs Travis said with a wink which made Carys smile a little. 'You'll be quite the local celebrity now.'

'Celebrity!' Carys said. She hated the word. To her, it smacked of naff reality shows and people who were famous for contributing absolutely nothing to the world. She didn't want to be a celebrity. Unless...

'You really think it will be good for Amberley?'

Mrs Travis nodded. Just you wait and see.'

She was right too. No sooner had the gates opened than a steady stream of cars could be seen along the driveway. Carys, hiding out in the safety of her office, watched as crowds of people made their way to the entrance. Some of them were even holding newspapers. Carys gawped in amazement. Was this good or really very bad indeed? She couldn't tell. At least Richard wasn't anywhere near the house to see.

The telephone rang. Should she pick up? It could be another paper and she was terrified of saying the wrong thing again and Mrs Franklin wasn't in yet to intercept for her.

'Hello,' she began hesitantly and then cleared her throat. 'Carys Cuthland.'

'Oh, Carys!' It was Phoebe. 'I've just seen the papers and it's just too awful! How are you? Has Richard seen it yet?'

'I'm afraid he has.'

'And was he terribly upset?'

'You could say that.'

'Oh, dear! And it's all my fault,' Phoebe said.

'It isn't your fault at all.'

'At any rate, Natasha Bryant is hereby expelled from the YBGs, that's for sure. I've talked to Serena and she agrees completely. It's completely unacceptable conduct. I can't believe she used to be our friend and confidante.'

'Oh, Phoebe. I don't want you to lose a friend over this.'

'A *friend!* A fiend more like! I should have known we couldn't trust her. I always knew there was something sneaky about her.'

Carys couldn't help but smile. Phoebe trusted everyone and never had a bad word to say about anyone. She would allow the very devil himself to join the YBGs if he asked, believing him to have been misrepresented and maligned.

'The question is, what are we going to do about it?' Phoebe asked.

'There's not much we can do, is there? The damage is done now.

You can't unprint a story. Anyway, it seems to be bringing in the tourists. I've never seen so many people visiting on a Monday morning.'

'Really? Well, that can't be bad news,' Phoebe laughed. 'And are you going to mingle?'

'No!' Carys yelled.

'I think you should. They'd love that. Tell all their friends they'd met a duchess.'

'Phoebe, you are dreadful.'

'Listen, I've got to dash. I'm seeing an estate agent.'

'Another property on the horizon?'

'No, just seeing an estate agent - Phillip.'

Carys grinned as Phoebe hung up and, as soon as she placed the receiver down, the phone rang again.

'I do hope you're making the most of this wonderful publicity,' Valerie Buckley-Stewart's voice ordered down the phone.

'Valerie! It's just awful. I was just telling Phoebe that the place is crawling with visitors.'

'You lucky thing! We're as quiet as a churchyard. You must have stolen all our tourists.'

Carys smiled. She'd have to tell Richard that one. That might cheer him up a bit if he thought he'd got one over on Barston.

'But I think it's awful.'

'It's absolutely nothing to worry about, darling. You know you've made it when you become public enemy number one in the local rag.'

Carys couldn't quite see the logic in that comment.

'Trust me. The public will love you. They won't blame you at all.'

'Well, I'm going to be hiding in my office for the rest of the week until it's all died down.'

'Oh, my dear! You mustn't do that. Everyone will want to see you. They'll expect you to make an appearance. They'll be very disappointed if you don't.'

'That's just what Phoebe was saying.'

'And very astute of her. You've got to get outside this instant and mingle. Let them know how upset you are over this story. Get them on your side. They'll love you for it.'

Mingle, mingle, mingle. That's what Phoebe and Valerie had said but Carys wasn't at all sure about their advice as she stepped out of the private entrance and walked out towards the main gardens. There was a crowd of people admiring the flowers and, from what Carys could see, most of them were carrying cameras.

'There she is!' someone shouted from behind a clump of hollyhocks.

'It's really her! It's the duchess!'

Carys gulped as a stampede of tourists charged towards her. She was too stunned to do anything but stand absolutely still.

'Can I have my picture taken with you?' a lady asked, thrusting her camera into her husband's hand and linking her arm around Carys before she could protest. 'You're much prettier than your photo in the paper,' the lady told her.

'Will you sign my guidebook?' another asked. 'To Melanie.'

Carys took the pen that was handed to her. Valerie Buckley-Stewart had been absolutely right - she was a celebrity. She tried to smile but didn't dare trust herself to say anything.

'You mustn't take any notice of the papers,' an elderly gentleman said. 'Fish wrap, that's all. Don't you go worrying your head.'

'Thank you-'

'I'm going to write in and give them what for - sticking their nose in where it isn't wanted. It's disgusting.'

'What's the world coming to?'

'It's a disgrace.'

'*Disgrace!* Somebody laughed. 'Get it? Dis-*grace?*'

Nobody seemed to get it but Carys smiled politely.

'I hope that husband of yours has learnt from it,' another lady said.

'Enid!' her husband chided. 'That's enough.'

'I'm only speaking my mind. If the story is true, then he needs a good talking to - leaving his young bride to cope on her own all day.'

'It really isn't as bad as-'

'You men have no idea what us women have to adapt to when we take you on.'

Her husband rolled his eyes. He'd heard it all before.

'All I'm saying is, it can't be easy moving into a monstrous house like this. No disrespect intended.'

And on it went. Carys nodded and smiled and signed guidebooks and did very little really until everybody had calmed down and decided to move on. A duchess was only a human after all.

She was just retracing her steps back to the safety of the house when another group of tourists appeared out of nowhere.

'*There she is!*' someone cried and a dozen pairs of feet hurtled across the gravel driveway in pursuit of their prey.

Carys picked up speed and only just made it to the door in time, her heart hammering inside her chest. This was terrible! She had to get away.

And she knew just the place too.

CHAPTER 23

'Without further delay, Fabio kissed Rosa fully on the mouth and she responded with a low moan. He made her feel beautiful and she hadn't felt beautiful in such a long time.'

Carys closed *Places of Passion* at the end of chapter sixteen and smiled across the room at Great Aunt Violet. Less than ninety minutes ago, she'd sneaked out of Amberley wearing a pair of dark sunglasses and a woolly hat despite the summer sun. She thought she'd be too recognisable in Ash's old tweed cap as that's what she'd been wearing in the photographs gracing *The Cuthland News*. She had felt silly, though - as if she were pretending to be a famous actress escaping a mob - but it had worked and here she was in the safety of Aunt Violet's town house. It was a wonderful haven away from Amberley. She knew that she was a coward to run away but she really felt that it had been the only option. There was no hiding even in her office as the phone had been ringing constantly and Mrs Travis always seemed to know which part of the house she was in if she tried to disappear to an obscure drawing room.

'I'm not at all sure about this Fabio character,' Aunt Violet said after a pause, bringing Carys back to the present. 'I think he's hiding something.'

'But Johnny isn't right for Rosa either. He proved that when she found out about his ex-wife and the way he treated her.'

'Sure she was telling the truth?'

Carys frowned. She hadn't thought of that.

'And what about Danny? The psychologist.'

'Too dependable,' Aunt Violet said. 'Not exciting enough for our Rosa.'

Our Rosa. It had become a familiar phrase throughout Carys's readings at Aunt Violet's. It was as if the writer had created the character purely for their entertainment and that she belonged to them and them alone.

'Oh, my goodness!' Carys suddenly exclaimed. 'I've just remembered. I saw a poster in *Bellwood's Books* as I drove by - Marissa

Dahling is coming to Carminster to promote her latest novel, *Escape From Paradise*. It's the next Rosa Cavallini novel in the series.'

'Another book after this one?'

'Yes. She's writing a series of five, I believe.'

'That's the best news I've had in a long time. We won't want for anything to read for the foreseeable future.' Aunt Violet's pretty face creased into happy wrinkles.

'And she'll be at Bellwood's tomorrow night. She'll be doing a reading and a signing and I thought we could go along.'

For a moment, Aunt Violet looked dumbstruck. 'But I haven't left the house for four years,' she said in a small, matter-of-fact voice.

Carys wasn't deterred. 'Then it's about time that you did.'

When Carys returned to Amberley, it was mid-afternoon. There were still great hordes of tourists milling about the place but she managed to sneak in the private entrance just as somebody shouted, 'Over there! It's her!'

There was a big pile of messages waiting for her on her desk which showed that Mrs Franklin had turned up some time after she'd left.

"*Vive!* rang. Want exclusive interview."

"*Cuthland Life* would be interested in a four-page article with photographs."

"*The Mirror* called. Wants quote for feature: *Aristocrats or Aristocrap?*"

"Reddings Coaches wants to book two parties a week after a surge of interest!"

"A Mr Forsyth from Pennington Bridge called. Said you mustn't let the press get you down and that you're doing a marvellous job."

Carys smiled. At least there were some sweet people left in the world.

She fended for herself for the rest of the day, answering the phone and being as polite as was possible with journalists who tried to snare interesting quotations from her.

By the time evening came round, she was exhausted and felt that she'd achieved very little. The Montella exhibition was moving along well and her guidebook for the ghost tour was in production but the day had bled away, leaving very little time to gather her thoughts.

'I must say,' a disembodied voice said from the armchair by the fireplace, 'it has been quite an exceptional day.'

Carys couldn't help laughing as Georgiana settled slowly into partial solidification. 'You can say that again.'

'Those photographs of you really weren't all that bad, you know.'

'You've seen them?'

'Of course I have. It is my job to keep up-to-date with everything.'

Carys frowned in puzzlement. 'I looked like a fishwife.'

'You did not! You looked-' Georgiana paused, her nearly translucent face tipped gently sideways in contemplation, 'you looked like a true lady of the country.'

'That's what I was afraid of.'

'I do not think any woman is ever truly satisfied with her image. There is always a little something which could be improved upon. A line, a little blemish, the curve of the lips.'

'I guess you're right.' Carys nodded slowly. 'Although your portrait in the Montella Room is perfect, don't you think?'

Georgiana sighed. 'As near to perfection as I will ever get.' And then she gave a smile, a beautiful enigmatic smile.

'What is it?' Carys asked.

'Nothing,' Georgiana said but the smile, if anything, had grown.

'What are you hiding?'

'I assure you, I am hiding nothing. Why do you ask?'

'Because you've got a strange look in your eyes and I want to know what it is,' Carys said. And then something occurred to her. 'You've got something to tell me, haven't you?' She peered closer at Georgiana. 'And it's something to do with your portrait, isn't it?'

Georgiana's pretty mouth gaped open and her eyes sparkled merrily with mischief. 'Whatever gives you that impression?' she said quite innocently.

'Is that what you've come back to tell me?'

'What are you talking about?'

'Lara Claridge said you'd probably have something to tell me.'

'Are you still harping on about what that woman said?'

'But you do have something to tell me, don't you?'

Georgiana's face softened again. 'I may have.' And then she vanished in a blue mist leaving nothing behind but a faint echo of laughter. How wonderful to be able to do that whenever the fancy took her. Carys wished she could vanish into thin air when the going got tough. How easy that would make life.

She tried to think back to what Mr Morris had said about the portrait the day when he'd paid a visit to Amberley to make arrangements for the exhibition at The Bretton Gallery in Carminster. It had been built in 1850 by the sixth Duke of Cuthland who had taken the Grand Tour a little too far and found himself in possession of far more paintings and sculptures than could be reasonably displayed at Amberley. He had bequeathed them to the county, leaving a sum of money to erect a museum in his family's honour. It was a beautiful place with marble floors and sweeping staircases, richly painted walls and enormous windows looking out on the gardens. From time to time, the museum would show the Montella paintings as a nod to its connection to the Bretton family.

Carys had accompanied Mr Morris around Amberley as they had chosen half a dozen paintings which would form the backbone of the exhibition. There was Leo Montella's famous *Family Triptych* showing three generations of Bretton men. There was the sweet portrait of Catherine: Georgiana's second daughter, holding a posy of wild flowers. There was the handsome portrait of James, Georgiana's husband whom, she'd assured Carys, wasn't half as handsome as the artist had portrayed. 'He had the meanest of eyes and a nose the size of a marrow.' And then there were three paintings of Georgiana.

'Aren't three rather too many for one exhibition?' Carys had asked.

Mr Morris had shaken his head. 'Not when they are the best.'

One of them hung in the Music Room and showed Georgiana sitting in a pretty chair by the window, a lute lying supine on a table behind her. It wasn't a particularly striking painting but there was a peace about it: an aura of calm which caught the eye and stilled the mind.

'It's the first portrait of Georgiana by Montella,' Mr Morris pointed out. 'But the later works are of more interest.'

They'd then gone to the Montella Room where there were four further portraits of Georgiana.

'These are the two I'm most interested in.' He pointed to Carys's favourite of Georgiana wearing her beautiful blue dress, holding the red rose. 'Stunning,' he said. 'Painting perfection. And this one.' He pointed to a smaller, more intimate portrait of Georgiana with one of her sons.

'I've never really looked at this one before,' Carys confessed, looking at Mr Morris who was peering over his glasses to study the portrait.

'There is something very intriguing about it.'

'What?' Carys asked.

'The expression on her face. Look.'

Carys looked. It was typical Georgiana - with a pretty, knowing smile and a naughty light dancing in her eyes. 'Isn't it just like the others?'

Mr Morris shook his head slowly. 'I don't think so. Look at her hands.'

Carys looked again. Little William was standing in front of his mother and her arms were draped over his shoulders. 'I'm not sure I can see -'

'The palms are open.'

'Yes,' Carys said, looking yet again. 'They are.'

'Shouldn't her hands be holding her son?'

'Why?' Carys clearly wasn't reading the portrait at all and was about to enquire further when Mr Morris's mobile rang.

She walked around the room until he had finished and then he apologised, saying he had to run but that he'd be in touch very soon.

She escorted him out and they chatted amiably.

'I always get excited about Montella,' he confessed. 'He painted his best work for the Brettons. Of course, he painted for many other great families of the time: the Churchills, the Russells, the Spencers, but one has the feeling that he was happiest here with the Brettons.'

Carys watched Mr Morris as he got into a rather ancient Volvo and drove down the driveway, dwelling on his words. *He was happiest here with the Brettons.* and Georgiana had certainly looked happy in Leo Montella's portraits of her.

Turning quickly, she headed back to the Montella Room and looked at the portraits once again. The smile, the eyes, the hands. And Georgiana's naughty little laugh when Carys had mentioned the painting. It was so obvious. Why hadn't she thought of it before?

Georgiana and Leo Montella had been in love!

CHAPTER 24

Carys stayed in her office until late in the evening, popping upstairs briefly to check on Cecily and Evelyn after dinner.

'It's all right,' Nanny said. 'I'll put them to bed. I know you have a lot to do.'

Carys didn't confess that she wasn't actually working in her study. She was there in the hope of Georgiana making an appearance and also in the hope of avoiding Richard. It seemed an age since his eruption over the newspaper that morning and his bad mood had probably abated by now but she didn't want to risk it so she took the coward's way out and hid.

She sat at her desk for what seemed like hours without really accomplishing anything. She was thinking. Thinking of her new family and responsibilities, thinking of Natasha's betrayal, and thinking of Georgiana. Where was she?

Peering into the evening shadows around the bookcases, she half expected to see her materialising in her bright blue cloud. How she longed to confront her now she believed she knew her secret. But she obviously didn't want to talk.

Carys picked up the pile of phone messages from journalists who'd called earlier that day. What was she meant to do with them? Should she bin them or could she use the contacts for some good publicity for Amberley? Best not to take a chance, she thought, in case she messed up again, and yet she didn't want to throw them away and so opened her top drawer.

And frowned. For there, sitting neatly and tidily, as though it had never left, was Francesca's diary. Carys turned around as if she might spot Francesca sneaking down the driveway. She felt very unnerved by the fact that her uncommunicative mother-in-law had managed to enter her office - several times now - without her knowing. What exactly was going on? It was becoming very clear that Francesca meant Carys to have the diary but why couldn't she just hand it over herself in person?

She opened the cover again to see if there was a note or something and, sure enough, there was a single sheet of cream writing paper neatly folded in half. Carys unfolded it and read the neat blue writing.

'This is for you. Please keep it. F.'

At least that was *some*thing, Carys thought. Not exactly warm or affectionate, rather distant and laced with mystery, but it was communication nevertheless. But why did she want her to have it? Was there some secret message in it like Mr Morris believed there was in the Montella portraits of Georgiana?

Carys took it out of the drawer and promised she'd read it properly this time.

And she did. There were some entries she'd already read before so she skimmed through those but there were others that were new and really rather startling.

'I think it's always hard to admit that you're not the most important thing in the life of the person you love but I've come to realise that I come a very poor second to Amberley. H warned me about that before we got married but I didn't believe him. How could anyone put a house before a human, I thought? Well, I know now. I hardly see him and, when I do, he's so tired he can barely keep his eyes open let alone ...'

The entry ended but Carys could finish it herself because that was the position she was in now.

She read on, and it was almost like having Francesca in the room with her, telling her, personally, of the years she'd spent as mistress of Amberley.

'There are days when you dread waking up. There is always so much to do and your time is never your own. What will be waiting for me today? A leaking roof in a tenant's cottage? A problem with a member of staff, or the shop, or the park? Would somebody have discovered that an antique was in dire need of repair or that something somewhere in the house had fallen or collapsed? I sometimes want to run away but, even in a house this size, you can't run far. Somebody, somewhere knows where to find you and they usually come armed with a list of things to do!'

Carys smiled. Yes, she knew exactly what Francesca meant. Is that why she'd wanted her to have the diary? Was it her way of saying, *I know what you're going through. Don't worry. It's perfectly normal.*

She closed the book. She'd read some more very soon but it was getting late now and, truth be told, she still didn't like wandering around Amberley late at night even though she was already on first-name terms with its resident ghost.

Switching the lamps off in her office and closing the door behind her, she began the slow walk to their private apartment. Her office, of course, was at the very end of a corridor which meant a long dark walk at this time of night as only a few essential lights were kept burning. Richard's words, 'our electricity bill is more than a lot of people's annual wages' rang in her ears and she hadn't dared to challenge him. Instead, she had to brave the semi-darkness and the spooky shadows of Amberley.

Crossing the hallway and the family entrance, she caught sight of the cloistered courtyard. It was the oldest part of the house and held a spectral beauty at night, its arches and tracery casting phantom-like shadows on the grass. Then, it was through the pretty Yellow Drawing Room where she switched another lamp off before continuing her journey. Two more public rooms were passed through and then she took a narrow staircase which was softly carpeted, leading to a long landing where a vast collection of porcelain was kept. Carys loved examining the tiny teacups and pretty plates and thought it such a shame that they were hidden away in a part of the house where the tourists couldn't see them but Richard had assured her that they were a small part of the Amberley collection which went on regular walkabout - touring the museums up and down the country. And, indeed, with her involvement in the Montella exhibition, she was beginning to learn that nothing stayed at Amberley for long.

After the porcelain passageway, she turned into another corridor which stretched along the front of the house with long views out towards the woods and the hills during the daytime. Now, there was nothing but blackness to greet her.

Finally, after approximately a quarter of a mile, she sneaked up a creaky staircase to their private apartments. The girls had been in bed for hours and she had a feeling that Richard probably had been too.

Carys opened their bedroom door slowly and, sure enough, Richard was in bed. He'd left her bedside lamp on but looked as if he'd been asleep for hours. She washed and undressed, shivering in the chilly room even though it was still summer. She was secretly dreading her first winter at Amberley, convinced she'd be wearing a coat, hat and boots indoors. Just the other day, she'd been wearing two layers of fleece and had been in danger of electrocution from the static when she got undressed.

'Richard?' she whispered as she got into bed.

'Hmmmm?'

She dared to snake her arms around him and he felt so warm and good. She kissed his shoulder.

'You asleep?'

'Doing my best,' he muttered.

Carys bit her lip. 'Am I forgiven?' she whispered.

There was a pause: an awful, gut-wrenching pause, which made her wonder if she'd have to pack her bags, return to her town house and denounce her title of duchess.

'As long as it doesn't happen again,' Richard said at last, squeezing her hand and sinking his head further into his pillow.

'It won't,' Carys said. 'I promise.'

Carys got up extra early the next morning. So early, in fact, that she surprised Richard by accompanying him to his estate office and giving herself a quick tour.

'I just want to see where you spend most of your time,' she explained when he kept looking at her quizzically but she went and blew it when she attempted to tidy his desk and he threw her out.

'Don't forget, I'm out tonight,' she said.

'Out?'

'With your Aunt Violet. I told you. We're having a girls' night out.'

Richard looked perplexed, shook his head, and then shut the office door on her.

So, it was back to her own office where she managed to make a good deal of progress with a stack of post, organised the final stages of the transportation for the Montella exhibition and set up several meetings with estate tenants in the hope of getting to know everyone and find out how she could progress in the future. A thoroughly exhausting, fulfilling day.

After eating tea with Cecily and Evie in which Cecily had managed only two words: 'No' - twice - Carys took a shower and changed into a pretty summer dress in forest green and wrapped a gold fringed shawl around her in lieu of a coat.

Great Aunt Violet had been rummaging through her wardrobe too and looked stunningly pretty in a floral blouse and cherry red skirt. Tiny diamante droplets swung from her ears and her eyes sparkled with joy.

'I can't remember the last time I had an evening out,' she said as Carys helped her down the stairs. Carys hadn't realised just how frail Aunt Vi was. Her limbs were as delicate as new branches and her failing eyesight made her almost completely reliant on Carys.

'Just a few more steps. Nearly there,' Carys encouraged. 'You're doing brilliantly.'

'Should have moved years ago,' Aunt Violet mumbled as she proceeded. 'But an old person's bungalow wouldn't have my view, would it?'

'It certainly wouldn't.'

'I do love this old house but I'm afraid it doesn't love me any more'

'Houses aren't always easy to get along with, are they?'

Aunt Vi chuckled. 'Listen to me complaining when you have that great monster, Amberley, to cope with.'

Carys was a bit surprised at Aunt Vi's summation of Amberley. After all, it was her ancestral home.

'Oh, it's not that bad,' she lied.

Aunt Violet smiled and gave a little chuckle. 'You brave, brave girl,' and she shook her head, leaving Carys to wonder what exactly she meant.

There was quite a crowd outside Bellwood's Books. Carys had never been to a book signing before and she had to admit that it was all rather exciting. The queue to get into the store was made up of an eclectic bunch of young, old, male and female. Marissa Dahling's popularity seemed truly universal. There were enormous posters up in the shop window and teetering towers of books on every available table - not just of her latest title but of her whole backlist.

Carys approached a shop assistant.

'Hello,' she said, 'I rang before about seats for me and my Great Aunt.' She nodded towards Aunt Violet, and they were ushered towards the front row.

'That okay for you?' the assistant asked.

'Perfect,' Aunt Violet said. 'What fun this is!' she said, clasping her hands over a tiny, bead-encrusted handbag.

Carys smiled and, in that moment, she felt great joy and great sadness, for she couldn't help thinking of all the Great Aunt Violets there must be who would derive so much pleasure from so simple a thing as a book reading but didn't have anyone to take them.

I must try and do more for Aunt Violet, she thought. And then, the excitement began as the manager of the store held up his hands in a bid for silence.

'Ladies and gentlemen. Thank you for coming here tonight to our special author event. It isn't everyday that we can welcome an international bestselling author to Carminster and I'm very proud to welcome her to Bellwood's. She's sold over fifty million books world-wide and is published in over thirty languages. Her books have been turned into successful films and she's currently producing one of them for a Broadway show. Please welcome Marissa Dahling.'

There was a deafening round of applause as Marissa Dahling appeared and took a seat behind a small desk laid with several stacks of her books, a small microphone and a bottle of water and a glass.

Carys took a sideways glance at Violet whose tiny eyes were almost popping out of her head.

'Marissa Dahling!' she whispered.

Carys nodded. She must be in her late forties, Carys thought. Strikingly beautiful, with alabaster skin and sunshine yellow hair swept up into an elegant chignon, she wore a gold choker from which a heart dangled and her fingers dripped with diamonds. Success sat well with Marissa Dahling.

She introduced herself not as a bestselling author but as a wife and a mother. 'And a relentless observer of human weakness.'

There was a ripple of nervous laughter from the audience who were, perhaps, worried that she might look into the very heart of them and pluck out their mystery.

She talked about her family, her travels, and her passions which included horse riding in the Grand Canyon and buying local honey from wherever she visited, believing it kept her 'young, loving and full of energy'.

Aunt Violet nudged Carys. 'We must get some straight away. I want to look just like her.'

Carys smiled.

And then Marissa Dahling read an extract from her latest novel, *City of Broken Hearts*: another thrilling tale of love, lust, and betrayal.

Aunt Violet was hooked, her face a perfect picture of concentration as she lost herself in the opening chapter.

'We must have that book!' she whispered to Carys when the reading ended and everyone applauded.

'I'll find us a copy.'

Questions and answers followed and Carys felt Aunt Violet giving her arm a gentle squeeze.

'Carys, dear,' she whispered. 'Will you ask a question for me?'

Carys raised her eyebrows. 'Really?'

Aunt Violet nodded.

'Well, I-' what could Carys say? She'd pledged to give Aunt Violet the best night out ever and if that meant overcoming her nerves by raising her hand and asking a question, so be it.

'Of course,' she said. 'What do you want me to ask?'

'Will you ask her if her heroines are based on her and if she herself has met so many wonderful lovers?'

Carys's face flushed scarlet. She couldn't ask *that*. Surely Aunt Violet was teasing. She turned to look at her but she looked completely in earnest.

'Go on, dear. Before she gets up.'

Carys bit her lip nervously, her mind whirring. How was she going to phrase this? Could she really do it? She'd always been so shy when it came to this sort of thing. Even at school, she'd rather have risked the wrath of the teacher by asking her neighbour for help rather than putting her hand in the air. And she was in the front row too - where everybody could see her!

But, if it made Aunt Violet happy ...

She put her hand in the air.

'Yes, lady in the gorgeous golden shawl I've been admiring all evening.'

There was a titter of laughter around the room and Carys blushed again. 'I - er - was wondering if you base your heroines on - erm - yourself and if the men in your stories - if they were - if you'd met them - in real life.'

Marissa Dahling smiled and her beautiful eyes twinkled in naughty delight. 'And your name is?'

'Oh,' Carys said, not having expected to be questioned herself. 'Carys,' she said in as small a voice as possible.

'Well, Carys,' Marissa said, seeming to boom her name into the microphone so that everybody knew who'd dared to ask such a naughty question, 'I like to think that my heroines have my zest for life - my energy and vitality. I suppose they are all a little like me. And my heroes? Well, let's just say that I've met one or two in my time!'

Everybody laughed and there was a short round of applause before questions were wrapped up and Marissa agreed to sign books for anyone who'd bought them. Immediately, there was an almighty rush for the tills as people grabbed armfuls of books and then stood in line to get them signed.

Carys and Aunt Violet found a copy of *City of Broken Hearts* and looked over the stacks of her backlist. The Donna Carrera trilogy: *Sunsets and Starlight*, *Heaven's for Fools*, and *Hearts for Hire*, looked particularly tempting with their simple white covers with embossed motifs.

'I didn't realise she'd written so many,' someone said.

'This is her twenty-first,' a shop assistant said with a huge smile. 'We're selling any three titles for the price of two tonight and Ms Dahling will be pleased to sign any bought here this evening and any from your own collection.'

Carys heard Aunt Violet rustling in her handbag and turned to see her producing an enormous woollen purse which looked as if it hadn't seen the light of day for a decade or two. She walked over to the display and picked up the complete Donna Carrera trilogy and, together with *City of Broken Hearts*, took them to the till to be paid for.

A moment later, she joined Carys again. 'Go on, Carys. Get my books signed for me,' Aunt Violet smiled.

'Of course!' Carys said. 'There's quite a queue, though, it might take a while. Will you be all right waiting here?'

'There's a nice seat over here,' one of the shop assistants said, leading Aunt Violet to a quiet corner.

Carys got in line behind a teenage girl who was holding a heap of Marissa Dahling paperbacks, their spines cracked and their covers curling from hours of pleasurable reading. One looked as if it had even taken a tumble into a bathtub. She caught Carys's eye and smiled.

'I'm so excited,' she said. 'I've read all her books, have you?'

'Well, no, but I probably will now.'

'She's amazing!' the girl enthused. 'I've messed up two relationships now because I'd rather stay in with a Marissa Dahling book than go out on a date.'

Carys grinned and then peeped through the queue to the table where Ms Dahling was sitting and signing. Did she know how much her fans adored her?

And then, before she knew it, it was her turn.

'Ah!' Marissa said, with a bright smile. 'Carys, isn't it?'

Carys nodded. 'Hello.'

'What a lovely name. Shall I make the dedications to you?'

'Oh, no, actually, it's for my aunt: Violet.'

'Another lovely name,' Marissa said. 'I may name one of my future heroines after you or your aunt.'

Carys could feel herself blushing again as she willed herself to say something. 'I've been reading your books to my aunt,' she said. 'We love them.'

Marissa looked up after putting a final flourish on her fourth signature. 'Thank you.'

'I'm sorry if I embarrassed you with my question.'

'No, not at all. I enjoyed answering it. I'm sure it was the question everybody wanted to ask but they didn't have your courage.'

Carys smiled. She liked Marissa. 'Thank you so much,' she said, taking the books handed to her. 'I'll look forward to reading these.'

'Did you get them all signed? What was she like? Was she nice?' Aunt Violet asked, leaping off her seat like a jack-in-the-box as Carys approached.

Carys opened one of the books and Aunt Violet inspected the artistic dedication and signature in beautiful black ink.

'Goodness! To me!'

Carys nodded. 'All four.'

'I can't thank you enough,' Aunt Violet said, linking Carys's arm as they left the shop. 'It's been a perfect evening.'

'And it's not over yet,' Carys said. 'You haven't forgotten we're having a spot of supper at The Garden Room?'

'My goodness!' was all Aunt Violet could say.

By the time Carys had seen Aunt Violet safely home later that evening and returned to Amberley, she was very pleasantly exhausted. A perfect evening indeed. She felt that nothing in the world could spoil her mood.

But she hadn't banked on what was laying in wait for her the next morning.

CHAPTER 25

Carys wasn't a violent person by any means but she had the feeling that if she ever saw Natasha Bryant again, she would floor her. It was the day after the book signing and Carys was just penning a response to an enquiry about whether somebody could have their wedding photographs taken in the grounds of Amberley without actually getting married there when Mrs Travis came into her office.

'I'm sorry to disturb you, Lady C, but I thought you might like to see this.'

'What is it?' Carys asked, looking up from her desk.

'It's the local paper. Mr Reeves brought it to me. I don't think Lord C's seen it yet.'

Carys's eyebrows rose. This sounded ominous. Mr Reeves was Amberley's butler and the unofficial clippings master of anything to do with Amberley as he read all the local newspapers.

'Well,' Carys said, taking the paper, 'at least I'm not on the front page.'

Mrs Travis pursed her lips. 'No,' she said. 'It's on page five.'

Carys frowned at her sombre voice and quickly flicked through the pages. 'Oh!' she yelped in shock. 'How?' It was all she could muster.

'It was that book signing you went to,' Mrs Travis said, stating the obvious.

'But I didn't see anyone-' Carys was going to say that she didn't see anyone taking photos but then she remembered being half-aware of flashes going off every now and then. But they'd been fans, surely? Anyway, how had the papers known she'd been there?

And then she remembered. That question! She'd had her name boomed out across the audience. Well, there weren't too many people called Carys, were there? And if that appalling Natasha woman had been there -

Yes! Sure enough, in bold, rather smug-looking letters, Carys thought, was written, *Story by Natasha Bryant*. Of course she'd been there. Marissa Dahling's visit to Carminster was a big event.

'What an absolute bitch!' Carys said and then covered her mouth in shame. 'Sorry, Mrs Travis.'

'Not at all,' she said stoically. 'I always thought that one was a bit of a trollop!'

For a moment, Carys felt like laughing, but it didn't last and her eyes returned to the story and the photograph of her standing with Marissa Dahling. And on to the headline: *Duchess Seeks Advice from the Queen of Romance.*

When bestselling author, Marissa Dahling, gave a reading at Bellwood's Books last night, she didn't expect to be cross-questioned about her love-life by the Duchess of Cuthland. The duchess, who recently confessed to marital problems, seemed keen to know if Ms Dahling's heroes were based on her own experience with men. Ms Dahling is, of course, famous for her sexy novels filled with passionate affairs and handsome men and beautiful, jet-setting women.

'This is completely outrageous! I can't believe they've printed such rubbish.'

'I tell you, my lady, it's gone downhill something dreadful since that Natasha was taken on board.'

Carys shook her head in utter dismay. This was the second time Natasha Bryant had made her look like a fool.

'What are we going to do?' she asked. 'How are we going to hide this from Richard? He always looks through the papers.'

'Yes, my lady, *looks*,' Mrs Travis said cryptically.

'What do you mean? He's bound to notice this. Look! My picture's the size of a postcard and is on a facing page, for goodness' sake!'

Mrs Travis looked pensive for a moment as if she was working something out in her own mind first. 'He rarely reads it so why couldn't we take out this offending page and replace it with the one from yesterday. I'm sure he won't notice.'

'Are you sure?'

'Well, we can hope. And, as long as nobody else tells him about it-
'

'It's worth the risk. I don't want him seeing this. It'll probably mean divorce! Do you still have yesterday's paper?'

'We keep all the papers, my lady, for at least a month.'

'That's great. Then this might just work.'

Mrs Travis nodded. She looked as pale and anxious as Carys was feeling.

As she left the room, Carys, who'd handed the newspaper back minus the offending pages, sat down at her desk feeling completely drained. She'd been duped - *twice!* She read through the shoddy story which was trying to pass itself off as journalism and then folded it neatly before hiding it in the third drawer down on the left-hand side of her desk. That, she believed was the least ostentatious of drawers. If you were snooping for something in somebody's desk, the third drawer on the left-hand side would not be your first port of call, would it? One would, she believed, go for the top drawers first. Then the second drawer would be inspected then, perhaps, the bottom drawer. No, she thought, the third drawer, right at the back underneath some leaflets she'd collected, would be the safest hiding place.

Once she'd tucked it away, she drummed her fingers on the perfect polished desktop, wondering if she should ring Natasha up and have it out with her. But where would that get her? It would do no good whatsoever and it would give Natasha the pleasure of knowing she had riled her. No, she'd have to let it go, even though it made her heart pound with fury.

One thing was certain, though: from now on, she would have to remain vigilant at *all* times.

'You're looking rather pale,' a voice said, startling Carys some two hours after she'd hidden the latest newspaper disgrace in her most secret of drawers.

She looked up to see Georgiana's beautiful blue mist descending into her favourite armchair.

'Georgiana! Where have you been? I've been worried sick. I was beginning to think I'd made you up and that you didn't really exist at all.'

'Oh, I've been around,' she said enigmatically.

Carys instantly forgot her previous anxiety at Georgiana's absence. It was so good to see her again and have someone to talk to.

'You won't believe what's been going on here.'

Georgiana raised a hand in the air. 'You do not need to explain, Carys, dearest. I have been watching from afar and I think the whole thing is simply appalling.'

'You mean, you know about Natasha's story in the paper?'

Georgiana nodded. 'I do.'

'You never cease to amaze me,' Carys said. 'So, what do you think we should do?'

Georgiana looked pensive for a moment. 'Absolutely nothing.'

Carys sighed.

'For the time being,' Georgiana added. 'I have a feeling a situation will present itself before too long when we can reassess the matter.'

Carys frowned, wondering what she meant but it didn't look like Georgiana was going to explain. And then she remembered something.

'Mr Morris from The Bretton Gallery was here the other day, looking over the Montella portraits of you.'

'Oh, yes?' Georgiana said, brushing some invisible dust from her blue gown.

'Yes,' Carys continued, 'and he was very taken with that portrait of you - in your blue dress.'

'Well,' Georgiana smiled, 'most men are.'

Carys narrowed her eyes. 'No, not like that. It was something quite different.' She paused, as if trying to make Georgiana sweat a bit but it didn't seem to be working. Perhaps if Carys watched *The Bill* rather than *Emmerdale*, her interrogation skills would be slightly more honed than they were. 'He seemed to think you're hiding something - like the Mona Lisa.'

Georgiana batted her eyelashes and continued to examine her dress for imperfections which weren't there. 'Really? How strange.'

'And I agree with him,' Carys said, getting up from her chair and walking around her desk to perch on the front so she could be a little bit closer to her suspect. 'I must say, I wouldn't have noticed it if he hadn't pointed it out to me but-'

'Carys, you really should not listen to these - these - quacks! First that awful Lavinia Claridge-'

'Lara.'

'And now this tiresome Mr Morris. Some people do not have lives of their own and so they constantly meddle in those of other people.'

'But Mr Morris isn't meddling.'

'Then what, precisely, would you call it?'

'Taking a vested interest.'

'Oh! What nonsense.'

Carys stared at her. She was smiling. She was doing her best to hide it but Carys could definitely see that the corners of her mouth were turning up into a naughty little smile which was daring to tickle her cheeks.

'Come on,' she said, lightening her tone. 'You can tell me.'

'Tell you what, exactly?' Georgiana asked but her voice was perceptibly higher now, as if she knew she'd been found out and there was nowhere to hide.

'Tell me what that painting's all about.'

There was a pause. Georgiana was now pleating the silky blue material of her dress between her busy fingers. 'It is nothing but a portrait - commissioned by my husband. That is all.'

'It is not. And you know it!' Carys said boldly.

Georgiana looked momentarily shocked: her eyes wide and her mouth a little circle of surprise.

'Come on, Georgie,' Carys said, a little laugh in her voice. 'You know all there is to know about me. I don't hide anything from you.'

Georgiana clasped her hands together and, for a moment, her eyes looked quite serious and she looked as if she might be about to confess.

'I won't tell a soul,' Carys whispered. 'Your secret will be safe with me.'

'It better had.'

'Then you'll tell me?'

Again, there was a pause. And then, Georgiana nodded. 'I promise I will tell you. After our first ghost tour.'

CHAPTER 26

The day of the first ghost tour arrived far too quickly and, even though Carys had poured hours of work into the project, she still didn't feel ready.

'What made me think I could do this?' she asked, panic creasing her forehead.

'You will be fine,' Georgiana assured her.

'I won't. I've forgotten everything we went through - dates, names, furniture makers - *every*thing!'

'It's only stage fright,' Georgiana said. 'I believe it's the rush of adrenalin you need in order to perform well.'

'I'll be sick! I know I will. I'll be sick in one of those great urns by the fireplace and everyone will be horrified and leave in disgust and nobody will ever visit Amberley again.'

Georgiana laughed. 'Calm down. Come on, now. Deep breaths. Relax.'

Carys tried to do as she was told. 'Deep breaths. Oxygen is good.'

'Yes.'

'I've got to relax.'

'Yes.'

'Calm. I need to be calm.'

'That's right.'

There was a moment's pause when Georgiana seemed to be winning.

'I can't do it!' Carys suddenly said, her eyes wide with fear and her face as pale as a cloud.

'Come and sit down,' Georgiana said. They were in the Yellow Drawing Room and the sun was streaming through the windows as if in encouragement. 'Is it not a beautiful day?' Georgiana said.

Carys took another deep breath and looked out of the window. Everything was the bright emerald of summer. If only she could spend the day walking around the grounds, she thought. A good long walk through the woods and around the lake with the dogs and then back for a lazy lunch and a read in the private gardens - far away from the prying eyes of tourists.

'This is the sort of day people visit in droves,' Carys said, panic rising again.

'Let's hope so! Isn't that what we have been working towards?'

'I suppose so.'

'Would you not be terribly disappointed if nobody showed up?'

Carys sighed. 'I suppose so.'

'I mean, it was such a good idea and, after all your hard work, it would be a shame not to make the most of it. And Richard will be so proud of you if it is a success - which I am sure it will be.'

'All right! Enough with the bolstering,' Carys laughed and Georgiana breathed a sigh of relief.

'I meant to tell you earlier, you look fabulous.'

'Georgiana!'

'No! I mean it.'

'You don't think I'm too duchessy?'

'Not at all.'

'Because I did wonder - what with the pearl earrings and the suit.'

'It's a very pretty suit. Not too duchessy at all.'

'Because I'll never be one of those tweed and pearl duchesses,' Carys went on.

'I believe you,' Georgiana said, looking up and down at Carys's pretty ensemble. She was wearing a pale pink suit in a material as far removed from tweed as it could be, and the jacket had pretty piping around the sleeves. Her hair was newly-washed and loose and her make-up had been applied with the lightest of touches.

'I don't look middle-aged, do I?'

'Dear girl, I've never seen anyone look less middle-aged.'

'And I don't want people to think I've just walked out of a copy of *Cuthland Life*.'

'Carys!'

'What?'

'Will you stop! You're talking rubbish,' Georgiana said. 'I know what you need,' she continued, walking over to a cabinet by the fireplace.

'What?'

'A small glass of fortification.'

Carys's eyes widened in astonishment as she watched Georgiana pour her a whisky. She didn't know ghosts could do that.

'But, I don't drink spirits.'

'This spirit thinks you should.'

Carys couldn't help but smile.

'Go on. It will do you the world of good.'

Carys took the glass and drank a small mouthful. As she swallowed, she felt the warmth of the fiery water and blinked hard. 'Well!'

'Good?'

She swallowed some more. 'I haven't quite made up my mind.'

'And you've run out of time,' Georgiana said. 'Look.'

Carys looked out of the window and saw a crowd of people.

'Oh my goodness. They're here already.'

'It is time.'

Carys checked the clock on the mantelpiece. It was time. Roberta Ellis, one of Amberley's long-serving room stewards, and the only person to volunteer for the ghost tours, was busy handing out tickets. She would take the second tour, it had been decided. Carys was jumping straight in at the deep end with the first tour.

'Then I should greet them, shouldn't I?'

'Unless you want me to,' Georgiana said, her naughty eyes sparkling.

'And you know what to do?'

'We have been over this hundreds of times. Trust me. I'm a professional.'

'Okay,' Carys said, flapping her hands as she tried to calm down. 'Just as we planned.'

'Just as we planned,' Georgiana repeated.

Carys watched as Georgiana floated out of the Yellow Drawing Room humming a little tune that Carys didn't recognise. She was glad that she, at least, was enjoying this.

Taking a deep breath, Carys walked through the hallway and out of the private door, crossing the gravel driveway to meet the first party of the day.

'Good morning,' she said, her voice sounding much brighter and more optimistic than she had hoped. 'I'm the Duchess of Cuthland and I'd like to welcome you to Amberley Court and to the very first ghost tour.' Her eyes scanned the crowd of fifteen people and she was pleased to see a good mix of men and women, young and old. They'd decided that fifteen would be the maximum you could keep an eye on at any one time, and would allow time for questions as they went around.

'The house you see today was built on the site of a priory and we still have part of the old cloister which we shall walk around later. The original building dates from the early sixteenth century but the east front was remodelled in the early eighteenth. The windows vary in date from 1500 to the nineteenth century so it really is a bit of an architectural jigsaw.'

There were a few smiles which made Carys relax a little. She felt she just might be able to do this after all. She smiled, taking in the crowd of people and really wanting to make them all feel welcome. Until she saw... *No.* It couldn't be, *could* it? Carys peered closer at an elderly lady who was standing behind a young couple. She had thick glasses on and her curly grey hair sprang out from under a purple beret but, from under her curly hair, there was a glimpse of red. And she was anything but an old lady.

'Er - excuse me a moment,' Carys suddenly said. 'I've just got to check we're -' she paused, 'okay for beginning the tour.' And, with that, she dived back into the house.

'Georgiana?' she called. 'Are you there?' Carys ran into the Yellow Drawing Room. 'Georgiana!'

'Whatever is the matter? Are you not meant to be with the tour group?' Georgiana said, suddenly appearing in her blue cloud.

'My goodness! You're never going to believe it.'

'What? What's happened?'

'It's her.'

'Her who?'

'Natasha! She's here - undercover - dressed as a little old lady.'

'Really?'

'I mean, I just don't believe it. The cheek of the woman. And to think I wouldn't recognise her.'

'And you are *quite* sure it's her?'

'Sure? Of course I'm sure,' Carys hissed. 'I'd recognise those beady, searching eyes anywhere, and the shifty way she was lurking at the back of the group. And she was carrying the most enormous bag. I bet she'd got notepads and tapes and cameras in there.'

'Then I would confiscate it.'

Carys's eyebrows rose. 'You would?'

Georgiana nodded. 'Large bags are not permitted on the tour for fear of breakages.'

'That's brilliant. Why didn't I think of that?'

'Because you've got quite enough to think about.'

'That's very true. Oh, Georgiana! What are we going to do? Even if we take her bag away, she'll still make up some horrendous story and Richard was so cross with the last one, I feel as if I'm on my final warning.'

'Don't panic,' Georgiana said looking thoroughly panic-stricken herself. 'Let me think for a moment.'

'As long as it's only a moment,' Carys warned, chewing her lip as Georgiana looked pensive.

A few tense-ridden minutes passed and then Georgiana spoke.

'I have it,' she said.

'What?'

A mischievous smile danced across her face and, for a moment, she looked just as she had in the famous Montella portrait. 'Do you trust me?'

'Of course I do. Now tell me what we're going to do,' Carys said.

'You, my dear, aren't going to do anything any different from what we have already planned.'

'Well, what are *you* going to do, then?'

Georgiana gave a little laugh. 'I'm going to give that reporter the most surreal experience of her life.'

'So, if you'd like to follow me into the entrance hall,' Carys said a few minutes later, after having briefed Roberta on their intruder. 'We have to insist that large bags be left at the front desk here and, if you can switch all mobile phones off, then we can be assured that they won't interfere with any supernatural vibes.'

There were a few excited murmurs from the group.

'But I have valuable things in here,' Natasha protested in a really bad imitation of an old lady's voice.

'It will be quite safe here,' Roberta assured her, taking the bag from her. 'You can collect it after the tour.'

'I should also remind you that no photographs can be taken inside the house but you're very welcome to take them in the garden later,' Carys said politely with a bright smile that was aimed at all fifteen members of her tour group - bar one. 'Now, if you follow me, we'll begin in the hallway.'

Fifteen pairs of feet shuffled behind her and she began the tour, recounting dates, pointing out paintings and answering the staggering number of questions which she hadn't expected.

'Are there really ghosts here?'

'How many are there?'

'Have *you* seen any?'

Nobody seemed at all interested in the fine portrait of the fifth duke or the pair of walnut side chairs.

Moving on to the Red Drawing Room, Carys tried to distract them with the history of the dinner service but they weren't having any of it.

'Where are the ghosts?'

Carys smiled, realising that she'd have to veer away from the safety of Amberley's history and move onto the more exciting topic of the spirit world.

'As many of you know,' Carys began, 'I have only recently moved into Amberley. I'm still getting used to it - still managing to get lost - and still experiencing all it has to offer. But I have been lucky enough - if that's the right expression - to witness some interesting things.'

For a moment, nobody said a word. They were completely and utterly spellbound by Carys and what she was saying. It was a strange, almost powerful moment. This, she thought, must be how a good teacher feels when they have their students in the palm of their hands.

'What kind of things?' a young woman asked from the front of the group.

Carys paused. 'More of a feeling than anything,' she said. 'A feeling that I wasn't alone; that there was somebody with me.'

'Have you seen anything?' the young woman asked.

Carys and Georgiana had discussed this at great length and it had been decided that it would be totally insane for Carys to tell people of her new best-friend who came and went in a bright blue cloud and who gave her advice. They would keep things vague, mysterious and wonderfully enticing.

'Only shadows in the shadows,' Carys said enigmatically. 'But other people have seen things - up and down the centuries.'

'Then why haven't we heard more stories about Amberley being haunted before?' a voice piped up from the back - Natasha's 'old lady'.

'Perhaps because so much rubbish is published in newspapers today that it doesn't leave much room for half-decent stories,' Carys said with glee, causing most of the group to laugh.

Natasha frowned which was most unbecoming on her artificially lined face. 'I've heard Amberley has financial problems. Are you sure this isn't some sort of publicity scam?'

Carys's eyebrows rose in surprise at her brazen question. 'I have yet to hear of an historic house that doesn't have financial problems. If you know of one, I'd be very interested to know who runs it because perhaps they could give us some tips.'

Again, there was a ripple of laughter through the group.

'There may be some establishments that are unscrupulous in what they offer to the public but Amberley Enterprises is not in the business of extorting money from people under false pretences. That doesn't mean I can guarantee you'll all see a ghost today but I am hoping you will experience something wonderful for the price of your ticket. Now,' Carys continued, 'shall we go on?.'

After her words, there was an air of respect and of expectation too as they continued their tour of Amberley. Carys told them of Flemish tapestries, linen fold panelling, and all things made of marble and mahogany. In fact, she barely recognised herself or knew where all this information was coming from. It was as though Georgiana's confidence had bolstered her own or perhaps the steely presence of Natasha had encouraged Carys to do the very best job she could.

'And here she is,' Carys said, as they reached the Montella Room, standing underneath the portrait she'd come to love so much. 'Georgiana, wife of the fifth Duke of Cuthland. There are several portraits of her by the Italian artist, Leo Montella, but none painted with such delicacy as this.'

There was perfect silence for a moment as sixteen pairs of eyes gazed up at Georgiana's portrait.

'Some of you might have heard of The Blue Lady.'

'The ghost? Is this her?' the excited young woman asked.

'This is her,' Carys confirmed.

Then, right on cue, the door leading from the Montella Room into the Reading Room slammed shut.

'Oh my God!' the young woman exclaimed as everyone's heads spun around. 'Is that her?'

Silence fell upon the room like a sudden cloud and there was a sense of hushed expectancy. What would happen next? Were they about to witness a visitor from the spirit world?

'Just a draft,' Natasha dismissed.

Somebody tutted loudly and somebody else told her to shut up.

'I have a right to voice my opinion,' Natasha went on.

'Not when it spoils the enjoyment of everybody else,' someone said.

'Quite right.'

'Hear, hear.'

Carys cleared her throat. As much as she was enjoying seeing her arch enemy being verbally lynched, she knew she'd better put a stop to it before it all got out of hand.

'Amberley might be very old and certainly has a number of drafts but no draft could be strong enough to slam that door,' Carys pointed out confidently.

'See,' the young woman said. 'It was a ghost.'

'It was a cheap trick,' Natasha said.

'Shall we see?' Carys said, moving towards the door to open it. 'Is there anybody there?' she asked in a silly voice causing some laughter.

'Shush!' the young woman said, quite sure that they were about to make contact.

'This is ridiculous,' Carys heard Natasha muttering.

And then, suddenly, the door at the other end of the Montella Room slammed shut. Everybody span around, mouths open and eyes wide, including Natasha.

'What was *that?*' somebody asked.

'It's her again, isn't it?' the young woman said. 'I can feel it.'

'Nonsense,' Natasha said, rolling her eyes heavenward behind her fake glasses.

'Then how do you explain that?' the young woman turned on her.

'It was simply another door slamming. Doors slam. It happens every day.'

'Not in this house,' Carys interrupted. 'Doors as heavy as ours don't just slam.'

'Then somebody slammed them,' Natasha said as if she was talking to a group of backward children.

'The same person who slammed this door just a few seconds ago?' Carys challenged. 'Because I can tell you that it would be impossible for somebody to get to the other side of this room in that time without climbing out of a window and running around the house which we would have seen from the window here and would have taken too long anyway.'

Natasha sighed in exasperation. 'Then you must have two door-slammers in your employment.'

Carys frowned in bemusement. 'I don't recall seeing *Door Slammers* on the Amberley payroll,' she joked, again, causing laughter.

'And it has gone rather cold in here, hasn't it?' the young woman said.

'That's a myth,' Natasha countered. 'You're merely imagining things.'

'Look, lady,' a burly man in his thirties stepped forward, frowning at Natasha, 'I don't know why you came on this tour if you're such a sceptic but you're spoiling things for the rest of us so I, for one, would be grateful if you'd keep your thoughts to yourself.'

Carys tried to hide a little smile as Natasha's eyes narrowed.

'Hear hear,' somebody else said.

'Shall we go on with the tour?' Carys suggested, opening the door which had slammed first and leading them through to the Dining Room. Natasha was the last to leave the Montella Room and, as she entered the Dining Room, Carys noticed that she had turned a peculiar shade of white.

'Are you all right?' Carys asked.

'Y-yes. Perfectly,' Natasha said, clearing her throat.

The rest of the tour group turned to look at her.

'Because you look awfully pale.'

'I assure you, I'm perfectly fine.'

'Good,' Carys said, her eyes quickly darting into the vacated Montella Room where she saw the faintest hint of a blue mist.

'There are four dining rooms at Amberley and this is the one used to entertain important guests. The Cuthland family have always been great supporters of the arts and Richard Burton and Elizabeth Taylor have dined in this room as have the playwrights Oscar Wilde and Arthur Miller. But, perhaps the most famous diner here was Queen Victoria.'

'WHAT?'

Everyone turned to face Natasha who had blurted out the strange exclamation.

'Queen Victoria,' Carys repeated.

'What was that?' Natasha asked, looking around.

'What was what?'

'That - just now! I felt a hand on my shoulder. Somebody squeezed my shoulder!'

'It wasn't me, love,' the burly man said.

There was a ripple of laughter but Natasha wasn't joining in.

'But there's nobody behind you,' Carys pointed out. 'Are you sure you didn't imagine it?'

'I did NOT imagine it,' she said, her head shaking furiously.

'It's her,' the young woman said.

'Will you stop talking nonsense?' Natasha exploded.

'Er - ladies and gentlemen,' Carys said, raising her hands in a bid for calm, 'I think we should, perhaps, move on, don't you?'

They left the Dining Room and Carys took them through one of the old servants' passageways and into what Georgiana had described as the bowels of Amberley.

'Now that's what I call a drop in temperature,' somebody said.

'These passageways are no longer used, as we - thankfully - have modern kitchens upstairs now, but they would have been teeming with life not so long ago,' Carys said, careful to avoid naming any dates she couldn't be sure of. *Long ago* and *in the past* seemed to be enough historical accuracy.

'So your own staff don't come down here?' somebody asked.

'Just to keep things clean,' Carys said. 'But, personally, I prefer to be upstairs. It is a little spooky, don't you think?'

Right on cue, the sound of footsteps was heard from further along the passageway.

Carys frowned.

'What's that?' somebody asked. 'I can hear footsteps.'

'Me too.'

'Who is it?'

Fifteen pairs of eyes turned to Carys for an answer.

'Well,' Carys said, 'there shouldn't be anyone else down here except us.' She glanced quickly at Natasha, half-expecting her to say something sarcastic, but she was looking as spooked as everybody else.

'They've stopped,' somebody said.

Carys took a deep breath. 'We have to go this way anyway, so we'd better take a look.'

Now, there were fifteen pairs of feet echoing down the passageway and it became impossible to hear anything else. Carys led the way, turning left into one of the old kitchens where there was a large table and an ancient range. And then Carys began.

'When I first came to Amberley, I didn't think to venture downstairs to these rooms. To be honest, I had no idea they were here. But, I was later told about a young kitchen maid who used to work here,' Carys said, repeating the story that Mrs Travis had recently told her. 'Her name was Martha and she fell in love with one of the stable boys. It was in the days when it was strictly forbidden for members of staff to form relationships with each other but she didn't heed the warnings from her colleagues and was found, one night, in the stable boy's quarters.'

There was a collective gasp from the tour group and a few giggles too.

'Both were dismissed and it was later heard that Martha lost the baby that was conceived at Amberley and died shortly after herself, and some believe that she haunts these kitchens to this day, crying for her baby and her lost love.'

There was a sad and stony silence.

'That's so heartbreaking ,' one of the ladies said at last.

Natasha, who was stood at the back of the tour group, nearest the door to the passageway, suddenly turned white.

'Are you all right?' Carys asked.

'Y-yes,' Natasha stuttered.

'Did you hear something? I thought I heard something,' the young woman said, turning to Natasha. 'A - a - crying.'

'I didn't hear anything,' the burly man said.

'Neither did I,' another lady said, frowning in frustration.

Carys kept her eye on Natasha. 'Did *you* hear something?'

'N-no, of course I didn't. What's there to hear?'

'I could've sworn-' the young lady said.

'Shush!' the burly man said. And everybody listened in silence. But there was nothing but silence to hear.

Suddenly, Natasha shivered.

'I felt that too,' the young woman said. 'It came from somewhere over there.' She pointed to the end of the passageway.

Everybody moved out into the passageway but there wasn't anything to see, hear or feel any more.

'Onwards and upwards,' Carys said, leading them down the passageway until they came to a door which led to a staircase at the back of the house. This was one of the servants' routes to the bedrooms, Carys explained, reminding them that servants were expected to do their work almost invisibly.

'Unfortunately, we don't have the luxury of quite so many staff as the Bretton family once did.'

Carys led them across a landing and up another staircase before entering the Long Gallery and was delighted to hear low murmurs of appreciation at its grandiose beauty.

'This is the Long Gallery,' Carys began, 'It used to be used for walking in on a winter's day and dancing in on a summer's evening,' she continued, using the same words that Richard had when he'd shown her around that day which now seemed so long ago. 'Obviously, it's used as a library now.'

'How many books are there?' a young man asked.

'Fifteen thousand,' Carys said, thrilled at the ease at which she could answer such questions.

'This is part of the regular tour, isn't it?' Natasha said, obviously regaining some of her earlier impudence, having forgotten her fright downstairs.

'It is, yes. After all, it is one of Amberley's finest rooms. But you'll notice we have it to ourselves today. Please feel free to wander around but I would ask you not to take the books down from the shelves as they're very fragile.'

Carys watched as the group broke up and wandered around the room at their own pace. Some gazed up at the fine plaster ceiling, some walked over to the windows to look out across the gardens and one stood awkwardly alone pretending to peer at the spines of books whilst reaching for something in a pocket. Could it be a hidden notebook and pen, Carys wondered?

'Find anything interesting?' Carys dared to ask.

Natasha looked up from the shelves and shook her head.

Gosh, Carys thought, it really was an appalling disguise. Hadn't she noticed that her red hair was peeping out from under the grey wig?

Carys stared at her for a moment. 'You know,' she said, 'I'm sure we've met before, haven't we?'

Natasha looked dumbstruck for a moment. 'I'm sure we haven't.'

'You haven't visited Amberley before?'

'No. Never,' Natasha said, quickly and unpleasantly.

'It's just you look so familiar but, then again, I do see so many people, I could be mistaken.' Carys smiled sweetly and turned to join a couple by the window. No sooner had she joined them than there was a loud thud. Carys spun around and saw a large leather-bound book on the floor by Natasha's feet.

'I - er - didn't touch it.'

Carys frowned. 'It's very important that you don't handle the books.'

'I said, I didn't touch it.'

The burly man stepped forward. 'There's one on the floor,' he said.

'I know there's one on the floor, you great oaf, but it wasn't put there by me.'

There was a moment of frosty silence and then everybody began to speak at once.

'It's her! She's back - The Blue Lady.'

'Look, lady, I've just about had enough of you ruining our tour.'

'What would I want with these useless books? They're not worth the paper they're printed on.'

'These are valuable heirlooms and you have to respect them.'

'I've never met such a rude lady.'

'I've never been so insulted in my life,' Natasha said, her voice rising angrily above everyone else's. 'There's something going on here. I've been the victim of some trick and I intend to find out exactly what.' And, with that, she strode out of the room. The rest of the tour group stared in wide-eyed disbelief, their mouths dropping open as they heard a series of screams coming from the direction in which she'd gone.

'What an extraordinary lady,' Carys said.

'Thank goodness she's gone,' the burly man said. 'I thought I was going to have to knock her for six.'

'So did I,' Carys said, and everybody laughed. 'Right, shall we continue?'

Twenty minutes later, the tour had ended and everybody agreed it had been a stunning success and promised to tell all their friends and family.

As Carys stood by the front porch, waving goodbye to everyone, she knew Roberta would be in the middle of the second tour and that she herself had a good long break until the next one that afternoon. She smiled to herself. Even with the intrusion of Natasha, it had all gone far more smoothly than she could ever have hoped and this gave her a glow of confidence. She was actually looking forward to the next tour group.

'And so you should.'

Carys did a double take as she walked into her office a moment later. 'What?' she asked.

'Feel proud of yourself,' Georgiana said, drifting out of her blue haze and settling into the armchair by the fireplace.

'My goodness,' Carys flopped into the chair next to Georgiana's. She didn't feel like sitting at her desk. 'I can't thank you enough for what you did.'

'What did I do?' Georgiana asked.

Carys grinned. 'You know what you did.'

'What?' Georgiana looked puzzled. 'I'm afraid I don't know what you are talking about.'

Carys frowned. 'On the tour,' she said. 'With Natasha - like we agreed.'

Georgiana looked at Carys for a moment, her eyes vague and uncomprehending. 'Carys - I do not know what you mean.'

'Rubbish! That was you, wasn't it?'

There was a moment of silence when the two women just stared at one another. And then Georgiana burst out laughing.

'You rotten thing!' Carys said. 'You had me going there for a moment.'

'You should have seen your face,' Georgiana laughed. 'What a picture.'

'Don't ever do that again. I thought we had another ghost to contend with.'

'Heaven forbid.'

Carys sighed and shook her head, and then she bit her lip. 'You don't think things will backfire with Natasha, do you?'

'I don't think you need to worry about her any more She's learnt her lesson.'

'I hope so.'

Georgiana nodded. 'I must say that I was a little concerned with that young woman in the white trousers. She seemed very in tune with the spirit world. I felt sure she was going to spot me.'

'I did too. She was definitely on to you.'

'Good publicity, though.'

'And everybody went away delighted in the belief that they witnessed something ghostly.'

'They *did!*' Georgiana said. 'Now,' she said, getting up. 'I suppose I should make my presence felt on the next tour.'

Carys looked a little apprehensive. 'Don't go over-the-top,' she said. 'I don't want you terrifying Roberta. Remember, she has no idea that there really is a ghost at Amberley.'

Georgiana gave a winsome smile. 'You can rely on me,' she said, and Carys watched as she vanished in her blue mist to cause magic and mayhem amongst the next Amberley tour group.

CHAPTER 27

Carys was just getting into her stride on her second and last tour of the day when Richard charged through the Montella Room at great speed.

'Carys!' he yelled across the room, interrupting her in mid-spiel.

'Richard?' She turned around to face him and immediately saw that something was wrong - horribly wrong.

'Carys,' he repeated, waving something at her. Her eyes widened in horror. It was the newspaper.

She gave him a pleading look, and raised her hand to acknowledge the tour group. Had he not seen them?

'I need to speak to you,' he said, disappearing into the next room and not even giving her the chance to object.

She turned to her tour group and bit her lip. She'd planned for all sorts of unexpected occurrences on the tour: what to do if the fire alarm went off and how to cope with breakages, but nothing had prepared her for being interrupted by an irate husband.

'I'm afraid something's come up,' she said. 'If you'll bear with me a moment, and - er - please feel free to look around.' She cast her eyes around the Montella Room. They'd be quite safe there, she thought. They weren't likely to start taking the portraits off the walls, were they?

She took a deep breath and left the room.

'Richard,' she said in a hushed voice once she'd closed the door behind them both. 'I'm in the middle of a tour. Can't this wait?'

'No, it can't,' he said. His face was an angry shade of red which was most unbecoming. 'I suppose you've seen this?' He flung the newspaper at her unceremoniously.

Having no choice, Carys took it from him. There was no point trying to feign ignorance. 'Yes,' she said. 'I've seen it.'

'Somebody left it in the office and I was idly flicking through whilst on the telephone. You see, I'd already read it here, hadn't I? In the privacy of my own home. Yet I hadn't seen this page before. Now, forgive me, but I'm sure I'd have remembered a picture of my wife in the newspaper.'

Carys sighed. So much for Mrs Travis's attempt at sabotage. 'I can explain,' she said but she didn't think she was going to be given the chance.

'This is getting to be a regular occurrence, isn't it?'

Carys flapped her hands, doing her best to calm him down. 'Richard - shush! They'll hear you next door.'

'I don't give a damn if they hear me.'

'You're not making any sense. You're blaming me for something that was completely out of my control and yet you're making a complete fool of yourself in front of my tour group.'

'What?' he stared at her and, for one awful moment, she didn't recognise him at all. Who was this rage-ridden man standing before her? He was wearing the same checked shirt and slightly faded trousers as usual but, other than that, he seemed a stranger to her.

'My ghost tour. Remember? I told you about it and you gave it the go ahead.'

He shook his head as if he'd never heard of such nonsense before.

'I'm doing this for you - for Amberley,' she continued, 'but I don't seem to be getting any support.' Carys could feel her heart hammering inside her chest. They didn't seem to be communicating at all and this knowledge made her feel very uneasy.

'I have to go,' Richard said dismissively.

'And so do I,' Carys said, angry that Richard should suggest that he had somewhere else he should be and something more important he should be doing. Well, so did she.

'We'll talk about this later,' he said, his back towards her.

For a moment, she watched him go. She had no doubt whatsoever that he'd be raising this issue with her again but the thing that filled her with the most dread was the fact that she didn't want to be around to hear it.

She returned to the Montella Room and was aghast at the fifteen faces that turned towards her as she entered. From their expressions, she knew that they had heard every single word.

Carys cleared her throat. 'I - er…'

'If you don't mind me saying, love,' a little old lady in a pink hat said, 'that was completely over the top - I mean the way your husband reacted.'

'Excuse me?'

'We've all read the story,' a young man explained rather bashfully.

Carys could feel herself blushing. 'I see,' she said. 'Listen, I'm rather embarrassed by all this.'

'There's no need to be,' the little old lady said. 'We're all friends here, aren't we?'

The group nodded their heads in unison.

'Oh,' Carys said. All of a sudden, she felt rather lost. 'I don't know what to say.' She could feel herself swaying slightly, as if she was about to faint.

'Are you all right?' the pink-hatted lady asked.

'I feel a bit - light-headed.'

'Here,' a young lady of about nineteen pulled out one of the chairs from the table that was used at the weekly Amberley Enterprises meetings.

'Thank you.' Carys sat down and wasn't at all surprised when the other chairs were pulled out and most of the tour group sat down with her. 'Just give me a moment and we'll continue with the tour.'

'Hang the tour,' the young lady said and Carys looked up in surprise. 'You've got to sort this problem out first.'

Carys blinked hard. Had she heard correctly? She looked around the table at the faces that were watching her. This wasn't what she'd expected from being a tour guide. She was meant to be cool and confident and, most importantly, in control. Yet she felt utterly powerless, as though Richard's words had stripped her of every ounce of self-confidence.

'If you don't mind me saying,' the young lady continued, 'I wouldn't let a man of mine speak to me the way your husband speaks to you.'

There was a general murmur of agreement from around the table.

'She's right, dear,' the pink-hatted lady said. 'It was completely uncalled for. Especially when you explained that it wasn't your fault.'

For a moment, Carys bent her head and covered her face with her hands. They'd heard everything! She suddenly had an image of them all huddled up with their ears pressed against the door.

'*Shush!* Listen.'

'What's she saying?'

'Did you hear that?'

'He didn't really say that, did he?'

'I - I wouldn't treat you like that,' a young man's voice said. Carys looked up. He was sitting next to the young lady who'd pulled the chair out for her.

'You're such a sweetheart,' the young lady said, ruffling his hair. Was it her brother?

'It's that Natasha Bryant's fault,' he continued, his big eyes shyly concerned.

'She hasn't helped,' Carys whispered. 'Oh, God! It's all such a mess.' Carys could feel her eyes vibrating with sudden tears. Where had they come from? She didn't want to cry. She *couldn't* cry. Not in front of a room full of strangers. She had to pull herself together. She was the Duchess of Cuthland, for goodness' sake. Duchesses didn't cry in public - they didn't make a spectacle of themselves. They -

A wave of insecurity washed over Carys. Who was she fooling? She wasn't a duchess. She was plain old Carys Miller from Stanton Street. Had she really thought she could just step into the role of duchess? Had she really been so stupid as to think she could pull it off?

'I've got to go,' she said, attempting to stand up. She immediately felt a hand on her shoulder. It was the pink-hatted lady.

'You're going nowhere,' she said.

Carys looked at the faces staring at her. She knew they all meant well but she was beginning to feel rather trapped by them. There was only one way to distract them: get up and continue the tour as if nothing had happened.

Carys pushed her chair backwards. 'I think we'd better-' she paused. That sounded far too hesitant. She needed to take control again, if only until the end of this tour. 'Right, everyone,' she said, 'let's continue.'

But nobody moved. Each and every face was looking at her with sympathy and understanding. They didn't give a damn about the tour.

Carys bit her lip, willing herself not to be swept along by them. 'I think you'll find the next room very-'

'Uninteresting,' the young woman interrupted. 'Really, don't worry about the tour. We've all had a great time, haven't we?'

Again, there was a collective sound of agreement from around the table.

'We've seen some wonderful rooms-'

Carys shook her head. It had been an appalling tour. They hadn't even witnessed Georgiana's spooky door slamming routine yet.

'I'm so sorry,' Carys said, giving up at last.

'There's nothing to apologise for,' the pink-hatted lady said, giving Carys a gentle squeeze on her shoulder. It was such a well-meaning gesture, imparting strength and support but, sometimes, such gestures can have the opposite effect to that they intended, and Carys suddenly realised she was crying. She hadn't meant to - really she hadn't but, once she started, she couldn't stop.

'My dear girl,' the pink-hatted lady said, thrusting a tissue at her.

'I'm - s-so - s-sorry,' Carys stumbled, blowing her nose loudly and dabbing her eyes, wondering if the little mascara she'd put on that morning had migrated south.

'No need to apologise,' the young woman said. 'It would be much worse if you *didn't* cry.'

Carys tried to work out how that could be possible. She'd been humiliated in the local press - again; humiliated by her husband, and now she was humiliating herself by crying.

'Are you all right?' the bashful young man asked.

Carys looked up and nodded. 'Thank you, yes,' she said. 'I don't quite know what happened there and I really do apologise. I'd be happy to refund the price of your tour.'

'We'll not hear of it,' the pink-hatted lady said.

Carys bit her lip. She felt just awful that she'd let everybody down.

'Then, how about a cup of tea and a slice of cake?' Carys said, feeling a little brighter at her idea.

The group looked at each other and then smiled right back at her.

'Good,' Carys said, hoping that Mrs Travis would be amenable to her request. 'I'll go and arrange it. We'll have it here.'

'Oh,' the pink-hatted lady said. 'What a treat. Wait till I tell my friends.'

As long as that was all she told them, Carys thought, dreading it getting into the local press that she'd burst into tears on the ghost tour. Natasha Bryant would have a field day with that.

Twenty minutes later, with a table cloth spread and extra chairs brought in, everybody settled down to enjoy their tea and a choice of lemon or chocolate cake.

'It's not like any tour I've ever seen,' Mrs Travis muttered under her breath but Carys chose to ignore her and, once the door was shut and Mrs Travis safely out of the way, Carys spoke.

'I can't thank you all enough for your kindness,' she said. 'You've all been so understanding.'

The group smiled back at her. The bashful young man, who'd managed to obtain the chair next to Carys, dared to lean forward and place a hand on hers.

Carys immediately blushed and this caused everyone to laugh.

'I must have a photograph,' the pink-hatted lady said, opening her handbag in excitement. 'Only I don't know how to use this.' She produced a beautiful digital camera and waved it about hopelessly.

'Allow me,' a gentleman said.

'Oh, would you, dear? So kind,' the pink-hatted lady said, instantly posing next to Carys for her picture.

'As long as I don't see it in the *Cuthland News* under a dubious headline,' Carys said and everybody laughed again.

Finally, it was time to say goodbye to everyone. Carys led them through to one of the private doors and the group slowly left, each one stopping to shake her hand.

'Good luck,' the man with the digital know-how said.

'Be strong,' the pink-hatted lady said, giving her a hug.

'Be sure to stand up to him,' the young woman said.

'I've got a spare room in my flat - if you need it,' the bashful young man said, blushing furiously.

'Tim!' the young woman shouted, grabbing hold of his arm and dragging him away.

Carys couldn't help but smile as she watched the group walk down the driveway. They had to be the nicest bunch of people she'd ever met and now they'd gone, she felt quite bereft.

'What do I do now?' she asked herself.

CHAPTER 28

It was probably just as well that Georgiana hadn't put in an appearance on the last ghost tour. Carys wondered whether she had boycotted the tour deliberately, realising that her specialised skills weren't required. But where was she now? Why hadn't she shown herself? The tour party was long gone and Carys felt in desperate need of some company.

Carys had automatically sought refuge in her study after the tour, closing her door against the possible intrusion of Mrs Travis. She couldn't face questions now. No, she thought, now was a time for answers.

'Georgiana?' she whispered into the silence and then sighed when there was no sign of her. Where had she gone? Carys felt there was nobody else she could talk to. Her old friend Louise always seemed so busy these days and she didn't feel it was right to talk to Phoebe about problems she was having with Richard. Other than Georgiana, there was only one person she could talk to about it all, and that was Richard himself.

For a moment, Carys paused in front of the large mirror above the fireplace and gazed at her reflection. She always looked so tired these days. She pinched her cheeks in an attempt to encourage a bit of colour into them but it didn't work. That little trick only seemed to work in the movies. She ran her fingers through her hair and then found a lipstick in her jacket pocket and attempted to brighten her face up that way.

There. It would have to do. At least she wasn't in jeans and Wellingtons today which must please Richard a little.

Opening the office door, Carys gauged that the coast was clear for a quick departure from the hall. She wasn't in the mood for household concerns. She wanted to get out and get to Richard as quickly as possible. She knew she wouldn't be able to relax until she'd seen him and had spoken her piece. The dear pink-hatted lady and young woman on the tour group had been right - Richard was completely out of order speaking to her that way. She'd been so upset, her mind had, for a few brief moments, concentrated on one simple solution: to run away. Quick and easy. But could she really do that? Quit her marriage? She'd made a lifelong commitment and you couldn't simply bolt at the first hurdle you faced together.

Leaving the house, she walked, determinedly, towards the estate office. She'd only ever been in there once as she knew better than to bother Richard when he was working there but she didn't care what she interrupted today. He'd interrupted her at work - over a matter which really was nothing to do with her. Now it was her turn to make her presence felt.

She took a deep breath and entered the offices.

'Your grace!' Richard's secretary said, looking up from her desk in the tiny reception area, obviously surprised to see her. 'His grace is in a meeting,' she said but Carys wasn't going to be swayed.

'It's all right. He'll see me,' she said with a little more confidence than she felt. With that, she charged through to the meeting room where, she saw through the door, the whole of the Amberley estate workers seemed to be congregated. For a second, she lost her nerve. What was she doing? She saw Richard, pouring over a heap of papers and talking ten to the dozen, flapping his hands about as he tried to explain something.

Carys took a deep breath and knocked on the door and entered.

Everybody looked up and, when they saw who it was, stood up.

'Your grace,' they said in unison, making Carys feel like a head teacher who'd just disturbed a class of pupils at work.

'Please, sit down,' she said, noticing that Richard was the only one who hadn't stood up.

'Richard?' she said. 'Can we talk?'

He stared at her for a moment, his eyes narrowed in perplexity. 'What is it?' he asked, obviously not wanting to interrupt his meeting.

She motioned to outside and, for one horrible moment, she thought he was going to just sit there and she'd have to leave. It was a battle of wills and they locked eyes for a moment but Carys was determined not to back down. And it worked.

'Excuse me, gentlemen,' he said, standing up and following Carys out of the room. 'What's going on?' he asked once the door was safely closed behind them. 'Are the girls all right?'

'The girls are fine, Richard.'

'What is it, then?' he said, obviously thinking that nothing else could be important enough to warrant interrupting him.

'It's us.'

'What do you mean, *us?*'

'I'm not happy.'

'Carys, we'll have to discuss this later. I'm in the middle-'

'And that's *exactly* the sort of thing that's making me unhappy, Richard!' she said, trying not to get hysterical. 'I feel I can never talk to you. There's always something more important to do or someone more important to see. But I'm your wife! I should be number one. Yet I feel I come a long way down your list of priorities.'

'It's just a busy time of year,' he explained, scratching his head.

Carys shook hers. 'There's always an excuse, isn't there? And it's not just that. All this media rubbish is getting to me. I wasn't quite prepared for that. And I was even less prepared for the way you'd handle it. I've never been so embarrassed in my life as when you stormed into the middle of my tour group before. There was no excuse for it. None!'

'Carys-'

'It's not my fault. That's what I want to say.'

'Carys! We'll have to talk about all this later,' he said.

'Later. It's always later! But I'll be tired later. And you'll be tired. And the girls will be around and we won't talk, will we?' Carys stopped, suddenly feeling exhausted.

'I'm sorry. I've got to go now,' Richard said. His voice was calm and steady, a striking contrast to Carys's which had been spiralling out of control.

'How did I know you were going to say that?'

He placed a hand on her shoulder briefly but then turned and went back to the meeting room. Carys stood for a moment, completely numb. What had happened there? Had he listened to her? Had he really paid her any attention at all? She decided he hadn't. His head was full of Amberley. She was just a blip on his radar and he wasn't tuning into her.

'Everything all right, your grace?' his secretary asked as Carys walked back through reception.

Carys nodded, hoping her latest embarrassing conversation with her husband hadn't been overheard.

Leaving the office, She headed towards the walled garden. The sun felt warm and she took her jacket off and walked around the place she had such dreams for. She really had come to love Amberley and had foolishly believed that it was beginning to love her back. But it could never really be her home, could it? These houses weren't meant for women - they were men's houses. Women were merely visitors - coming and going through the ages, providing the next male heir. The roses that she could smell were not her roses - they were her husband's and if he wanted to dig them up then he would. If he wanted to dig up the whole of the walled garden and get planning permission for a block of flats then he would. Carys's voice was only noise. She had no real voice at all, did she?

She must have lost all track of time wandering around the gardens because, when she got back to the house, Mrs Travis was waiting to pounce.

'Oh, Lady C. The girls are in the kitchen having a spot of tea. I didn't know where you were. Are you all right?'

Carys nodded. 'Can you keep an eye on them for me?'

Mrs Travis looked a little put out. Babysitting Cecily and Evelyn wasn't in her job description.

'Just until Lord C's back.'

'When will that be?' Mrs Travis asked.

Carys shrugged her shoulders because she didn't know. 'I've got a call to make,' she said, quickly walking through the house to their private quarters before Mrs Travis could protest.

She didn't really have a call to make. She just needed to be alone. She didn't want to hear about Cecily and Evelyn's bickering or be asked about dinner or told that she had a dozen phone calls to return.

For a moment, she sat down on the end of the bed and looked around their room. It was beautiful, of course, like everything else at Amberley with its picture window, walk-in wardrobe, glorious fireplace and beautiful paintings but, at that moment, she didn't feel it was home and that thought made her intensely sad.

She got up and walked across to the wardrobe and reached in for her small suitcase.

'What are you doing, Carys?'

Carys spun around, surprised to see Georgiana watching over her. She'd never appeared in her bedroom before and it was rather unnerving.

'You gave me such a shock.'

'And you, my dear, are giving me a shock. What are you doing?' Georgiana repeated.

'I'm packing.'

Georgiana sighed. 'Well, I can see that much.'

Carys turned to face her. 'I'm going away.'

'What do you mean?'

'I'm leaving Amberley.'

Georgiana frowned. 'And nobody knows, do they?'

'That's right,' Carys said, surprised at how calm she sounded. Now that she was packing - doing something - she felt a little more in control.

'It isn't the answer, Carys.'

She shrugged. 'I don't know what the answer is,' she said. 'And I certainly can't seem to find it here. Not at the moment.'

'So you are leaving.'

'Yes.'

Georgiana sighed loudly. 'And how is that going to solve anything?'

'I don't know,' Carys said, her voice rising slightly.

'Running away has never-'

'Look, Georgiana, I don't mean to be rude but I'd just like a little space at the moment. I don't need your advice, okay?'

Georgiana didn't speak and Carys continued rifling through her wardrobe for a few essentials.

When she turned, Georgiana had vanished. She hadn't even said goodbye. Carys hoped she hadn't offended her; she'd never spoken sharply to her before.

'Georgiana?' Carys whispered. Could she hear her from her own dimension? 'I'm sorry. I didn't mean to shout at you.' Carys frowned. She felt even worse now but, still, she kept on packing until her little suitcase bulged. She could almost hear Georgiana remonstrate, 'Do you really need all that? How long are you planning on being away?'

'I don't know,' Carys said. 'As long as it takes.' And she left.

Mrs Travis was obviously being detained in the kitchen by Cecily and Evelyn and Carys ignored the ringing telephone and the barking dogs as she walked towards the door. Someone else could answer it and someone else could walk them.

Her little Marlva was waiting for her and she threw her suitcase onto the backseat, starting the car quickly before anybody saw what she was doing.

The tourists had left long ago and most of the staff had too. Amberley was quiet, the stretches of emerald lawn and the staff car park had emptied and there was nobody in sight. At this time of day, it was a beautiful place to be, Carys thought, but she couldn't be there now. It hurt too much so, watching the rosy façade of Amberley receding in her rear view mirror, she headed down the tree lined driveway and left the estate.

CHAPTER 29

Carys didn't really have a direction in mind. She just drove over the moors into Eastmoreland and soon found herself driving by the entrance to Barston Hall. For a moment, she wondered if she should pop in and see Valerie Buckley-Stewart. If Barston was anything like Amberley, there'd be plenty of guest bedrooms and she'd be sure to get some good advice from Valerie but it somehow felt like she'd be betraying Richard by going there. Barston was the opposition, after all, and he'd probably never forgive her if he found out she'd turned and run there.

She followed the road down into the valley, taking the picturesque route back towards Carminster. Her window was wound down and she could smell the rich peaty moorland which rolled away to the very horizon in purple splendour. It was easy to forget one's troubles here, Carys thought, as she heard the unmistakable song of a skylark. Nature had a way and calming a racing mind and unfurrowing a creased brow and Carys could feel herself relaxing as she drove.

Until she caught her first glimpse of Carminster cathedral spire. She swallowed, thinking back to their wedding day and, at once, her mind was racing again. What had happened to them? What had become of her dream of living with the man she loved? She couldn't understand it; it had all gone so horribly wrong.

She drove into town, becoming instantly entangled in the one-way system which was full of workers leaving for the day. The Carminster streets were narrow and interminably slow but Carys finally found herself in the street where Louise lived and found an elusive parking space not too far from her tiny terrace.

It was strange but she actually felt nervous showing up unannounced. *Don't be silly*, she chided herself. *That's what friends do.* But she hadn't spoken to Louise for ages and she did feel awful about that.

Taking a deep breath, she rang the doorbell and was greeted a few seconds later by an out of breath Louise.

'Carys? What a surprise.'

Carys let herself be hugged whilst musing on her friend's words. *What a surprise*, she'd said. Not, *What a lovely surprise*. Perhaps she was reading too much into it.

'How are you?' Carys asked.

'I'm fine. Come on in.'

'Are you okay?'

'Yes, why?' Louise asked.

'You're rather red.'

'Am I?'

They walked through to the sitting room and Carys soon saw why her friend's complexion was bright red for, sitting in a winged armchair as if he owned the place, was Martin Bradbury - Louise's ex. He nodded to Carys but didn't actually say anything. They'd never bothered to hide their mutual hate of each other.

Carys's quick glance noted the stubbled face which he'd obviously been scrapping against Louise's pretty complexion, turning the delicate skin raw. Honestly. Couldn't he even bother to shave?

'I - er - was just passing,' Carys said, realising now that she couldn't possibly stay.

'It's so good to see you. I was just talking about you, wasn't I?' Louise said to Martin but he'd hidden himself behind a copy of *Racing News*. 'Well, I was. I was just saying, I wonder how Carys is? Can I get you a cup of tea?'

There was a time when Louise would have just got on with making her a cup of tea. Now, the question seemed awkward, anxious.

'No,' Carys said. 'I can't stop long, I'm afraid. Just wanted to touch base.'

'Oh,' Louise said, looking a little crestfallen.

'But we'll get together soon, yes?'

'Of course. Lunch?'

'Brilliant,' Carys said, making a hasty retreat for the door. She didn't bother saying bye to Martin but she hugged Louise and promised she'd call.

As she got back into her car, she couldn't help feeling let down. Louise had always been there for her but she couldn't expect her to put her own life on hold on the off-chance of her needing to pop round and vent steam. The world didn't stand still for you and you alone.

So where was she to go now? She couldn't bother dear Aunt Vi, could she? The poor old lady wouldn't want worrying. And then Carys realised something: there was another person she knew who'd understand how she was feeling.

She turned the car around and headed back to Amberley.

It seemed strange to enter the estate via the west gate but it was no less beautiful a view. The driveway was narrower and lined with young trees. Beyond, were golden stretches of grass where the deer grazed. It was peaceful here - far away from the visitors, the estate workers and the delivery vans.

And there it was: Cuthland House. For a moment, Carys could perfectly understand its attraction. It was beautiful and not exactly your average retirement home. It was a home fitting for the widow of a duke - the woman who had lived in a family home that would never belong to her and had born an heir who would move her out as soon as his time came. It was the home for the dowager duchess of Cuthland. Her mother-in-law. Francesca.

'Francesca,' Carys said. It was a beautiful name but it struck terror in the very heart of her. They'd never shared more than a few words, never discussed anything of importance and didn't know anything about each other apart from what she'd learnt through reading her diary.

'The diary,' Carys said. She still hadn't talked to Francesca about the diary. Why had she given it to her? Did she expect Carys would want to talk to her?

Parking her car, Carys got out and opened the garden gate, walking up to the front door. The lights were on and she could hear the faint sound of a television. Taking a deep breath, she knocked on

to wait long for Francesca to open the door.
ot quite knowing what else to say.
in silence, her beautiful dark eyes giving
id something most unexpected - she

you.'

tes whilst
gave

Carys a chance to look around. The living room was not over-large like the ones at Amberley but had the feeling of cosiness one associates with a cottage. It overlooked the garden and the window was still open a little, the cool evening air lifting the bright white curtains.

The furniture was small, neat and very feminine: pretty side tables with cabriole legs, chintzy armchairs and an arts and crafts fireplace. It was a comfortable room and it was stuffed with photographs. Carys got up and looked at them, smiling at the ancient pictures of Henry and Francesca. They'd been such a handsome couple: he so darkly handsome - much as Richard was now - and she so beautiful with her raven hair, dark eyes and snowy complexion. There were photos of them on their wedding day, on their honeymoon at the estate in Scotland, with friends, at society dos with Francesca wearing the most beautiful ball gowns and looking like Elizabeth Taylor, and then there were the photographs of the young family: Richard climbing one of Amberley's oldest trees, Phoebe on her beloved pony, Jamie hugging a hairy terrier, and Serena looking uncommonly feminine at a wedding.

Along the mantelpiece were the more recent photographs of Cecily and Evie - the obligatory school photographs with gappy-toothed smiles, and triumphant pony club pics with the girls sporting their rosettes. There was also a wedding photograph of Carys and Richard. For a moment, Carys was a little taken aback. It seemed strange that she should have a place in such a collection and it surprised her to realise that she was as much a part of this family now as any of them.

'It's a lovely photograph,' Francesca said, coming into the room and placing the tea tray on a low-lying table. 'You remind me so much of myself at your age.'

Carys's eyes widened.

'You have that same expression - the ? excitement and pure terror,' Francesca sai'

'I do?' Carys said, looking at

'All day. I was watchi

Carys swallo

she began, 'th

France

said.

the door.

She didn't hav

'Hello,' Carys said,

Francesca regarded her

nothing away, and then she

smiled.

'Come in,' she said. 'I've been expecting you

Carys sat in the pretty living room for a full five minu
Francesca clattered around in the kitchen with tea things. It

one that suggests both

d.

the photograph again.

ng you.'

ved. It was a strange notion - to be watched. 'It was,'

e strangest day.'

sca sat down in an armchair by the fireplace. 'I know,' she

Carys sat in a matching chair opposite and took a sip from a blue and white china cup which Francesca motioned towards. It was funny but she'd been so worked up about talking to Francesca for such a long time but, now that she was actually here, she felt strangely calm.

There was a few moments of silence before Francesca spoke. 'You read it, then?'

'Yes,' Carys said, knowing, immediately, that Francesca was referring to her diary. 'Why did you want me to have it?'

Francesca looked pensive for a moment, as if rehearsing her answer in her mind first. 'Because it was just the sort of thing I could have done with when I married Richard's father.' She looked across at Carys and a tiny smile lighted her face. 'How are you coping?'

Carys hadn't expected the smile nor had she been expecting that question and she immediately felt tears springing. Oh, no, she thought. Please don't go and cry. Not in front of a dowager duchess - mother-in-law or not, it would just be too embarrassing. So she quickly blinked away her tears and nodded.

'I don't believe you, Carys,' Francesca said quietly.

Carys's mouth dropped open but she found that words eluded her.

'It's all right,' Francesca said. 'You can talk to me. It won't go any further - unless you want it to.'

Carys stared at her.

'Well, I-' she began nervously. 'I don't think I'm coping very well. It just seems to be one thing after another. Have you seen the papers?'

Francesca nodded. 'Pay them no attention. They'll always be interested in you. You're young and attractive. They're going to bother you. It's human nature.'

'But Richard's been so angry about it all.'

'But it wasn't your fault.'

'I know!' Carys all but screamed. Finally, someone could see things from her point of view.

'Did you tell him that?'

'Yes!'

Francesca sighed and shook her head. 'Bloody Bretton men,' she said slowly, and Carys couldn't help but laugh. She couldn't have put it better herself. 'They think the whole world revolves around them and their house.'

'But it does,' Carys said in frustration.

'So what's the answer?'

'I was hoping you'd be able to tell me,' Carys said.

'Ah,' Francesca said, taking a sip of tea before continuing. 'Let me see. I was married to Henry for thirty-six years - all of those spent living at Amberley Court. And, do you know what? I don't have a single piece of advice to give to you. I really don't.'

Carys frowned.

'All I can say is, if you're really unhappy, you must leave; if you think you can cope then stay.'

Carys looked at Francesca. Was she joking? She didn't appear to be. 'That's it?'

'That's it. We're all different, you see. I stayed and learnt to cope as so many other wives before me. Amanda couldn't cope and so left. There's no middle ground and you can only decide for yourself.'

Carys swallowed hard. It was as simple as that. The answer was there and it didn't involve waving a magic wand or wishing for things to be different. She just had to make up her mind.

Francesca put her cup down and leant forward slightly. 'What would you like - in a perfect world?'

Carys sighed. 'I'd like Richard to notice me.'

Francesca nodded. 'Then there's only one way to achieve that.'

'What's that?'

'For him to notice you, he'll have to notice your absence first. So I suggest you take a little holiday.'

'But I've got nowhere to go,' Carys said, thinking of her failed visit to Louise's.

'You don't need to go anywhere. You can stay here.'

'Here?'

'With me. We needn't tell a soul. You'll have a good break from life at Amberley and we'll make Richard sweat a little - come to his senses - that sort of thing. What do you think?'

Carys began to smile. 'Are you sure this isn't all rather underhand?'

'I'm not sure at all,' Francesca said. 'But I think it could be a lot of fun. The Bretton women will be taking charge of things. At long last.'

CHAPTER 30

It felt funny waking up in the guest bedroom at Cuthland House; funny to wake up without Richard. Not that Richard was ever actually around when she awoke. He was up at the crack of dawn, occasionally joining her and the girls for breakfast after he'd already put in an hour at the office.

Carys swung herself out of bed and, finding a set of towels which had been left out for her, took a shower in the guest bathroom before dressing and heading downstairs.

Francesca, like her son it seemed, had been up for hours.

'Did you sleep all right?' she asked as she put away a few cups.

'Yes, thank you, I did.'

'It's one of the blessings of this house,' she said. 'I've slept really well since moving here.'

'You mean you didn't up at Amberley?' Carys asked.

'Not really. Not *completely*. I usually woke during the night. That old house makes some strange sounds, doesn't it? Have you heard any strange noises?'

Carys bit her lip. Now was the time to confess, to share. 'Oh, you know,' she said, wondering if her mother-in-law would take the lead in this particular conversation and maybe confess to a ghostly sighting or two.

'Yes,' Francesca said slowly. 'That old house certainly has a lot to say. All those squeaks and groans. Used to drive me mad. I'd pace up and down for hours. I never got used to it.'

Carys nodded. So she hadn't heard any *supernatural* sounds, then?

'Help yourself to breakfast,' Francesca said motioning to the table where there was toast and marmalade, fresh croissants, a pot of tea and one of hot chocolate. Carys didn't feel that she deserved such a wonderful spread. After all, she had walked out on this woman's son.

Then something dawned on her. Richard hadn't called. He hadn't even noticed she'd gone. Carys frowned at the thought.

'What's wrong?' Francesca asked.

'He hasn't realised I've gone, has he?'

225

'I wouldn't take it personally,' Francesca said. 'That's the thing with a house like Amberley. You can lead a completely separate life from your partner. Sometimes, I'd go for days on end without seeing Henry. The only proof I had that our paths had really crossed was his crumpled pillow in the mornings.'

Somehow, that didn't make Carys feel any better.

'He'll call,' Francesca said.

'But what will you say?'

'Nothing.'

'But he'll find out I'm here, won't he? My car-'

'He never comes out this way. Believe me, this part of the estate is almost completely forgotten.'

'But the staff - somebody will tell him, surely.'

'I don't think so,' Francesca said. 'You can relax here for a while. Just you, me and the baby.'

Carys's mouth fell open and Francesca smiled.

'Don't look so surprised,' she said. 'I could tell the minute I saw you.'

'But I'm not-'

Francesca's eyes widened. 'Are you sure?'

Carys looked confused. 'I'd know, wouldn't I?' But then she began to think. The tiredness, the dizzy spells, the weepiness. She'd put it all down to her new life and settling in. Could she really be pregnant?

Francesca sat down opposite her. 'Don't look so worried,' she said. 'We'll go to a chemist and find out.'

Carys nodded. She felt completely stunned.

'I wanted to apologise to you,' Francesca said, immediately capturing Carys's attention. 'I know I've not been the most friendly of people and I wanted to say sorry for not spending more time with you when you first came to Amberley.' She shook her head. 'I don't know what it was,' she said. 'Perhaps it was the knowledge that my time was finally coming to an end. You know that feeling of a chapter closing? Your arrival meant that a new generation was taking over Amberley.'

'But didn't you have all those feelings when Richard married Amanda?'

Francesca gave a little shake of her head. 'It's funny but no, I didn't. I can't say why. Life continued pretty much as it always had. Even with the arrival of Cecily and Evelyn. I think I was so excited about becoming a grandmother that I didn't think of anything else. But there was something more permanent about your arrival.'

'Permanent?'

'Yes,' Francesca said. 'I had the feeling that you were the real start of the future. Perhaps it was all tied in with Henry's death, I don't know. Anyway,' Francesca said, waving her hand in frustration at her own ineloquence, 'I hope we can be friends now.'

Carys smiled. 'I like the sound of that,' she said.

Carys stayed at Cuthland House for another three days but she realised that she couldn't stay there forever, however welcome she'd been made. She had to face the future full on.

'I'm going back,' she told Francesca who was sitting in the garden reading a copy of *Social Whirl* which she herself had graced many a time.

'What, now?'

Carys nodded.

'Do you want some company?' Francesca asked, closing the magazine.

'No, thank you. I'll probably be best doing this alone.'

Francesca smiled. 'Well, let me know how it goes and, if you have any trouble with Richard, send him straight to me.'

Carys grinned. It was good to have Francesca on her side.

Carys decided to walk. She could pick the car up another time. It was a gorgeous summer's day. The sky was a perfect blue and cloudless and everything shimmered with summer light. She walked down the driveway and was just about to take a short cut across the fields when she saw a figure running towards her. It was Mrs Travis and the sight of her running was rather startling.

'Mrs Travis!' Carys exclaimed once the red-faced housekeeper had reached her. 'Whatever is the matter?'

'Oh, my lady! It's Cecily,' Mrs Travis said. 'She's gone missing.'

'Missing? What do you mean?'

'Nobody's seen her since last night and her bed looks unslept in.'

Carys gasped. Where could she be? She remembered Francesca's warning when they'd stayed up late talking the night before: 'Look after her,' she'd said. Carys had thought that Cecily didn't really need looking after. She'd always shied away from her attention and seemed so independent and strong.

'Everyone's out looking for her,' Mrs Travis explained, breaking into Carys's thoughts. 'Have you seen her?'

'No,' Carys said. 'I've not seen anyone.'

'I was just going to check the dowager duchess' house.'

'But I've just come from there.'

'And she wasn't there?'

'No.'

'Oh my good lord,' Mrs Travis said. 'Where can the girl have got to?'

'I'll help you look,' Carys said.

'Oh, will you, my lady?'

'Of course I will.'

'I'll go this way,' Mrs Travis said, her chest heaving in anxiety.

Carys nodded and decided to head across the fields. Where could Cecily be and why had she run away? Carys thought long and hard. If she was a child living at Amberley, where would she run away to? If she hadn't slept in her bed, surely she'd have chosen somewhere sheltered.

'The yew bower?' Carys wondered. It was certainly sheltered but it was also a little on the spooky side and she didn't think she'd head there if she was Cecily. The new stables? Cecily certainly loved her pony but surely they would have looked there already.

Carys wracked her brains as she walked. There wasn't anywhere to shelter in the walled garden other than an ancient greenhouse with broken windows, and the other gardens were equally bereft of accommodation. And then something occurred to Carys. Maybe Cecily hadn't let the house at all. Hadn't she only recently been discussing with Francesca how easy it was to go whole days without being seen there?

Carys headed across the fields towards Amberley. Everybody seemed to be outside, combing the estate for Cecily. Carys, it appeared, was the only one to think of looking indoors.

Walking through to the Yellow Drawing Room, she listened to the comforting tick of the clock. The kitchens? No, too cold. The library? Nowhere to hide and the chairs were too uncomfortable. Most of the rooms in Amberley weren't very child-friendly at all. Stuffed full of antiques, they made play rather difficult and Carys couldn't think of a single room she'd choose to hide in if she was a child. Unless …

'The attics!' she suddenly exclaimed. They'd be warmer than the kitchens, far away enough for it to feel as if you were running away and not so precious that you might break something.

Carys headed up to the, as yet, unexplored rooms. She'd only ever taken a quick peek at the long dusty corridors and been told that there were enough bits of old furniture up there to furnish the whole of Cuthland but she'd always had so much to do with the rest of the house without worrying about what was commonly referred to as 'the storage floor'. Now, she entered the low-ceilinged floor with a sense of anticipation, hoping her instinct was right.

'Cecily?' she called out softly, entering room after dusty room, her eyes gazing quickly at heaps of rickety chairs, three-legged tables, mountains of ancient coats and strange kitchen appliances.

'It's Carys. Can I talk to you?'

She moved from room to room, careful to duck to avoid knocking her head on the low beams and doorways.

'Cecily? Are you there?'

Carys sighed. What a mess everything was, she thought. When she'd first met Richard, she'd little suspected that, just a few months down the line, she'd have become a duchess, found herself pregnant, would have left the family home and lost her step-daughter. But she was determined to put everything right now. She loved Richard more than she could have thought possible. They'd *have* to make things work. Love couldn't be thrown aside just because a few office hours got in the way.

A sudden noise from the next room brought Carys back to the present and she went to investigate, treading lightly on the old squeaking floorboards. It was slightly larger than the other rooms and had a little window which looked out across the lake. There was an old dolls' house in the corner - a gorgeous Georgian wedding cake of a house - and Carys was surprised to discover that it had been left uncovered and yet wasn't covered in dust.

She took a closer look. It looked absolutely new - as if it had only recently been played with. Carys peeped into the little windows at the rooms it housed. It reminded her of Barston Hall and she could well imagine many happy hours had been spent playing with it.

Then, there was the tiniest squeak from a floorboard behind her. Carys bit her lip and slowly turned around and there, standing behind the door, was Cecily, looking at her with fearful eyes.

'Cecily!' Carys cried. 'What are you doing? Everyone's out looking for you. We've all been so worried.'

She looked up at Carys but didn't say a word.

'Are you all right?' Carys asked softly and Cecily nodded. She was wearing her nightie with a light cotton jumper on top. Carys approached her slowly and smiled. 'What are you doing up here? Were you visiting the dolls' house?'

Again, Cecily didn't reply.

Carys swallowed. She'd never found herself in a position quite like this before and wasn't sure how to proceed. Should she skirt around the issue and cajole Cecily into returning downstairs with her? Should she drag her away from the attics vowing not to give her any pocket money for a month? Oh, dear, Carys thought. Neither of those seemed appropriate.

Taking a deep breath, she decided to be blunt. In her experience, children responded best to honesty.

'What made you run away?' she asked.

Cecily's lip wobbled for a moment but then she spoke. 'You ran away first and it was because of me.'

Carys frowned. 'Whatever do you mean?'

'Evie said it was my fault that you left.'

Carys couldn't believe what she was hearing. 'But that's nonsense. Cecily? Do you hear me? That's complete nonsense.'

'Why did you go, then?' Cecily asked, tears threatening to spill at any moment.

'For lots of reasons,' Carys said. 'And none of them had anything to do with you.'

Cecily shuffled about uneasily from foot to foot and Carys noticed that she was wearing her favourite pink sandals.

'Where did you sleep?' Carys asked, looking around and not seeing anywhere she'd fancy bedding down for the night.

Cecily left the room. 'In here,' she said and Carys followed her into a smaller room in which was placed an old chaise longue, the fabric faded and torn.

'Were you warm enough?' Carys asked, the maternal side of her instantly showing itself.

'I was okay.'

'It doesn't look very comfortable to me.'

Cecily shrugged and Carys knelt down beside her, thinking that she must be as nervous talking to her as Carys had been when calling at Francesca's.

'You know,' she began, 'it can't have been very easy for you when I came here. It wasn't very easy for me either. I mean, how many women suddenly discover that they're going to be a step-mother to two girls?' Carys paused. 'There have been a lot of changes, haven't there?'

Cecily nodded.

'And I'm guessing that it's not going to be easy getting used to them. Maybe that's the reason I ran away too. I got scared for a while. I didn't know how to cope.' Carys gave a little smile. 'But I realised that this is my home now and I want to be here more than anything else in the world. I want to be with your daddy and I want to be with you and Evie.'

Cecily listened but her eyes were cast down.

'Do you think you could help me?' Carys asked. 'I'm going to need lots of friends to help me. Would you be my friend, Cecily?'

Cecily didn't answer for a moment but she slowly looked up and saw Carys smiling at her and she nodded.

'Good,' she said. 'Now, how about some lunch? I'm absolutely starving!'

Cecily nodded again and then did something completely unexpected: she put her hand in Carys.

Carys bit her lip in an attempt to stop tears from flooding. 'Come on,' she said. 'I'll make us some pancakes.'

Leaving the attic rooms behind, they walked, hand in hand, down the long staircase back into the main house. At once, Carys could hear voices in the hallway.

'I suppose we should let everyone know we're all right.'

'I'm nervous,' Cecily said in a shy voice.

'Me too,' Carys said, squeezing her hand. 'Take a deep breath.'

Cecily did and Carys echoed it.

'Cecily!' Richard shouted as soon as they appeared. 'Where have you been?' He swooped down and picked his daughter up, swinging her around and kissing the crown of her head feverishly.

'Oh, my goodness,' Mrs Travis joined. 'Thank heavens you're safe.'

Carys stood and watched. Once again, she seemed to belong in the background.

'I've been so worried about you.'

'I'm all right, Daddy. Carys came and found me.'

'But where were you?'

'In the attic.'

'The attic? But it's horrible up there.'

'It's not. It's quite warm and there's lots to do,' Cecily said matter-of-factly.

'But you've been gone hours.'

'I know,' she said. 'I was beginning to get hungry.'

Richard squeezed her, flattening her nose against his chest. 'Then we will get you something to eat.'

'Carys is going to make me pancakes,' Cecily said with a smile, looking around to her step-mother who immediately blushed.

'Pancakes?' Mrs Travis said incredulously. 'You'll be needing a good bath before you eat anything, Miss Cecily. Look how grubby you are.' And, with that, Mrs Travis led Cecily away, leaving Richard and Carys alone.

CHAPTER 31

'Carys!' Richard said, his voice not much above a whisper. The smile that he'd bestowed on Cecily had vanished and his face was as white as ash.

'Hello,' Carys said, her voice quiet too and her face allowing only the tiniest of smiles.

'I've been so worried. I woke up and you weren't there.'

'But that *always* happens to me,' Carys said before she had time to think. It sounded so accusatory and she hadn't meant to jump in like that.

'But at least you know where I am.'

Carys hung her head. 'I was at your mother's.'

'Were you? She didn't say a word.'

'No.'

'Why didn't you call?'

'I needed to get away. Just be me for a bit. It's hard to do that here.'

Richard frowned. 'But there's acres and acres and endless rooms to escape to.'

'But they're not mine.'

Richard stared at her. 'Yes they are. When you married me, you took on the role not only of my wife and step-mother to my girls but mistress of this house.'

Carys flinched. He made it sound like an impossible job description.

'It needs you, Carys,' he added gently.

She looked up at him. His eyes were wide and soft and she felt her own begin to vibrate with tears.

'*I* need you,' he said, and it was absolutely the right thing to say - or the wrong thing - because the tears fell before she could stop them.

'Carys!' He crossed the space between them in an instant and kissed her. 'I'm so sorry. I'm so sorry,' he whispered in her ear.

'I'm sorry too.' she said. 'It all went wrong.'

'I know.'

'I didn't know what to do.'

'Shush! Don't worry,' he said, hugging her close. 'It's okay now. We'll sort things out. I promise.'

Carys blinked her tears away and looked at him. 'Why's everything so complicated?' she asked. 'Why can't it be easy for us?'

'As long as there's Amberley, I'm afraid life's always going to be a little hectic.'

Carys smiled. 'Always Amberley.'

'But you do love it, don't you?' Richard asked, looking worried.

'I love it more than I could have imagined.'

He looked relieved. 'Than we'll work things out.'

'But you work too many hours,' Carys told him. 'I hardly see you.'

'That will change.'

'Will it?' She looked at him, aware that it was easy to make such promises at such a moment.

'From Monday.'

'What do you mean?'

'Jamie's coming to work for me.'

'Jamie? I thought he was in Tibet.'

'He's coming back - broke. I'm giving him a job. He'll be taking over a few things which means I'll be able to spend more time with you and the girls.'

'Really?'

'Really.' Richard smiled. 'We'll have to smarten Jamie up a bit and I'll have to train him. He's never really shown an interest in the estate until now - much too busy on his travels - but he sounded ready when I told him.'

'That's brilliant.'

'It is, isn't it? I'm just surprised I didn't think of it earlier,' Richard said, looking a little bit pleased with himself. 'Come on,' he said, taking Carys's hand.

'Where are we going?'

'I'm taking you to bed.'

And he did.

They made love, slowly and tenderly, as if it was something they had all the time in the world to do. Amberley Enterprises had to wait. The phone calls, the paperwork, the crumbling plaster in the east wing, the blocked drains in the old stable yard, the irate tenant farmer whose roof needed repairing - all had to wait whilst the duke made love to his duchess.

'I have something to tell you,' Carys said, propping herself up on the pillows so that she could see Richard's face.

'Yes?' he said sleepily, opening his eyes to look at her.

'I'm pregnant.'

Richard's eyes widened and he looked at Carys as if she might be joking. 'That was quick,' he said.

'No!' she laughed. 'It dates from - well, I'm not quite sure yet.'

'But you're sure you're-'

'Oh, yes. I did a test at your mother's.'

'Does she know?'

'She was the one who told me.'

Richard laughed. 'Sounds like mother.'

'She's absolutely delighted.'

Richard leant forward and kissed her again. 'So am I.'

'We'll have to tell the girls.'

'Of course.'

'Can I tell them?' Carys asked.

Richard nodded. 'They'd like that. They'll be choosing names for us.'

Carys snuggled back down into the bed which felt the very height of luxury at that time of day when both of them should have been elsewhere.

Richard took her right hand in his and kissed each finger.

'When should I tell them?' Carys asked.

Richard smiled. 'Whenever you like.'

'After our second honeymoon?' Carys suggested.

Richard's eyebrows rose. 'It's funny you should say that,' he said. 'Because I've been thinking we should have a little trip away.'

Carys smiled. It was exactly what she'd been hoping to hear.

CHAPTER 32

A certain sense of peace seemed to fill Carys over the next couple of weeks. The Montella exhibition was all moving along smoothly and the ghost tours were finally into credit and Carys opened a little bank account for her walled garden fund. Jamie had returned from finding spiritual enlightenment in Tibet, had been bought a suit by Richard and was in the process of learning all there was to know about Amberley Enterprises.

'It's really rather exciting,' he said in the kind of calm manner that could only come from having spent a month in a monastery. Richard was delighted, as was Carys, because he was spending less time at his desk and more time with his 'girls'. He went out riding with Cecily and Evie, took them on a shopping spree to Carminster, played crazy golf with them and even attended one of their ballet classes.

With Carys, he slept. Like he'd never slept before. She made him switch of his alarm clock, made love to him and made him breakfast - every morning and in that order. They took the dogs out together for wonderfully long walks around the estate although, admittedly, it was quite hard for Richard to switch off.

'That gate needs fixing,' he'd say or, 'I must tell Mr Brodie to order some more fencing.' And he'd get out the little notebook that was ever present on his person. But Carys had to admit that it was a big improvement on the Richard of a few weeks ago.

Carys was also enjoying a much easier relationship with her step-daughters. Cecily had definitely had a change of heart since Carys's return, deciding that her step-mother wasn't quite as bad as she'd first thought. Evie was as sweet as ever and they were both terribly excited about the news of Carys's baby.

'I hope it's a girl!' Cecily said.

'I want a baby brother!' Evie said. 'Called Richard. After Daddy.'

'Carys gets to choose the name, silly!'

Carys smiled her way through these exchanges, teasing them that the new baby was going to have a truly outrageous name like Ignatius or Ebenezer. She even went as far as to consult the Bretton family tree. She'd always been fascinated by family trees: the shapes and patterns they made and the endless striving and thrusting down into the new generations - new branches, new beginnings - and to which she was to add another little branch.

It was funny how names were repeated too: some like William, Elizabeth, Anne and George never seeming to go out of fashion. Whilst other names stood out, declaring their uniqueness with a strange sort of pride. Conibear, for instance. Who had he been? Where had that name sprung from? What colour eyes had he had? Had he had the famous Cuthland dark eyes? Perhaps that was where they'd began - with Conibear Cuthland, the tenth duke.

Family trees were so very male, she thought, examining the Bretton's in the front of the Amberley guidebook. But who were the women? Who was Diana Bellwood, the wife of the seventh duke? Who had her family been before she'd exchanged Bellwood for Bretton? Was she well-known in her own right or always referred to in terms of her husband? And Dorothy Hewson who'd given Amberley four boys and four girls? So many lives lived out under this one roof. So many stories to discover.

And then her eyes alighted on one she did know: Georgiana Lacey.

'Georgiana.' She said the name aloud. It would be a wonderful gesture to name her child - if she was a girl - after one of the first friends she'd made at Amberley. Carys sighed suddenly. She was worried; she hadn't seen Georgiana since she'd left Amberley to stay with Francesca. She sincerely hoped that she hadn't sent her away forever when she'd been so rude to her last time they'd met.

Carys closed the guidebook and walked to the Montella Room where she stood in front of Georgiana's portrait.

'Where are you?' she whispered.

'I'm right behind you!' a voice said.

Carys turned and smiled at the happy face of her ghostly friend.

'*Georgiana!*' She walked forward and, before she realised what she was doing, embraced her friend. 'Oh, dear.'

'It's all right. Don't worry. I'm only vapour, you see,' Georgiana quickly explained.

'How strange. I'm sorry,' Carys said, feeling rather flustered at having tried to hug a spirit. 'I was so excited at seeing you. I've missed you so much.'

'And I have missed you too.'

'I was so scared you wouldn't come back.'

Georgiana looked surprised. 'Why would I not come back?'

'Because I was so horrible to you.'

'Oh, please don't worry about that. As long as everything is all right now?'

Carys nodded. 'I think it is. I mean, I know it is. Jamie's working for the estate now and that's taken so much pressure off Richard.'

'So you can spend more time together.'

'Yes. It's wonderful. Everything feels just right.'

'And have you anything else to tell me?' There was a naughty sparkle in Georgiana's eyes and Carys instantly blushed.

'We're going to have a baby.'

Georgiana clapped her hands together and beamed. 'That is wonderful!'

'In April.'

'A spring baby? So romantic.'

'I've just been looking at the family tree for inspiration. I don't know where to begin. What did you call your children, Georgiana?'

Georgiana smiled wistfully. 'Well, my first precious daughter was Little Georgiana. Then there was Catherine and Mary and Alice.'

'So many girls!'

'And a very nervous time for me, I can assure you. I felt like Anne Boleyn - that my time to provide a male heir was rapidly running out.'

'So what happened?'

'I had William,' Georgiana said softly, her eyes looking dreamy and lovelorn. 'Dear, sweet William.'

Carys smiled. 'He's in some of the portraits, isn't he?'

Georgiana nodded. 'Of course,' she said and she gave Carys a knowing look.

'What?' Carys asked.

'He was special,' Georgiana said.

'Well, he was the long-awaited son, wasn't he? After four daughters, I mean.'

'No,' Georgiana said, 'it was more than that.'

Carys was puzzled. 'What do you mean?'

Georgiana didn't answer for a moment. 'I adore those portraits of me and William. Leo Montella has captured something very special, do you not think so?'

'Oh, absolutely. They're wonderful paintings.'

'Leo Montella. Is it not a beautiful name?'

Carys nodded. 'Yes, it is.'

'And he was such a beautiful man. Have you ever noticed that some men are attractive whilst others are handsome? Well, Leo was *beautiful* - truly he was. He had eyelashes that were longer than any woman's - and so dark.'

Carys smiled but there was a little part of her that couldn't help wondering where this conversation was going.

'You were musing on the dark eyes of the Bretton's before, weren't you?' Georgiana said.

'How did you know?' Carys asked, suitably unnerved.

Georgiana waved a hand dismissively. 'They didn't begin with the tenth duke, you know. Nor the ninth nor the eighth. They didn't begin with a duke at all.'

Carys's own eyes narrowed. 'What are you saying?'

Georgiana looked around the room but there was only her and Carys and the bright faces from the portraits present.

'You must not tell a soul. Promise me you will not tell a single soul.'

'I promise,' Carys said and Georgiana beckoned her to come closer.

'My sweet William was not my husband's child,' Georgiana said in an excited whisper.

'What?'

Georgiana nodded. 'He was Leo's child.'

'Oh, my goodness!' Carys said, covering her mouth with her hand. 'You've got to be kidding.'

'I am most certainly *not* kidding.'

'You had an affair with the artist?'

'Oh, Carys, don't sound so outraged! Women *did* have affairs back in history. They aren't the prerogative of the modern woman, you know. And you have been suspecting it for some time, haven't you?'

'But I - but - you were *married*.'

'Yes.'

'You were respectable.'

'Most certainly.'

'And you had an *affair!*'

Georgiana laughed at Carys's shocked face and decided she'd

better try and explain. 'I loved my husband. I really did. We were best friends. But Leo was the love of my life. I cannot really explain it any other way.'

'I can't take this all in. Is this what you've been wanting to tell me? You said there was something, didn't you? Or Lara Claridge did. I forget now, I'm so confused. Is this why you came back?'

'I didn't just come back. I have been here all the time. I have never truly left Amberley. It's rather a hard place to leave, isn't it? I think you recently discovered that.'

'Is Leo here too?' Carys asked, looking around as if she might spy the ghostly figure of the renowned artist in the room bearing his name.

'No, no. He's not here.'

'But this is all so - so-'

'*Wonderful!*' Georgiana interrupted.

Carys laughed. 'Unexpected!' She shook her head as if trying to clear her thoughts.

'And Charlotte too.'

'What?' Carys's mouth dropped open.

'My daughter, Charlotte. She was Leo's too.'

'*Two* children?'

Georgiana nodded, her eyes alight with joy. 'Two.'

'Did your husband know?'

'Of course he didn't. He would have been truly appalled. It would have broken his heart.'

'He accepted them as his own?'

'But of course.'

'But-'Carys stopped, seeming to think of something for the first time. 'They weren't Brettons.'

'No.'

'William - he became the next duke, didn't he?'

'He did.'

'But he wasn't a Bretton.'

'No,' Georgiana confirmed again.

'So all the dukes after him weren't descended from Brettons either,' Carys said, her face quite pale.

'No,' Georgiana said matter-of-factly. 'They were descended from Montellas.'

'Oh, my goodness. And nobody else knows this?'

'Not a soul.'

A nervous little laugh escaped Carys. 'But they're so proud of their family history stretching right back to the first duke.'

'I know,' Georgiana said. 'I'm afraid I rather corrupted their family tree, didn't I?'

Carys shook her head. 'So the dark hair, the dark eyes-'

'Are Italian.'

'Why hasn't anyone noticed?'

Georgiana shrugged. 'I am a firm believer that people only see what they want to see.'

'Gosh! This is so *huge*.'

'But not uncommon.'

'What do you mean?'

'I'm quite sure I'm not the only lady who had a dalliance.'

'You mean there are other men who've inherited titles which aren't really theirs?' Carys said aghast.

'Well, I cannot prove anything but it's not completely out of the question, is it?'

'I'd never really thought about it. I just assumed-'

'That's it. Everybody assumes and the world continues happily enough.'

Carys laughed again. 'What am I to do with such knowledge?'

Georgiana gave her a warning look. 'Absolutely nothing.'

'Can you imagine if people knew? Can you imagine what Natasha Bryant would make of it in the local paper? Imagine the faces of the tour groups if they were told. Amberley - passing to the child of a painter!'

Georgiana tutted. 'You make him sound like a tradesman,' she admonished. 'He was an *artist*. And a very respected one at that.'

'And your husband never knew?'

'No, James, never knew. Leo did, of course. That's why there are so many portraits. It was a legitimate way for him to spend time with his children and they're such wonderful portraits, are they not?'

Carys had to agree. She'd never seen such lovely paintings. 'But not to be a Bretton - a true Bretton.'

Georgiana sighed. 'It isn't the end of the world when you think about it. He was still my son and what was wrong with him inheriting the title? Why shouldn't *my* family make a contribution to the Bretton family tree - a *real* contribution? You, I believe, have had such thoughts yourself.'

'Well, I must admit to wondering about the role that women play.'

Georgiana nodded. 'I didn't plan any of it, Carys. It was all - well - wonderfully spontaneous and it was not my fault that Leo's love gave me a son and heir whilst James's did not.'

Carys and Georgiana looked at each other and then they both burst into sudden laughter, filling the Montella Room with merriment.

'I'd never have guessed in a million years,' Carys said at last.

'Come on, now,' Georgiana said. 'I've seen you looking at the portraits. You cannot tell me you didn't suspect *some*thing.'

Carys looked pensive. 'I always thought there was a rather special quality about the paintings, I must admit, and I can see that naughty sparkle in your eyes.'

Georgiana smiled prettily. 'We had something rare and very beautiful and I so wanted to share it with you.'

Carys smiled back at her. 'I'm so glad you did.'

A voice shouting suddenly broke into their secret conversation.

'Come on, Carys! We're leaving.'

'Oh, my goodness. It's Richard. I totally forgot.'

'What is it?'

'We're leaving - for Scotland.'

'Now?'

'Yes. A sort of second honeymoon. I don't know where the time's gone.' Carys suddenly looked panicky.

'You had better hurry.'

For a moment, Carys was torn. As much as she longed to get away with Richard, she didn't want to leave Georgiana but she didn't suppose it would be fitting to take a ghost away on a second honeymoon.

'Go on, then,' Georgiana said, flapping her hands to hurry Carys along. 'What are you waiting for?'

Carys sighed. 'I guess I'll see you later,' she said with a tiny smile and she began to walk out of the room, stopping when she was at the door. 'You *will* be here when I get back, won't you?'

Georgiana looked anxious for a moment.

'Georgiana?'

'Actually, I was thinking of taking a little break too.'

'What do you mean?'

'Well, I can't stay here forever. I must leave you to make a home for yourself. I can see you're beginning to settle. I knew that awful Amanda would never make a go of life at Amberley. That's why I gave her a helping hand in leaving.'

Carys dared to grin. 'Oh, Georgiana!'

'But you - you appreciate a place like this. You belong.'

Carys bit her lip. 'I suppose I do. But I want you here with me.'

Georgiana shook her head. 'Ghosts who hang around too long tend to start meddling in the lives of the living and that can be a dangerous thing.' She saw Carys's sad expression and added, 'But I'll be around. I might just make my presence felt on the occasional ghost tour.'

Carys smiled and nodded and watched in awe as her friend slowly began to vanish in her blue cloud, leaving the faintest scent of roses hanging in the air, and then she walked through the house to where Richard was waiting for her.

'I've packed all our stuff already. Where were you?'

'Oh, just saying goodbye to the house.'

He ruffled her hair. 'You are funny. I thought you couldn't wait to leave.'

'I can't. But, now that we're going, I'm beginning to realise how much I'll miss it.'

He smiled and kissed her. 'I feel just the same.'

They walked out of the house and there, standing on the driveway was a sight Carys thought she'd never see: a brand new silver Marlva Panache.

'Who's is that?' she exclaimed.

'Ours.'

'Richard!'

He shrugged. 'I traded in the old Marlva County and did a bit of a deal.'

'But you need the Country for work.'

'Not really. Jamie's got his own and we can share that. And this is far more fun, isn't it? It'll get us up to Scotland in real style.'

Carys hugged him. 'It's wonderful,' she said. 'I love it!'

Then, like a pair of excited children, they got into the car, started the engine and drove away, glancing every now and then in the rear-view mirror at Amberley Court, content in the knowledge that they would be back home very soon.

ABOUT THE AUTHOR

Victoria Connelly was brought up in Norfolk and studied English literature at Worcester University before becoming a teacher. After getting married in a medieval castle in the Yorkshire Dales and living in London for eleven years, she moved to rural Suffolk where she lives with her artist husband and a mad Springer spaniel and ex-battery hens.

Her first novel, *Flights of Angels*, was published in Germany and made into a film. Victoria and her husband flew out to Berlin to see it being filmed and got to be extras in it. Several of her novels have been Kindle bestsellers.

If you'd like to contact Victoria or sign up for her newsletter about future releases, email via her website at www.victoriaconnelly.com.

She's also on Facebook and Twitter @VictoriaDarcy

ALSO BY VICTORIA CONNELLY

Austen Addicts Series
A Weekend with Mr Darcy
The Perfect Hero
published in the US as Dreaming of Mr Darcy
Mr Darcy Forever
Christmas with Mr Darcy
Happy Birthday, Mr Darcy

Other Fiction
Molly's Millions
The Runaway Actress
Wish You Were Here
A Summer to Remember
Flights of Angels
Irresistible You
Three Graces
It's Magic (A compilation volume: Flights of Angels,
Irresistible You and Three Graces)
A Dog Called Hope

Short Story Collections
One Perfect Week and other stories
The Retreat and other stories
Postcard from Venice and other stories

Non-fiction
Escape to Mulberry Cottage
A Year at Mulberry Cottage

Children's Adventure
Secret Pyramid

Made in the USA
Monee, IL
10 July 2020